Praise for *Taking 1960* by Rosa Sophia

"*Taking 1960* was a well written and intriguing mystery that kept me wondering until the end. The paranormal aspects of the book were extremely well done. This was a great debut novel and I definitely look forward to reading more of my fellow author's work."

— Rev. David P. Smith, www.davidduir.com, Author of *Honoring the Sacred Earth* and *Under an Expanse of Oaks*

"I really enjoyed this book. Not only did it have several elements that appealed to me, it kept me guessing all the way through. *Taking 1960* has a haunting quality that sticks with you after you've finished the last page. This book literally took me for a ride. If you're looking for something paranormal, *Taking 1960* is a book I would recommend highly. Look for more from author Rosa Sophia—she has entered the literary world with a splash."

— Toni Rakestraw, www.unbridlededitor.com

Check Out Time

Retail is Murder

By Rosa Sophia

Richard,
Thanks for being You,
for being such a wonderful
friend. I love our talks.
We will stay in touch!
love, your friend always,
Rosa Sophia
♡
3-2014

ISBN 978-1-61392-015-2
First edition: June, 2012
Printed in the United States of America

Oaklight Publishing, LLC
4306 Independence Street
Rockville, MD 20853
USA
http://oaklightpublishing.com

For my Dad,
and the guys on the night crew.

Author's Note

This novel was inspired by a number of people to whom I owe great thanks. First and foremost, I must thank my editor, J.W. Coffey. I also want to thank the people with whom I worked on the graveyard shift. You will meet a few of them in this story. You will also meet the Indie band Jargon, which was inspired by my wonderful musician friends in Pennsylvania. Obviously there were more than a few people who contributed to *Check Out Time*; you know who you are.

My friends, my coworkers—those who suffer from insomnia, those who find themselves in a grocery store at two in the morning stocking frozen vegetables—without them, this book could not have been written.

Most of all, I must thank my father, who was the main inspiration behind *Check Out Time*. In 2008, I was reunited with my dad. I had not seen him in fifteen years, and all I had was a smattering of brief memories. After parking my car for the first time at his house, I stood in the driveway and waited. Dad walked outside. I don't know why, but I thought he would be taller, or maybe heavier. The few memories I retained collided with this new image of my father. He looked tired, early fifties, blond hair almost to his shoulders, and I think he was wearing a stained blue T-shirt. Over the T-shirt was his tan work coat, and he was wearing old blue jeans and steel-toed boots. I remember thinking that he looked like he was going to cry because he was so glad to see me. That is how I will *always* remember him.

In October of 2010, my father suffered a stroke while riding his ATV in the mountains. As of this writing, he is still in a nursing home. I don't know if my father will ever be the way that I remember him again.

The character of Roy Vogler is based on my father. I started writing this story in 2008. In short, this story is fictional but the love I have for my dad is the foundation of *Check Out Time*. Although we had fewer than three years to get to know each other all over again, I treasure the time that I spent with him. My father helped to reignite my passion for working on cars, and his encouragement was part of the reason I finally decided to pursue a degree in the automotive field.

The greatest gift my father has ever given me are my two little sisters, Ashley and Alyssa. In 2008, I was reunited with the rest of my family, and I am very grateful. I will be sending a portion of the proceeds of this book to my family for the care of my little sisters.

Check Out Time is a dark mystery with quirky characters, and in a sense, it's also my way of expressing how glad I am that I have reconnected with my father.

I hope you enjoy reading this book as much as I enjoyed writing it.

— Rosa Sophia, August 14, 2011
North Palm Beach, Florida

CONTENTS

Prologue

The leaves on the oak trees rustled in a slight breeze. It was a mild summer day. Naomi had foregone traditional dress for a black tank top and a pair of blue jeans and sandals.

"We are gathered here today to mourn the loss of a beloved friend and mother."

Naomi stared down at her feet. She wasn't really listening to the pastor. She couldn't help but think that it was a little silly that someone who didn't really know her mother was leading the ceremony. She felt eyes on her back. Everyone was watching her. She was standing apart from the others. After a while, she began to notice that one man in particular was looking in her direction. He watched her with solemn, sorrowful eyes, his hands clasped over his black suit jacket.

After the funeral, Naomi went and stood in the parking lot. She made a point to avoid everyone. They came up to her and said a whole lot of things that she didn't really hear. They told her that it wasn't her fault, but she didn't believe them. They asked her if she was really going away, if the Penn Foundation was where she really thought she should be. It was what the psychiatrist at the police station had suggested, but Naomi wasn't bound to it. The law couldn't tell her what to do; they insisted that she was innocent, a mere bystander.

The man who had been watching her walked up beside her. "Hello," he said. The greeting sounded forced, as though he were afraid of her.

Naomi eyed him suspiciously. "Hi. Do I know you?"

The crowd was dispersing. There was a discomfort in the air that was almost palpable. The man beside Naomi shrugged. "You did know me, once." He caught her gaze and stared at her. He appeared as though he were on the verge of tears. "Do you need a place to live? I have plenty of room."

"Who are you?" Naomi took a step back. Part of her already knew who he was; the rest of her didn't want to believe it.

The man smiled weakly, his first attempt to comfort her. Then he spoke, and it was clear that he was afraid of her reaction. "I'm your father."

She didn't have a whole lot of choices. She could have had herself committed, but she didn't think that she really belonged there. She wasn't crazy. She knew it would take her a while to stop blaming herself for her mother's death, but that was no reason to institutionalize herself. She didn't have many friends in Quakertown, so she agreed to go live with her father.

She remembered the long drive to her new home. She remembered the way her father, Roy Vogler, squeezed the steering wheel with such force that she was afraid he might snap it in half. She wanted to ask him why he

2

seemed so afraid of her, but she couldn't bring herself to say it. He opened his mouth to speak several times, and then stopped. Finally, she asked him what was wrong.

"I . . . your mother . . . I mean . . . Naomi, I know she told you things. We didn't get along, that's true. She just didn't want you to talk to me, that's all. She never wanted you to meet me."

"How did you know where to find me?"

"You know Pete Miller?" When Naomi shook her head, Roy continued. "Miller's Auto Parts in Quakertown?"

"Oh," Naomi said. That store had been right down the street from her mother's house.

"Pete's an old friend of mine. We used to work together at a shop in Perkasie before I started my own business. All these years, I've had him keep tabs on you. I know it sounds strange. He would drive by your house every now and then, see you in the front yard when you were a kid. Make sure you were okay. He would call me and tell me. There was never much to tell, but at least I knew you were all right. And I had your address, which your mother would have never given me. Last week, Pete called me and told me that . . . ." Roy trailed off, pausing for a moment. "He told me he saw the ambulance at your house, the cops. He saw you on the front stoop, crying. He saw . . . ."

"I know what he saw." Naomi remembered getting into the back of that police car. It was an experience she never wanted to repeat.

"He told me when the funeral was, found it in the paper. And here we are. Naomi, I was so afraid you would run from me."

"I had a feeling you would come."

"So you expected it? And that's why you didn't run?"

"No." Naomi stared solemnly out the window. "I just thought I might see you."

"I know you're scared, Naomi. So am I. But it'll be all right, you'll see."

Chapter 1: Roy T. Vogler Learns to Cook
Eight Months Later

If you drove down Maine Street in Witchfire—passing Jim's General Store, Whellaby's Grocer, the local diner, and several very old Victorian-style homes—you would eventually come to an empty stretch of road that curved around until it manifested a dirt driveway. Oak trees flanked this particular driveway, all of them brimming with foliage in the simmering heat of the summer. The driveway passed over a wide creek where the townsfolk often went fishing. Today, only one man sat by the bank, mopping his brow. It was nearing a hundred degrees in Witchfire, a little town in Pennsylvania that hadn't seen such a sweltering summer in years.

There was a sign that marked what was at the end of the dirt driveway, but no one bothered to read it anymore. Most of the people that came this far into town were locals, so they already knew what was there without having to take a second glance at the sign. This was the home of Vogler's Auto Yard. The sign read, 'Junk Yard, Parts Dealer, Auto Repair Shop.' The sign also declared that state inspections could be carried out here, in the heart of Nacre Township, in the garage owned by Naomi's father, Roy Thompson Vogler. A lot of folks around town called him R.T. Naomi called him Dad.

A second garage stood a short walking distance away from the main garage. Each garage was built on a different side of the chain-link fence that surrounded a large junkyard. Naomi spent most of her time in the smaller garage, either working on her own car or helping her father with their hobby: restoring antique and classic cars. She had painted a colorful mural on the Eastern wall of her little hideout. Large letters read, 'Naomi's.'

Inside the little garage, she sat up so fast that she nearly cracked her head open on the rear bumper of the Buick she was trying to repair. Naomi had been taking another look at the exhaust pipes when a voice interrupted her lonely reverie.

She caught herself just before she hit her head, and then she slid out from under the vehicle and jumped to her feet. "Dad, you scared the hell out of me."

A man of rather short stature stepped into the shadow of the garage, escaping the heat of the sun. His blue T-shirt was wet with sweat and his jeans were stained with engine grease. His daughter looked no different. Her work clothes were a mess and there was dirt all over her face.

Naomi's father shook her head. "Like father, like daughter," he said musingly. "Come on, kid, I'm going to make lunch."

He patted her on the back. The two of them walked away from the smaller garage where Naomi had been working, past the much larger garage where the business was housed, and toward the old farmhouse that Roy called home.

"You're making lunch?" Naomi asked, as if in disbelief. "What? Burnt grilled cheese?"

"Nah. I figured out how to make salad and veggie burgers."

"No way!" Naomi exclaimed.

"Oh, come on. You knew I had it in me."

"I guess it took almost burning the house down to turn you into a good cook."

Naomi's dad sighed. "Must you be such a smart ass?"

"I learn from the best," she retorted.

Soon, the veggie burgers were simmering on the grill. Naomi and Roy nearly forgot about them; they busied themselves by talking about the Chrysler that Roy had been working on that day. When Naomi lifted the cover on the grill, the burgers were burnt.

"I guess it's about time R.T. Vogler learns to cook," Naomi said jokingly, "But I hope you realize that veggie burgers aren't like *real* burgers. They hardly take any time at all."

Roy's face grew redder than it already had been under the heat of the June sun. "If you don't like it, you do the cooking."

Naomi cringed. There had been a time when she had loved to cook. She had searched out complicated recipes and cooked in her spare time, enjoying the chemistry and the creativity of making something new. Memories

7

flashed through her mind and she recoiled, shutting the cover on the grill. "I think I'd rather just have salad," she decided.

Naomi and her father went into the cool house and sat down in the air-conditioned living room, where they ate lunch and drank lemonade. The house smelled like grease. Naomi, who wouldn't have believed it even if someone had told her, looked even prettier with dirt all over her face than she did without it.

They ate their lunch in silence, pausing either to burp or resituate themselves on the couch. Life might have been different for Naomi—

If her mother hadn't died.

Chapter 2: A New Life in Witchfire

Naomi had been living with R.T. for a little under a year. She had taken up residence in a small house trailer that sat in the back of the property, just in view of her father's house. Those months were all that Naomi knew of her father, all that she had *ever* known of him. Her mother and father had separated when Naomi was a tiny little baby, incapable of remembering Roy.

Naomi had long believed that she would never meet her father. In one terrible week, Naomi lost her mother and found her father. At that time, she had been the same age she was now—twenty-one. Next month would be her birthday.

If not for her father's quick intervention, she would have had nowhere to go. The day that they had met had been the day that her entire universe had shifted and everything she had once believed had been proven untrue.

Naomi didn't know why her mother had lied to her about Roy. She supposed that she would never find out. Upon moving in with her father, she found him to be exactly the opposite of what her mother had told her. He was a kind, loving man, who cried right in front of her one evening, even as a wide smile crossed his face and he thanked God for bringing his daughter back to him. He was honest, hard working, and a good mechanic. Naomi

9

chose not to speculate on her parents' relationship; after all, it was in the past.

The month before her twenty-second birthday, Naomi got a job at the local food store, Whellaby's Grocer. Her father had given her the 1986 Buick Park Avenue she had been working on in the garage. The car was her project vehicle. Once she made it drivable, she planned to take it to work with her every day. Until then, she would walk the mile and a half to Whellaby's on the days she was scheduled. There was only one catch—Naomi had gotten a job on the nightshift stocking crew. She would have to walk through town in the dark.

Naomi reclined on the dark blue vinyl seat and watched the cars pass by on Maine Street. She sipped her coffee. "Why does every town have a *Main* Street?" she wondered aloud. "Why couldn't they be more creative?"

There were two young men sitting with her. Up until now, they had been very quiet. Oliver was Naomi's best friend, one of the first people she had met after moving to Witchfire. He sat across from her, his black hair pulled back in a ponytail and his wire-framed glasses slightly cockeyed over his thin face. He shrugged. "What time is it?"

"Only seven. We've got plenty of time," Naomi said. "You okay, Geo?"

Geoffrey, the man sitting at Naomi's left, glanced up. "Sure, yeah. I was just thinking. You do know that Witchfire's 'Main Street' is actually spelled like the state of Maine, right?"

"Huh. I didn't realize that."

"I guess you've got an excuse. You're still pretty new here."

Naomi shrugged. "There are a lot of things I don't notice."

Oliver smirked. "I like to think I know you pretty well, Naomi. There's a lot of things you *do* notice, too, so don't try to play dumb. You always seem to know what's up with people."

"People, sure, but apparently not street names," Geoffrey pointed out.

Naomi had met Geo and Oliver at the same party one night, ten months ago. She had found herself unable to sleep. She had clambered out of bed, out of the trailer that she was still learning to call home, and into the night. She had walked down the dark dirt road, the moon her only light, the forest surrounding her. Eventually, she had reached the heart of town and found a little bar. The place was called Moonlight Joe's for a reason she couldn't fathom, and there had been a lot of noise emanating from the establishment on that particular night.

It turned out that a band had been playing there. It was a rock band that was apparently well known in the area. They were called Jargon and their lead singer was a stocky young man with pale skin, brown eyes and dark curly hair. The lead singer's name was Geoffrey Harp and after the show, the young man offered to buy a drink for a sad-looking young woman who was sitting in a corner booth, drinking by herself. The sad-looking woman was Naomi. Shortly after Geo and Naomi had gotten acquainted, another young man joined them. This man introduced himself as Oliver Windsor, a history major at the local community college.

That night, she made two of the best friends she'd ever had. As the three of them sat together at the Blue Plate Diner, known to locals as the Night Kitchen, Naomi couldn't help but feel incredibly grateful for their company. Both guys had helped her get a job at Whellaby's; the three of them would be working together on the night crew. Whenever they met at the Night Kitchen, Naomi would take comfort in knowing that for at least one night out of the week, she hadn't had to walk through town in the dark.

Chapter 3: Whellaby's Grocery Store

Naomi was walking down the lane to her father's house. It was foggy and strangely cold for summer. There was a bite in the breeze that made her uncomfortable. She felt as though someone were watching her.

She thought back to almost a year ago, her birthday, when she had invited a couple of friends over to her house for a 'party.' Naomi's parties were never much of anything, mostly because she didn't have that many friends. As a child, she had envisioned a 'sweet sixteen' like no other, but when she had finally hit sixteen years of age, she realized that she didn't have the number of friends that it took to throw a really great party. At sixteen, in fact, she hadn't had any friends at all.

When twenty-one rolled around, things weren't that much different. That was when she'd cut off her waist-length hair and decided to become a new person. She didn't feel any different as she walked down that dark lane, but she knew that things *were* different—more so than she had ever wanted them to be.

The darkness around her began to encircle her, closing in—she knew it wouldn't let go. The lane blurred. She felt a tear roll down her cheek. In the darkness, someone spoke to her.

"Naomi?"

13

Naomi's eyes opened. She blinked. She realized that she had fallen asleep. "What time is it?"

"It's time to go in to work. You just fell asleep on the bench outside. You must be pretty tired. It's freezing cold out here," Oliver said.

Naomi looked up. Sure enough, she was sitting on the bench outside Whellaby's Grocer. The sun had gone down. Dim lights illuminated the nearly empty parking lot. "I just had the strangest dream," she mumbled.

"Come on, guys," Geo called from the other side of a long line of parked shopping carts. "We're going to be late."

"Right." Naomi stood up and followed her friends into Whellaby's. It was going to be a very long night.

Naomi had been inside Whellaby's during the day, but never during the night. There weren't that many people in the store, but there were more than she expected to see at ten o' clock at night. Oliver took her to the manager's office. When they walked in, the manager was sitting behind his desk, a jug of iced tea in one hand and the store phone in the other.

"Just tell Mr. Whellaby the figures when you get a chance, Maureen!" The manager paused and glanced up. "I have to go. Just give him the information and get back to me later on. Call anytime, I'll be here all night," he finished sarcastically. Then he hung up the phone.

The night manager was a stocky man with an expression that said he was sick of the grocery business.

14

He had dark hair. Somewhere in his features, Naomi detected the background of an Asian man whose family line had been seriously watered down by Caucasian blood.

"You must be the new recruit." When he stood up, the night manager towered over her. Naomi had expected that he might want to shake hands with her, but instead he thrust his hands into his pockets and said, "Follow me. Oliver, you get in aisle seven with Ramsey."

"Sure," Oliver said. He caught the door to the office just as it began to swing shut behind Naomi. "This'll be fun."

Naomi experienced a wave of exhaustion as she followed the night manager down an aisle to the back of the store. She didn't know why she felt tired. Lately, she had been getting plenty of sleep. Perhaps it was the idea of staying up until six-thirty in the morning, working, that made her feel sleepy. Naomi had never worked a nightshift job before; it was all very new to her.

Some of the lights in the store had been turned off for the night to conserve energy, so it was dimmer in the building than usual. Naomi listened as her manager told her various details of the job—how many cases she was expected to stock per hour, when lunch break was and who was going to train her.

"Geo will show you the ropes in aisle nine," the manager said. His name was Keith Ryan, and Naomi could tell by his mannerisms that he had been working at Whellaby's for a long time.

15

Chapter 4: Taking the Buick for a Spin

During the night it was cool outside, but when the sun came up, the temperature rose into the high seventies. When Naomi started walking home at seven in the morning, groggy and exhausted from her first night of work, she felt the day grow hotter as the sun beat down on the asphalt. She hadn't been able to get a ride home. Geo's car was a mess. The head gasket had busted, the engine oil was the color of a cappuccino and the car itself was sitting in the garage at Roy's auto repair. Naomi would see it when she got home, wishing that she had a set of wheels that ran.

She was glad that she only worked a couple of nights that week. She wasn't used to staying up all night and even the walk home was tiring. Under normal circumstances, she would have enjoyed it.

The uniform polo shirt clung uncomfortably to her skin. The summer heat was unusually sweltering that morning. As she slogged along Maine Street, debating on taking a shortcut through the forest that dipped into a valley beside the road, she heard a loud honk.

Naomi turned as a pick-up truck pulled over and switched on its hazard lights. The early morning traffic slid by at thirty miles an hour as Naomi climbed into her father's old light blue Chevy. She dropped a plastic bag of snacks and drinks onto the floor of the truck and sighed as she leaned back in her seat.

"Hey, kid," her father said. When the passenger side door clanked shut, he turned off the hazard lights and merged into traffic. "How was your first night at work?"

"Exhausting," Naomi moaned. "I mean, I mostly just shadowed one of the guys, but I'm not used to staying up like this."

"I hear you. I wouldn't want to do it."

"What are you doing out so early?"

Naomi's dad rolled his eyes. "Eh, you know my buddy Truman."

"Truman?"

"Oh, you don't remember him? He came by the house last week."

"I do remember him. I forgot his name. What about him?"

"He called me about an hour ago saying he broke down near the freeway. So I went out there. Truman doesn't know a thing about cars. Here, one of his belts was loose. He took it to one of these big franchises to get it fixed and they didn't put the right tension on the belt. It slipped off while he was driving. He had a hell of a time steering the thing off the road. I put the belt back on for him and was on my way home and, lo and behold, I see my daughter lookin' like she's about to collapse on the side of the street."

Naomi rolled down the window and closed her eyes,

enjoying the feeling of the wind rushing against her face. "I sure am glad you showed up, Dad."

"It's a lucky thing. You going to work on the Buick today?"

"Later. After I sleep," Naomi mumbled.

When they got to the house, Roy had to wake up his daughter. Her head was hanging forward, her hands clasped in her lap. She slipped out of the truck and stumbled toward the house trailer, mumbling something about how she was too tired to eat. As the temperature climbed well into the eighties, Naomi turned on the air conditioner and climbed into bed, her head swimming, drowning in memories and sordid regrets.

Naomi dreamt of the usual things. There was a tall handsome stranger, emerging from the deep recesses of her desire to love and to be loved. In the dream, the man came to the front door of her mother's house. Naomi's mother called out to her, telling her that she had a visitor. She rushed down the steps and fell into the arms of a man who had no face, no name, and no real identity. As she allowed his hands to caress her, she suddenly grew afraid. Naomi drew back, but couldn't escape his touch. She fought him, pulling, pushing, and kicking, and when she woke up, she was drenched in sweat despite the coolness of her bedroom.

A fleeting image of her mother, dead, and lying on the linoleum of the kitchen, flooded her mind before she pulled herself out of bed and stumbled to the closet.

19

The clock on her nightstand told her that it was eight in the evening.

Naomi cursed out loud to herself; she had set her alarm for four o' clock that afternoon, but she had clearly turned it off in her sleep. She sat down on the edge of the bed and took a deep breath.

Her room in the house trailer reminded her of her bedroom in her mother's house. Her father had gone there and packed up her things for her. Naomi had been reluctant to return. She still blamed herself for her mother's death and hadn't wanted to walk through the kitchen where her mother had died.

The town of Witchfire was on the other side of Pennsylvania, at least an hour and a half from her previous dwelling in Quakertown. It was an hour and a half if you were driving fast in light traffic, two hours if you were consigned to traveling at the speed limit. Although Naomi had a couple of friends in Quakertown, she had chosen not to call them or visit them, partly because she never wanted to go back there. She also assumed that they must not be very good friends if they hadn't bothered to track her down after she had mysteriously disappeared. No one had made an effort to find her.

Naomi stepped out of her pajamas and her underwear. She walked naked to the closet and selected a pair of beat-up jeans, a t-shirt, underwear and a worn pair of socks. As she crossed the bedroom, stepping thoughtlessly in front of the window that faced the woods behind her father's

20

house, she cocked her head and listened.

Outside the trailer, something scurried. Nothing separated Naomi from the night air except for the half-open window and the torn screen. The other bedroom window housed the air conditioner, which she had turned off after opening the other window.

She could hear the crickets. A breeze shuddered through the tall grasses outside her window. Something moved in the thicket. Naomi hurriedly slipped into her panties and t-shirt. She pushed her shaggy hair out of her eyes and behind her ears. She peered out the window, but saw nothing amidst the early night shadows that hung soundlessly between the house trailer and the stretch of forestland.

Shrugging, she pulled on her jeans and socks and put on her steel-toed boots. She never left the house without her wallet. She attached the chain to her pants and clipped her key ring onto the front of her jeans. Then, forgetting the furtive sounds outside her window, she turned out the light, passed by her small living room and kitchen area and went out into the night.

The unnatural light in the garage cast a bright glow on the white Buick. The vehicle was up on the lift and the hood was open. Naomi's mind was elsewhere as she worked on the car, her thoughts drifting back to her recent dreams.

When it was time to take the car for a test drive, she lowered it, dropped the hood and climbed into the driver's seat.

Naomi could say one positive thing for the car, and that was that the CD player worked. She had installed it herself. As she backed out of the garage, the car seemed to be running all right. Her favorite song came on and she couldn't resist turning up the stereo.

The air conditioner didn't work, but Naomi didn't care. She rolled down the window and piloted the car down the long driveway that led among the tall oaks and sycamores.

The road wound past a little-known bridge that, although it couldn't support the weight of a car, was a perfect path to take through the forest. Naomi couldn't see it in the dark, but she knew it was there.

It happened more or less all at once. The wiring in the car needed to be replaced and sometimes the stereo would cut out. It did so now. The lead singer's voice drifted into nothingness and Naomi cursed as the steering grew tighter and the car almost refused to turn. Belts squealed and Naomi was forced to hit the brakes when a figure darted out in front of her. It looked like a man, but it was too dark to see his face. The headlights gave her a limited view of a dark blue shirt and black pants just before the man jumped headlong into the woods and disappeared from view.

Naomi put the car in reverse and backed up the way she had come. She couldn't steer very well, but once she

22

reached a straightaway, it was a little easier for her to back the car all the way up the driveway and toward the garage. Once she reached the front of the garage, she turned off the car and left it in the driveway.

The sight of the strange man running through the woods had chilled her. She turned off the lights in and around the garage and hurried back to the house trailer, where she locked the door, turned on all the lights and glanced momentarily at the dark house where her father lived. He often went to bed early; he was certainly asleep by now.

Naomi picked up the phone and called Oliver. Suddenly, she was reluctant to spend the rest of the night by herself.

Chapter 5: The Night Kitchen

Naomi drew the curtains on all the windows and busied herself with washing dishes in the little kitchen of the house trailer. When she had finished, she went into the living room and sat down on the couch. Her father had helped her acquire the furniture, and Naomi was very grateful for it. She had her own space; she had her own little house. Still, being alone sometimes made her nervous. Even though the curtains were drawn and the living room was very cozy with its thick carpeting, bright light, and blue lava lamp, Naomi couldn't help but feel as though she were naked in a room crowded with people.

When someone knocked on her front door, she startled and jumped to her feet. "Who's there?" she demanded.

"It's me, Oliver. You okay in there?"

Naomi breathed a sigh of relief and threw open the door. "Thank God," she mumbled. "I've been losing my mind in here."

"Everything okay?" Oliver wrapped his arms around her and gave her a playful kiss on the cheek.

Naomi crumpled on the couch, her head in her hands. Oliver sat beside her. "I guess everything's not okay," Oliver said, when she didn't reply to his question.

"No, it's not. I hate being alone and in the dark."

"Afraid of things that go bump in the night?"

25

"You could say that."

"I didn't see any boogie monsters when I got here." Oliver smirked.

"I'm serious," Naomi snapped. Her annoyed expression dissipated when Oliver began to rub her back.

"Sorry," he said. "Before I got here, I was watching Vincent Price—House on Haunted Hill. I guess it got to my head. *Spill.* I'm listening."

Naomi told him about her groggy awakening, about getting dressed and about hearing the strange noises outside her bedroom window. She explained that it had been too dark to see anything. She had eventually assumed that a skunk or one of the neighborhood cats had caused the noises. "So I went outside to work on my car," she continued.

Naomi told him about the issues with the Buick, about driving through the woods and about the CD player cutting out. She paused.

"Then what?" Oliver asked.

"Then somebody ran out in front of the car and I had to slam on the brakes, not that I was going very fast."

"You're kidding," Oliver interrupted.

"No, not at all. It was a man. I didn't get a good look at him."

"You don't think . . . ."

"I *do.* Oliver, I'm scared." Naomi's voice cracked.

Her friend put an arm around her. With his free hand, he held hers. "Maybe it was just a fluke . . . or

26

something," Oliver rambled.

"What kind of a fluke? It's after dark and some guy is running across the driveway in front of my car? There are woods on both sides; there are hardly any buildings near my father's shop. What was he doing out there? He was coming from the direction of the house."

"You think he was watching you?"

"I hate to say it, but what else could he have been doing? My father owns the forest around this place, too. There are no trespassing signs everywhere. He's the only one who goes hunting in these woods and that man wouldn't have been hunting."

"Naomi, calm down. It might not be what you think. Clearly, he was trespassing, but what if he was trying to break into the garage or something? Your dad has a lot of expensive equipment. You should wake him up and tell him about this."

"I'll wait until morning."

"Why?"

"Because I know that man wasn't here to steal from my father. *Something* was outside this trailer."

"An animal," Oliver said furtively. "A cat!"

"It was too big to be a cat, I heard it."

"All right. Enough guessing for now, okay?"

"Okay."

"Let's go to the diner."

Oliver led Naomi out to his car and the two of them drove off. In the passenger seat, Naomi shivered despite

27

the warmth. She couldn't help but think that something, *someone*, had been watching her through the window. Someone had seen her standing naked in her bedroom. No man had ever seen Naomi without her clothes on. It terrified her to think that some stranger had watched her get undressed, that a man had seen her body without her consent. She lapsed into a stony silence as Oliver drove down the main drag of Witchfire, toward the bright neon lights of the Night Kitchen.

Outside the diner, a man stood in the shadows strumming a guitar. When he wasn't playing, he would go in for a cup of coffee and a bite to eat. He felt most comfortable standing in the summer heat, leaning against the brick building, his guitar in his hands. A beat up overturned hat sat beside him. Inside it, coins glimmered under the dim light. The man played a song that he remembered from his childhood, silently mouthing the lyrics, and staring into the night sky.

A car pulled up. Two people walked up to the front door of the diner. The woman gave the guitarist a strange look before entering the diner. It didn't faze the musician, because he was used to strange looks.

Naomi and Oliver took a booth in the corner of the restaurant. The place wasn't as packed as it usually was on a Friday night. Naomi found herself searching the place for a man in a blue t-shirt. When she saw none, she sighed and leaned back in her seat.

"Try to calm down," Oliver advised.

The server, a woman who was used to seeing the night crew from Whellaby's Grocer throughout the week, came over to their table. "What'll it be for you two? Coffee?" she asked.

Oliver glanced at Naomi, who nodded. He looked up at the waitress. "Yes, for both of us. Thanks, Rochelle."

"Sure thing. You ready to order?"

"I don't think so."

"All right, I'll be back in a minute with your coffee." The waitress hurried away and Naomi slumped against the table, her chin resting on her forearm.

"How about we talk about something a little more cheerful?" Oliver suggested. Naomi replied with a short grunt, so her friend kept talking. "I only have to take two more classes before I get my degree," he said happily.

"That's fantastic," Naomi mumbled.

"You don't sound happy about it."

"Forgive me if I'm a little distracted. A man with a blue shirt just walked in."

Oliver turned. "That guy looks like he's in his seventies. He's got a cane, Naomi."

"He could be spry for his age."

"I honestly doubt that a man of seventy-something is going to be launching himself over brier bushes in the

29

middle of the night, much less trespassing."

"You never know. And it's not the middle of the night. It's not even ten o' clock yet."

"Still, I think you got my point." Oliver turned back and folded his hands on the table.

A moment later, the waitress appeared with their coffee. "Decide what you'd like yet?" Rochelle asked.

"I'll have a grilled cheese sandwich and some fries," Oliver said.

"All right. For you?"

Naomi looked up, blinking. "Perogies and a strawberry milkshake."

"I thought you said you hadn't eaten dinner?" Oliver pried.

"All right. I'll take the eggplant panini sandwich," Naomi said, rolling her eyes. "I guess I am pretty hungry."

"Is that all?" Rochelle glanced up from her notepad.

"That's it."

A moment later, when the waitress had disappeared into the kitchen, Oliver watched Naomi stare distractedly out the window. "I think Rochelle thinks you're a little weird. She's probably wondering why I'm hanging out with you," Oliver pointed out.

"She's got issues," Naomi mumbled.

"I think you're the one with issues. I wish you would stop worrying."

Naomi sighed. "I'm sorry, Oliver. You're right. That guy *could* have been a burglar."

30

"You should really call your dad and tell him," Oliver warned.

"I don't have a cell phone."

"Neither do I."

"That leaves us at an impasse then, doesn't it?"

Naomi went out front and checked the payphone, but there was a large 'Out of Order' sign hanging overtop it. When the food arrived, she ate with gusto, pausing between bites to breathe. After an hour or so of deep thought, Naomi came to the conclusion that Oliver had probably been right from the start. The man she had seen was most likely a thief. In the morning, she would tell her dad to be on the lookout.

Around midnight, the musician came inside and sat at the bar. His guitar was strapped over his back. He was the only one sitting there. The waitress brought him a pot of coffee without even bothering to ask him if he wanted any. Before the previous week, Naomi hadn't been in the Night Kitchen very often. It appeared that this strange man was a regular.

He was probably around Naomi's age, maybe a little older. He had curly hair that was pulled back in a ponytail and a playful smile as he joked with the restaurant manager. As Naomi finished her milkshake, she stared out the window. When she looked up after a few minutes, she saw the stranger leave the diner and walk out into the night.

31

Chapter 6: Watching Movies until Sunup

"So you didn't tighten the belt enough?" Oliver asked as they left the Night Kitchen.

"Yeah, it was something dumb like that. I thought I knew how tight it had to be, but I didn't torque it enough. I'm an idiot."

"You're not an idiot. You're just a human that makes mistakes. You can do more with cars than I can."

Naomi shrugged. They were driving down Maine Street at one in the morning, the yellow light of the dim street lamps flooding the inside of the car with an artificial glow.

"I'll tell you a secret," Oliver said.

"What's that?"

He grinned somewhat bashfully. "I don't know how to change my headlights."

"Oliver!"

As they drove down the winding driveway that led to the auto repair shop, and Naomi's house trailer, they saw no figures in the trees, and no strange men jumping through the bushes. Despite this, Naomi couldn't hide her nervousness.

"I don't want to be alone," she said.

"You want to watch some movies?" Oliver turned the tight corner in the driveway. In the short distance, they saw the pole light by the garage.

"That sounds good," Naomi agreed. "But nothing scary. None of your Vincent Price movies."

"Of course not." He parked the car under the pole light and turned off the engine. "Shall we?"

"Sure."

They both stepped out of the car and shut the doors. As they walked toward her father's house and the large side yard, they passed the Buick, the driver's side window still wide open. In the back of the property, the porch light on the house trailer guided them to the front door. Naomi unlocked it and they stepped into her living room, shutting the door tightly behind them.

While Naomi fixed a plate of snacks (some cheese and crackers) and got a couple of beers from the fridge, Oliver perused the framed photographs that hung on the walls. When Naomi walked out into the living room, Oliver pointed at one of the pictures.

"Is this your mom?" he asked.

"*Was* my mom, yeah," Naomi said.

"I'm sorry. I know you've told me that story before."

"It's okay. It's been almost a year. I'm kind of getting used to talking about it."

"That's good, I guess." He looked at the photo for a moment longer. Naomi's mother was standing by a tree during the summer, her curvy figure clothed in shorts and a tank top. Her short brown hair was decorated with a silver butterfly clip. She had been forty-four when she

34

had died. "Your mom was really pretty," Oliver said, hoping that the compliment would break the utter silence that had enveloped the room.

"Yeah, well." Naomi set up the DVD player and curled up on the couch. "It runs in the family," she said jokingly.

Oliver sat down on the couch and laughed. "Well, you're right anyway. It does seem to run in the family."

"Don't bother flattering me, Oliver."

Oliver shrugged. "What movie did you put in?"

"History of the World. I need a good laugh."

The two of them got settled and popped open their beers. They watched Mel Brooks' movies until the sun came up. When Naomi opened her eyes after a long nap, Oliver was gone. The television had turned itself off and she could hear birds chirping outside.

Chapter 7: Suicide

Two weeks after the strange man had run carelessly in
front of Naomi's Buick, Alexis Nevid was sitting in her
office smoking a cigar. She hadn't had much work lately.
Her last client had gotten fired just after hiring her. Due
to her great fondness for cigars, the client promised that he
would bring her as many Cuban cigars as she requested.
Every year, he would go fishing in Canada. He had just
come back from one of his trips with a fresh batch of
cigars. Alexis enjoyed the smokes, but wished that the
man had been able to pay her properly for following his
wife around.

Adultery cases—that was all she got these days. And
even those were few and far between. She often wished
that she'd stuck with the police force instead of going
solo.   Being a private detective wasn't all it was cracked
up to be. The only thing she really liked about it was that
she could make her own hours. She could say yes or no to
any client that walked into her office.

"At this point, I'd say yes to anybody for any
assignment," she mumbled. For a moment, Alexis stared
at the door to her cramped office. When no one came in,
she sighed and leaned back in her chair.

No sooner had she started talking to herself, a man
burst in and slammed the door behind him. Alexis shot

from her seat.

"Jesus Christ, you nearly gave me a heart attack!" she shouted angrily.

"Sorry, I'm in a hurry. I need you over there before the cops attract the press. The last thing I need is the Witchfire Herald spreading rumors about my store!"

"Your store? Wait a minute, you look familiar. Aren't you . . . ."

"Spencer Whellaby." He sat down in the chair across from her desk. "I can pay you as much as you like, just get over there right now before the press does! I can't handle this. I'm getting much too old for this kind of thing."

As soon as he'd mentioned money, Alexis was grabbing her bag and heading for the door. In it, she had her notebook and her camera. "All right, lead the way. You can tell me what's going on in the car."

Old man Whellaby drove like a teenager. He screeched around turns and sped down the main road, heedless of the speed limit. His recklessness was making Alexis nervous. She was even more upset when he admitted that the case she was being hired to handle revolved around a suicide.

"A *suicide*?" she exclaimed as she dug her fingernails into the seat cushions. "I'm a detective, for crying out loud! I've taken on a couple murder cases, but a suicide?

This isn't a case for a detective; this is for the mortuary to handle! Let me the hell out of this car!"

"You don't understand," Whellaby insisted. He pulled into the parking lot of the grocery store at five after six a.m. "The police say it was a suicide. I think it was a murder."

"Murder? Why?"

"Marty Timmson would have never killed himself. He was the happiest guy I know. He had a wife and a little daughter, one year old. All that man talked about was how damned perfect his wife was. Made the rest of us jealous."

"So what? No one ever expects a suicide." Alexis got out of the Lexus after Whellaby parked. "Some of the 'happiest' people in the world have killed themselves," Alexis argued. "I knew a kid when I was in college. He had a gorgeous girlfriend, a perfect family, and a full scholarship." She ran to keep up with Whellaby as they headed toward the group of policemen and the ambulance that was sitting in front of the store, its lights flashing. "That guy jumped off a bridge in our senior year," Alexis explained. "Nobody could figure out why. Who found Timmson, anyway?"

"One of the employees," Whellaby explained.

There were three men in blue standing on the sidewalk. One of them was wearing khakis and a t-shirt; he was the sheriff. Alexis caught her breath as they slowed to a stop beside the cops. The detective couldn't believe how quick on his feet Mr. Whellaby was.

"Good morning, Sheriff Bardnt." Alexis nodded in his direction.

"What are you doing out here, Ms. Nevid?"

"Following up on a case for Mr. Whellaby."

The middle-aged cop ran a hand through his thin hair. "There's nothing to follow up on," he said. "It was a suicide." He glanced over to the front door when several men with a stretcher and a body emerged from the store. "Manager of the store hung himself in the boiler room."

Alexis glanced at Mr. Whellaby, and then back at the sheriff. "Mr. Whellaby seems to think there was more involved. I would have liked to have seen the body before you moved it."

"No need. Had to get it out of there, anyway. The night shift is almost over, the morning people are just getting here and we can't have bodies hanging around for all the employees to see."

"You've made your point, Sheriff."

"If you're so insistent, you can take a look at the body once it gets to the morgue."

"I just might do that," Alexis said. "I'm a friend of Traci Corin."

The sheriff nodded knowingly. Traci ran the downtown mortuary. There would probably be an autopsy and Traci was likely to be the one to conduct it. Alexis would have a talk with her. She didn't think this case would go anywhere, but at the very least, she could get a bit of money out of Spencer Whellaby. He could afford it, after all. He was one of the richest men in town.

Naomi craned her head so she could see out the front door. She and the other employees were gathered at the front of the store. Naomi had the best view.

"What do you see, Naomi?" Geoffrey asked impatiently.

"Uh . . . ." She pushed her luck and took a few steps forward. A cop who was patrolling the inside of the store peered at her suspiciously. "There's a woman out there. She's got a badge on her shirt, but she doesn't have a uniform on. She's standing with some old man in a suit."

"Mr. Whellaby?" Oliver asked.

"Maybe," Naomi said.

She watched the cops and the woman for a moment. The woman was tall and a little muscular. She had long black hair and the features of a Native American. She looked annoyed; her hands were placed firmly on her hips. A black bag was slung over one shoulder and she was wearing a sleeveless black shirt and black jeans.

"That lady sure looks pissed," Naomi commented. She stepped back. "Wait, I think they're coming in."

The whole night crew, including Keith Ryan, stepped back and watched. The old man walked in followed by the exotic woman, her silver badge catching the florescent

41

light.

"I can't believe it. I'm two weeks into the job and they find a body," Naomi mumbled.

"Who found him, anyway?" Oliver wondered.

"I'm not sure. I'm just wondering when it would have happened. I guess while we were all working last night?"

Sheriff Bardnt looked at Mr. Whellaby expectantly. Somewhere near the front of the store, a customer was told to leave by a tired-looking cop. Behind the cluster of night crew employees, cashiers and customer service people stood staring or talking nervously amongst themselves. Some people had left at the first sign of a death, but many had stayed to feed their curiosity.

Mr. Whellaby grabbed a phone by the front check-out and switched it to the intercom so that everyone in the store could hear him. "Everyone, your attention please!" All eyes turned to him. "I'm closing the store, everyone go home." After putting the phone back, he turned around and talked with the strange woman. People began filing out.

Naomi was the last one to leave. She couldn't find any solid information on where the store manager had been found. So far, she had heard that he had hung himself in the back room, in the manager's office, in the seafood department, *and* in the deli. As she stood there glancing about, a cop turned to her, his hand on his belt.

"Ma'am, you'll have to leave, please."

"Oh," Naomi mumbled. "Sorry." She caught up with

42

Geo and Oliver in the parking lot. Oliver drove her home.

Chapter 8: All in a Night's Work

The store was closed for five days out of respect for Marty Timmson and his family. Naomi had heard that a lot of people went to Timmson's funeral and that there hadn't been a dry eye in the entire place. If there had been anything negative to say about Timmson, those words had died with him.

Naomi bit into a grilled cheese sandwich, chewed, and then wiped her hands on a napkin. "It's going to be weird, huh?" she said.

Across from her, Oliver and Geo agreed.

The Night Kitchen was busy as usual. It was nine o' clock, almost time to head to Whellaby's.

"You can't keep the only grocery store in Witchfire closed for too long," Geoffrey pointed out. "People need food and nobody wants to drive all the way to Montoursville." Geo finished his burger and sipped at his coke. "It said in the paper that he hung himself."

"It was worse than that," Oliver said.

"Worse?" Naomi finished her grilled cheese.

"Yeah, worse. You know what they say he hung himself with?"

Naomi glanced up. "What?" She watched the strange curly-haired man walk into the restaurant with his guitar and sit at the bar. Naomi looked back at Oliver.

Oliver leaned forward. His glasses caught the light, revealing small reflections in the lenses. "Bale wires," Oliver said.

"*What?*"

"Bale wires."

"I heard you, I just can't believe it. How does that work?"

"Simple," Geo said, grinning. He made the motion of choking himself and let his tongue hang out over his lips. His eyes rolled back in his head.

"Must you?" Naomi said, sighing. "I already have the image in my head, I don't need reinforcement."

At nine-thirty, when they were leaving the Night Kitchen, Naomi bumped into the curly-haired guitarist in the lobby. He turned his head to see whom he had collided with.

"Sorry. I didn't mean to bump into you." The guitarist had a nice, quiet, sincere voice. He smiled.

"No, it was my fault," Naomi said. "Have a good night."

"You as well."

The guitarist left through the door on the right hand side of the lobby. Naomi and her friends headed out through the door on the left.

In the back room at Whellaby's grocery store, two men were talking adamantly about the recent suicide. One of them was Ramsey, the young man who was training Naomi in aisles eight, nine, and ten.

Ramsey had thick and messy dark hair and he was beginning to sprout a scruffy beard. In his Whellaby's uniform and baggy black slacks, he looked a tad unkempt. His shirt wasn't tucked in and was hanging low over his thighs. He was looking through the back stock for aisle eight, the pet aisle, and piling cases of cat and dog food onto a U-frame.

One of Ramsey's coworkers, Shark Bite, was standing nearby. He was rambling about the suicide, saying that he didn't know where Marty Timmson had been found, but that he hoped it hadn't been in the men's bathroom.

Shark Bite was a middle-aged balding man whose black jeans always seemed as though they were pulled up too high. In his late thirties, his hobbies had included water sports. Shark Bite acquired his nickname by going scuba diving somewhere in the ocean and running amuck of an injured hammerhead. A huge and lengthy scar on his right arm was often put forth as evidence when people failed to believe his story. Presently, he was wearing his short-sleeved uniform shirt, which allowed for the unsightly scar to provide ample proof for anyone who happened to see him at a close range.

"I heard Timmson hung himself with bale wires," Ramsey said. He had a quiet voice and often had to repeat himself, but this time, Shark seemed to be listening.

"Bale wires? Is that what you said?"

"Yeah. In the boiler room."

"Where'd you hear that?"

"From Naomi and Oliver. I'm not sure where Oliver got it. He says he knows somebody that's good friends with Sheriff Bardnt's wife."

"That doesn't surprise me," Shark admitted. "In a small town, the only thing that surprises me is something like Timmson killing himself."

"It doesn't seem right, does it? Everybody said he was a happy guy," Ramsey mused.

"Yeah, well. That's what they always say about somebody who kills himself. Anyway." He stepped a little bit closer to Ramsey and lowered his voice. "Let's face it; neither of us liked Timmson all that much. Maybe it's better that . . . ."

"I wouldn't say that if I were you. The funeral was only yesterday."

"Sorry." Shark had always been one for speaking his mind. "But I don't care how many people say that Timmson was a nice, happy guy. I still say he was a real bastard."

Ramsey finished stacking the pet food just as Naomi walked into the back room with Oliver. It was ten-thirty. That night, all they had was a seven hundred piece load; that meant seven hundred cases of product to put on the shelves. The five-person night crew was used to loads of

48

up to a thousand nine hundred.

Naomi supposed that the recent lack of business was due to the body that had been carted out of the store only five days earlier. She knew where the boiler room was. The closed door at the end of the hall in the back room had become the equivalent of a puzzle piece to her. She didn't know where that little room fit into Timmson's living misery, and she didn't want to find out.

Naomi stood in the pet aisle staring at the shelf for five minutes. She began to feel conspicuous. Ramsey was putting all the dog treats on the shelf. He had his earphones on and Naomi felt a tinge of guilt crawl up her spine. Ramsey had been working at Whellaby's for a little over a year and he was a fast worker. Naomi had hardly been there at all. After a five-day gap, she had almost completely lost what little speed she had been building up. She also felt like an outcast.

Naomi was the only woman on the night crew. She had already caught on that no one on the night crew, not even her boss Keith Ryan, thought of her as female. Maybe it was her haircut, but it was probably the way she carried herself. It might have had something to do with the grease stains on her fingers. Then again, it was possible that everyone on the night crew was so undeniably eccentric that a woman lifting and throwing around boxes of heavy laundry detergent and motor oil didn't come close to seeming strange.

Naomi stared at the shelf some more. She had allowed herself to get lost in thought and now she couldn't remember what she was looking for. She turned the can around in her palm and peered at the UPC number on the back of the label. It was some kind of salmon cat food. She knew she could find its spot on the shelf by matching the UPC number with its duplicate on the label.

Just as she thought she might be getting somewhere, she heard footsteps and turned. Ramsey was standing there. He pulled off his headphones. "Need some help?" he asked.

"Yeah." She handed him the can. In the crook of her left arm, she held the rest of the case.

Ramsey managed to find the right spot within seconds. "There it is," he said, placing the can on the shelf.

Naomi rolled her eyes. "Sorry," she mumbled.

"That's okay. You're new." Ramsey returned to his work.

Naomi glanced up from the case of cat food just in time to see the Cat Lady park her cart at the end of the aisle. The woman meandered down the aisle clutching a collection of coupons.

The Cat Lady worked in a department store on the other side of town and spent more time at Whellaby's than the employees did. She was always on the lookout for the latest bargain and would come in three times a week, sometimes more, to use up all of her coupons. She toddled over to the cat food, her earrings jangling, and peered at the shelf. Naomi stepped aside.

"Hmm, let's see," the Cat Lady said. She glanced at her coupons and then began to pick cans off the shelf. "How are you tonight?" she asked.

Naomi smiled. "All right." It was a lie, but it would have been a waste of time for Naomi to tell the woman how she really felt.

"Say, I hate to ask, but I heard that someone . . . ."

"Yeah." Naomi nodded, shifting a case of cat food in her hands. "It was the store manager. He hung himself in the boiler room."

"Oh, my. Yes, I saw something about that in the paper." The Cat Lady shook her head sadly. "What a shame."

"Yeah," Naomi agreed.

The Cat Lady continued to talk, but Naomi wasn't listening. She was lost in a universe of thought and she wasn't sure that she wanted to turn back.

The night dragged on. With such dull work to occupy her hands, Naomi had a lot of time to think. She talked to a number of regular customers, including Kenny and Lisa, an interesting couple that often came into the store around midnight.

Nearing lunch break, an eccentric middle-aged man with brown hair, glasses and rotten teeth entered aisle nine and asked Naomi where he could find the canned fruit. As he sauntered away, a basket hanging from his elbow, his purple jacket swishing, Naomi couldn't help but notice how strange he was. As each day went by at her new job at Whellaby's Grocer, she began to think that all of the strangest folks in Witchfire were apt to only emerge at night, when they could slip off into the shadows, unnoticed by the general populace.

Chapter 9: Jargon at the Coral Reef Tavern

It was a Wednesday night. Naomi and Geoffrey were
scheduled off from work. Having voiced her opposition to
staying home by herself, Geo invited Naomi to his band's
performance at a bar on the other side of town. Now that
Geoffrey had gotten his car fixed, he could drive her. The
bar was relatively new, having only been a part of
Witchfire for a year or so, but it had become the hub of
social gatherings rather quickly, second only to the Blue
Plate Diner on Maine Street.

A crescent moon hung in the sky; a sliver that Naomi
thought resembled the sharp edge of her fingernail. It was
nine o' clock and Naomi was riding in the passenger side
of Geo's car. She was staring out the open window and
into the night.

"See something you like?" Geo asked, one hand on the
wheel and the other on the shifter knob.

"Only the moon," Naomi said. "It looks so delicate. It
looks like if I could reach it, I could snap it in half."

"Everything's like that," Geo said. "In a way."

"I guess so," Naomi mumbled.

"Are you okay?"

"Sort of. Life's been kind of hectic lately. It seems
like ever since my mom died, things have gone
disastrously downhill." She thought of the man in the

blue shirt and shivered. "There're thieves running around on my dad's property, managers hanging themselves left and right at Whellaby's."

Geoffrey had to laugh at Naomi's gross over-exaggeration. "It was only Timmson. Damn shame, but I would bet you fifty bucks that half the people in that store are secretly happy he's dead."

"Geo!"

"It's true. He wasn't exactly the nicest guy. People just say you're nice after you're dead because it makes them feel better about themselves." He paused, shaking his head. "I had a few of my own run-ins with Timmson, you know."

"You did?"

"Sure I did. Remember when I had that second job at the library? This was only a few months ago. I told them I needed off one night because I had to work at the library in the morning and play a show the next evening; I wouldn't have gotten any sleep. Timmson barked in my face that I'd better decide which job was more important. After that, I wouldn't even give him the time of day."

"It's not nice to speak ill of the dead," Naomi grumbled.

"But you see what I mean, don't you? He wasn't exactly popular."

"Yeah, yeah." Naomi looked out the window again and watched the shadows among the trees as they sped by Horizon Family Park.

Geoffrey took a right turn by the park and headed down Oak Tree Avenue. They passed several store fronts and a few houses. The post office sat nestled in between a few of those buildings, right next door to the fire department. About a quarter of a mile down the road from that was the Coral Reef Tavern, a tacky looking structure that had been built to look like some kind of undersea getaway.

While Geoffrey parked his car across the street from the bar, Naomi watched a group of girls walk into the establishment, their curvaceous bodies swaying in tight skirts or jeans, high heels clicking on the pavement. Naomi looked down at her own attire. She was wearing a pair of jeans that were stained with engine grease. Despite the fact that she had washed her hands after working on her car, there were still grease stains on her fingers and dirt under her nails. She was wearing a t-shirt that read, 'Avoid the Hangover, Keep Drinking,' and had a black hooded jacket with her in case she got cold later. Her wallet was attached to her pants by a chain and the outfit was complete with a pair of steel-toed boots. These were her garage clothes and she hadn't bothered to change.

The evening had brought with it a slight chill, so Naomi was comfortable. Despite this, she had a feeling that she was about to feel a little out of place.

"You didn't tell me I was supposed to dress up," she said.

Geo had been distracted momentarily by his satellite

55

radio. He turned off the car and looked at Naomi. "Huh?"

"Never mind," Naomi mumbled.

The bar was a lot bigger on the inside than it had looked from the street. The front door opened into a large foyer that was surrounded on all sides by fish tanks that had been built into the walls. Naomi stared distractedly through the tanks, watching the wavering shadows of people on the other side, their images distorted slightly by the water.

Geo's band had already set up most of the equipment. Geo led Naomi to a small table near the stage and went back to the car to get an amp and his guitar. Naomi ordered a beer and made herself comfortable.

As the show went on, Naomi sat alone at the little table, watching the people that danced and walked past her, drinks in their hands. Women in tight clothing moved to the beat, shooting flirty glances at the band members as they played. Naomi sat back and sighed, feeling all the more awkward in her jeans and t-shirt.

She glanced around the room as she listened to Geo sing. The bar was dimly lit, which lent to the undersea atmosphere. Fish tanks all around the room displayed ocean environments and brightly colored coral. The soft blue light played on the features of those who sat at the bar and talked, their cheeks flush from alcohol.

That was when Naomi turned her head and caught the eye of a man who sat on the opposite side of the room at the bar. She wouldn't have noticed him had it not been for the fact that he was staring right at her. When he realized that she had seen him, he smiled and turned away, his piercing blue eyes surveying the room and then saying hello to another man who walked up beside him.

Naomi shook her head. It was impossible that a man like that had been looking at her. He was very handsome, possibly in his late twenties. From what Naomi could see, he was wearing a dark blue t-shirt and a black button up long-sleeved shirt overtop. His blond hair was short and he had a neatly trimmed goatee and a warm, inviting smile.

Naomi thought sure that she was blushing. She had been sitting there for a little over an hour and a half, nursing the same half-empty glass of beer, and she knew from experience that alcohol was apt to play tricks on her mind. She looked behind her to see if there was another woman sitting nearby, but she didn't see anybody. She recalled the expression she had seen on the man's face. If she wasn't mistaken, it had been one of interest, intrigue and curiosity. Her first instinct told her that it had been curiosity of a sexual nature.

Naomi gulped down the rest of her beer. "That's impossible," she said to herself. Then she stood up and went to the bar. Without thinking, she sat almost exactly across from the blue-eyed man, who was talking to his

57

friend and holding an empty shot glass in his left hand. Naomi ordered another lager and waited for the busy bartender to bring her the drink.

In the meantime, a woman who had been sitting nearby stood up and headed for the bathroom. What happened next made Naomi wonder if she should grow her hair long.

A man tapped her on the shoulder. "Hey, man, are you saving this seat for your girlfriend?"

Naomi turned and looked him straight in the eye. "Excuse me?"

The older drunk appeared surprised. "Oh," he mumbled. "I thought you were . . . I thought . . . Sorry." Then he disappeared into the crowd.

Naomi sighed heavily. When the bartender brought her the lager, she took a long, grateful drink.

On the way out the door at one-thirty in the morning, Naomi crossed paths with the handsome blond. He said hello and looked as if he were about to introduce himself when Naomi pushed past him and into the humid outdoors. She met up with Geo by his car.

"Are you all right?" Geo finished a cigarette and dropped the butt on the pavement. "You look pissed."

"I am," Naomi grumbled. They both climbed into the car. "Some dude mistook me for a man."

58

"Huh?" Geo pulled out of the parking spot and headed down the street.

"Yeah. I look so masculine, apparently, that he thought I was . . . I don't know. That was ridiculous."

Geo turned down the radio and gave Naomi a meaningful look at the next stop sign. "You don't look like a man. He was just wasted. What about that guy who was giving you looks all night?"

"What guy?"

"The blond one."

Naomi gulped. "So I wasn't imagining that?"

"No, I saw him. He tried to say hi to you and you blew him off."

"Did I?" Suddenly, Naomi felt awful. She had spent so much time feeling badly for herself that she had completely refused to believe that any attractive man could be interested in her while she was wearing her greasy clothes and boots. She looked at Geo. "He really was looking at me, wasn't he?"

"Yeah, and not to sound . . . you know . . . but he wasn't that bad looking, either."

"No, he wasn't," Naomi admitted.

"Look, don't beat yourself up over this stuff. It's not worth it. You want to have a drink at your place?"

"Sure, I guess. Maybe that will make me feel better." Unfortunately, she knew it wouldn't.

Chapter 10: To Crawl From a Cardboard Baler

Naomi hadn't seen Roy in several days. In the morning, after sleeping off a hangover, she walked from her trailer to his house. She hadn't bothered to dress. She was wearing her pajamas and hadn't put shoes on. It was already hot outside and it wasn't even eight in the morning. She knew it would be cool inside the house.

Naomi crept in through the back door and greeted her father's house cat, Tammy. Then she went into the living room where she found Roy enjoying his morning cup of coffee.

"Hey, Dad."

"Oh, Naomi! Have a seat. I feel like I haven't seen you in ages."

Naomi shrugged and sat down on the couch. "Three days or so."

"Want some breakfast?"

"Sure."

Roy went into the kitchen. Naomi heard the frying pan clank against the stove. Then she heard his voice again. "Listen, the other day . . . ." He trailed off. "We're out of bread. I guess you'll have to eat your eggs without toast."

"That's okay." Naomi curled up on the couch, clutching her stomach. "Geo was over last night and we had a bit to drink. I'd rather not have a heavy breakfast."

"Understood."

"What was that you were saying about the other day?" Naomi sighed and closed her eyes.

"Oh, right. I think somebody tried to break into the garage."

"Huh?" Naomi's eyes popped open and she shot upright.

"It looked like somebody tried to pry open the back door. I wasn't going to bother telling you about it until now. I don't really know what to do about it. I told the cops, but there's nothing they can do except have a patrol car swing by the end of the driveway every now and then."

"Dad . . . ."

"Yeah, hon?"

"There's something I forgot to tell you." Naomi forced herself to stand up and go into the kitchen. She sat down at the table and told her father everything.

She told him about the strange rustling noise outside her window. She told him that she had felt as though someone were watching her. She also told him about her trouble with the Buick and about the man in the blue shirt darting across the driveway and into the woods.

Roy had forgotten about the eggs. He was standing there, open-mouthed, with a spatula in one hand when he realized that breakfast was burning. "Shit!" he exclaimed. He hurriedly turned around and flipped the eggs. "I hope you don't mind them a little black."

Naomi shrugged. "It's okay. I don't need breakfast just yet. I think what I really need is a glass of water."

"I'm worried about this, Naomi." Roy dumped the contents of the frying pan into the trash basket. "If you saw something, you should have told me." He looked her straight in the eye. "I don't like this one bit." He turned the heat off, put the frying pan back on the stove and sat down across from her.

"I'm sorry," Naomi mumbled. "Oliver even tried to get me to wake you up about it the other night, but I was thinking maybe it was something else. I mean, I thought there was someone just watching me. I didn't think there was a . . . ."

"Hey," he interrupted, "Nobody had better be looking at my daughter; I'd rather have everything in this place get stolen! Don't make it sound as if it's less important than somebody breaking into the garage. You're more important to me than anything, you know that." Roy slumped back in his chair. "I'd better call the police."

"Dad, you don't need to do that."

"What, and let some pervert sneak in here and watch you getting dressed? I don't think so." Roy stood up and went to the phone in the living room.

The image of the man in the blue shirt crossed her mind. She recalled the fleeting glance of his arms and his jeans as he'd jumped across the driveway. Then, Naomi thought of the handsome blond man she had seen at the Coral Reef Tavern. She gulped. "Dad, I'm going back to

63

the trailer," she called. She could hear him in the other room on the phone with the police.

Naomi slipped through the living room, down the short hallway and out the back door. She almost wished that she hadn't told her father about the rustling outside her bedroom window. She knew it was irrational, but she just didn't want to cause any trouble.

"Oliver. Did I wake you up?"

On the other line, Oliver grumbled. "Sort of. Don't worry about it. What's up, Naomi?"

"Somebody *did* try to break into my dad's garage. I told him that I was worried that someone had been watching me and he called the cops."

"Huh?" In his own bedroom across town, Oliver sat up, rubbing his eyes. "I thought we agreed that the person you saw in the driveway was probably just trying to rob the place? I thought you were going to talk to your dad the other morning and have him get new locks or something."

"I don't think it's that simple, Oliver."

"You sound panicky. Are you okay?"

"No." Naomi told him about the Jargon show at the Coral Reef Tavern and the strange man with the piercing blue eyes.

There was a long pause. "Naomi. Why do you think it's so strange that this guy was looking at you in the bar?

I'm not going to lie; the first time we met, I looked at you, too." Suddenly, Oliver felt a little awkward. "Anyway," he added. "It was just some guy."

"What if it was the man who was outside my window?"

"Naomi, you didn't even see anyone outside the window. You don't really know whether there was someone there or not. For crying out loud, it could have been a cat or a raccoon or something. It could have even been a deer; we do live in the country, after all."

"You're not helping."

"I'm sorry. You have valid fears, I know. But you could just as easily be *paranoid*. I know how you can get sometimes. It's easy to tell that you don't trust other people, and that you don't like being around them."

"I know," Naomi mumbled. "That's why I got a job on a night crew."

"See? You could just be imagining things. Of course, on the off-chance that you *aren't* imagining things, just close your curtains at night. Lock all your doors and, I don't know, ask your dad if you can get a Rottweiler."

"Do you work tonight?"

"Yeah. I've worked way too much this past week," Oliver groaned. "Do you need a ride?"

"Actually, I think I'll be able to take the Buick. I'm going to work on it a little bit today and hopefully get it finished. I think I'll feel a lot safer once I can lock myself in my own car."

"Whatever works. Are you going to be okay? I feel bad; I know I sound grumpy."

"Aren't you trying to quit smoking?" Naomi asked.

"Yeah. This is day five without a Newport."

"Then don't worry; I understand. I'll see you at work. Do you want me to bring that photo album I was telling you about?" Naomi was referring to pictures that she and her dad had taken during their recent trip to the mountains. A few months prior, Oliver had expressed interest in seeing them, but both Naomi and Oliver had completely forgotten about it.

"Sure. We can look at them at lunch break. I'll see you later, okay?"

"Okay. Bye, Oliver."

The evening was balmy, but there was a slight breeze. Roy double-checked everything on Naomi's car before allowing her to drive it. He advised her to call him if anything happened. Naomi put the key in the ignition and headed to work.

This time, no one jumped in front of her car and the Buick ran smoothly all the way to Whellaby's. There had been no gathering at the Blue Plate Diner tonight, as Naomi had wanted to get some extra sleep before work. Even so, working on her car had taken a good portion of the day and she had only found three hours in which to rest her head on her pillow.

She parked her car and yawned. Then she went inside
and got to work. It was two-thirty in the morning when it
happened. Naomi was halfway through stocking aisle ten
with Ramsey when they both heard a scream emanate
from the back room. Someone shouted. The voice
sounded unfamiliar and Naomi remembered the assistant
manager that had stayed late to mark down cartloads of
damaged goods. She dropped the case she had been
holding. She and Ramsey hurried toward the back of the
store. On the way, they nearly collided with Keith, the
night manager, who had heard the din as well.

When they arrived in the back room, there was a lot of
screaming coming from the cardboard baler. Naomi's jaw
dropped. She watched as Keith pressed the 'up' button.
The door on the enormous machine began to move
upward as the compactor rose. Inside the empty baler,
crumpled against the bottom of the machine, was the
assistant manager, screaming that Shark Bite had thrown
him in and turned on the compactor.

Chapter 11: The Man from the Coral Reef

Alexis Nevid had been sleeping soundly, until the loud ringing of her cell phone roused her from her troubled dreams.

"Hello?" she answered grumpily.

"Alexis, it's Frank. Frank Gibson."

"Frankie, what the hell are you doing calling me so late? What time is it, anyway?"

"Almost three in the morning. But don't worry, it's important." Frank was sitting at his desk at the police station, twirling a pencil between two fingers. He felt a chill run through him as he thought about the woman on the other line. He had known Alexis for years and they weren't close, but they were close enough that Frank had had plenty of time to develop a slight crush on her. He had hoped that if he supplied her with information, she might be grateful enough to go out with him. It was a long shot, but it was all he had. "Listen," he said. "You should get over to Whellaby's right away."

"The grocery store? Why?" Alexis yawned and sat up in bed.

"I heard along the grapevine that Mr. Whellaby thinks that Timmson didn't kill himself."

"So?"

"So, I heard you were investigating it. It's a laughing

69

stock here at the station, but if there's any truth to it, you might want to talk to the night crew."

"Why?" Alexis had a feeling Frank was baiting her and trying to see how excited she would get if he dropped little hints. She tried not to fall for it and kept her voice level.

"We just got a call from the night manager there. A couple of cops headed over, but you might be able to get there before them if you're quick. One of the employees attacked an assistant manager and walked out. If anybody was murdered, then any random acts of violence at that store should certainly be investigated. So I thought . . . ." There was a click. "Alexis? Are you still there?" Frank hung up the phone. "Shit," he mumbled. "That woman doesn't waste any time."

When Alexis got to Whellaby's, there were already a couple of patrol cars sitting in front of the building, their lights flashing. Alexis parked her car and slammed a fist on the steering wheel. "Damn it," she snapped. The cops had beaten her to the scene.

She reached into the back seat and retrieved her pin-stripe fedora. The night was little balmy, so she was wearing a loose black T-shirt and a pair of black jeans. She put on the hat and swung her long black braid over her shoulder. She made sure that she had her badge and headed into the store.

Truth be told, she hadn't done much work on Whellaby's case. She had looked into a couple things, such as Marty Timmson's history and she had asked around to try and find out if Timmson had any enemies, but she hadn't come up with much. She supposed that if there were any negative information to be found on the store manager of Whellaby's Grocer, she would likely find it in the grocery store itself. Until now, she had only talked to his friends and family about the incident. She'd had a lot of trouble trying to explain to them why a detective was investigating Timmson's death. For the most part, she had managed to wriggle out of the explanations. After getting nowhere, she had been ready to admit her failure to Whellaby.

Now, she was beginning to agree with Whellaby on the suspicious nature of Timmson's death. How does a middle-aged family man go from being perfectly content with his life to suddenly wanting to kill himself? Alexis had turned up no information whatsoever that might point to a mental illness. Still, she couldn't shake the feeling that she was missing something. Perhaps tonight, in the dimly lit grocery store, she would find an answer.

She could tell that the incident was pretty much over with when she saw two cops milling about near the self-check out lanes. One of them was drinking a cup of coffee. The only cashier in the store was standing there with her arms folded over her bosom. Alexis walked right up to the two cops.

71

"What happened?" she asked.

"Go home, Nevid," the fatter one said grumpily. "There's nothing to see here."

"Hey, Whellaby hired me, all right? Call and wake him up if you like. I have a right to be here."

"Sure you do, but you're not going to find anything. The evidence just left."

"Huh?"

"The guy who attacked the assistant manager walked out before we even got here."

Alexis clenched her fists. "If that's true, then what the hell are you doing here drinking a cup of coffee, for God's sake?"

"We've got people out looking for him, but there's not much we can do. We can arrest him for assault, if we find him."

"What the hell kind of cops are you?" Alexis snapped. Several feet away, the night cashier was watching with renewed interest.

"Like I said, Nevid, he ran off. You're welcome to talk to Rey Kustafik, though; he's sitting in the manager's office trying to collect himself. We already got a statement out of him, but he won't let anyone call an ambulance. He keeps insisting he's fine."

The cop, whose name was Edward Triston, finished his coffee and dropped the empty cup in a nearby trashcan. A couple of other police officers appeared at the end of aisle nine, talking quietly. When they walked past Triston and his partner, the four cops exchanged some words. They had already ignored Alexis. Before she could say anything else, they had walked out the front of the store and were getting into their patrol cars.

Alexis headed for the manager's office. She knocked on the door, but didn't wait for someone to open it. When she got inside, she found two men sitting there. Alexis recognized the night manager, Keith Ryan. He was lounging in his chair munching on some crackers, a gallon of iced tea sitting on the desk in front of him. In an armchair across from him, a portly man with a red face sat shaking like a frightened rabbit. Alexis didn't know exactly what had happened, but from what she had heard the cops say, she knew it had been pretty bad.

"Hi, I'm Alexis." She shook hands with the night manager and showed him the badge. "I believe we've met."

"Yeah, you used to shop here a lot," Keith remarked. "Have a seat." He gestured to a leather chair near the door.

Alexis sat down. The man sitting across from Keith had barely acknowledged her presence. "Mr. Whellaby hired me to investigate some things around here," she said. "Would you mind telling me what happened?"

Keith nodded. "According to Rey here, he told Shark Bite to get some pallets out of the back aisle. Shark told him no, they had a little argument and the next thing he knew, Rey was in the bottom of the baler and Shark had closed the gate."

"Shark Bite?" Alexis said, raising an eyebrow.

"Yeah. That's his nickname. His real name's Josh Carter. He's always had a bit of an anger problem, but I never thought it would go this far."

"I see. The cops told me he left."

"Yeah, walked right out." Keith looked at Rey. "Kustafik, are you going to press charges?"

"I . . . I really don't know," the man replied timidly.

Alexis couldn't help but notice that the man's pants were wet.

Keith looked back at the detective. "His wife's coming to pick him up. I don't think he'll be back."

"Do you mind if we speak privately, Mr. Ryan?" Alexis asked.

"Sure." He stood up and headed for the door. "Call me Keith. We can go upstairs to the break room. We'll let Rey calm down in here."

"Sounds good," Alexis said. She followed Keith up the stairs. They sat down in a little alcove where there were tables, chairs and vending machines.

Alexis told Keith why Whellaby had hired her and how the store owner suspected that Marty Timmson's hanging had been forced. Alexis wondered if Keith thought that Shark Bite was capable of trickery, or even murder. Had someone *forced* Marty Timmson to hang himself? And if so, could the murderer be Josh Carter? The thought itself was highly imaginative. How did one go about proving that a man who had committed suicide had actually been *told to do so?*

Downstairs, Naomi, Ramsey and the others had gotten back to work. Everything was okay, no one had been seriously injured and there was still a lot of product to put on the shelves. Apparently, the assistant manager, Rey Kustafik, had been very lucky. The baler had been empty when Shark Bite physically shoved him in, and although Rey had gotten a bump on the head, he had completely refused medical attention. When the compactor had gone down, there had been just enough space so that Rey wasn't crushed to death by the machine. Naomi had to wonder if Shark Bite had meant to kill Rey.

As she put a case of dish soap on the shelf, it was nearly four-thirty in the morning. Naomi was lost in thought when someone walked around the corner and spoke. She jumped a little and turned around. Standing there amongst the cardboard boxes was the strange blue-eyed man from the Coral Reef Tavern. Naomi gulped.

"I'm sorry, did I scare you?" he asked. There was a soft smile on his face, although he appeared slightly nervous.

Naomi stammered and shoved the rest of the soap up on the shelf. "Uh, no, not really," she mumbled.

"I was wondering if you could tell me where the pasta

sauce is."

Naomi tried not to look at him. "Aisle seven," she said quickly. Suddenly, she wasn't holding a case anymore, so she stood there and shoved her hands in her pockets. She had a feeling that she was blushing.

"Thanks." The blond man cocked his head. "Don't you remember me?"

"Um."

"I saw you at the bar the other night. I thought you saw me, but maybe you didn't."

"I did," Naomi mumbled.

"Well, I have to admit, I wanted to ask you to have a drink with me, but I'm not the kind of guy that hits on girls in bars."

Naomi felt as though her mind had just sunk into the bottoms of her shoes. "Um," she said.

"Would you like to go out with me Saturday night?"

"Um."

"I've seen you at Vogler's Auto Repair. Is that where you live?"

Naomi nodded. "Yeah."

"Shall I pick you up at seven?"

Five minutes later, Naomi stood there dumbly, staring at the spot where the blue-eyed man had once been. Somehow, she had said yes to him, and she realized that she had a date for Saturday night. Her mind reeled as she considered the possibilities. How had the blue-eyed man known where she worked, even where she lived? She hadn't even asked him his name, and she hadn't told him what hers was. Before the conversation had even started, the stranger had disappeared around a corner.

"Shit," Naomi mumbled. What if the blue-eyed stranger was the man whom she had seen running across her driveway?

Chapter 12: Frank and Alexis Look for Shark Bite

Adam had parked his rusty van in the lot and was inside the store shopping. When he had chosen four small cups of yogurt, he headed for the self-checkout. Once he reached the front of the store, he heard voices.

"I can't believe they let that guy get away." It was a woman's voice. When Adam rounded the corner, he saw her standing in between the self check-out and the front doors. As he paid for his items, Adam listened.

"They're small town cops, what can I say." The woman's male companion shrugged. He was probably about her age—mid thirties—with dark brown hair, olive skin and bags under his eyes. The woman looked fiery and widely awake, but the man was still yawning.

"Frank, I do appreciate you coming out here to check on things," the woman said. Adam's ears perked up. "It's possible that this Josh Carter is the missing piece to the puzzle. What if he knows something?"

"If he does, we won't know until we find him. And even then, all we can arrest him for is . . . ." Frank trailed off.

Adam had very sharp hearing. His eyesight may have been weakening over the years, but his hearing had seemed to grow stronger. He heard the cop mumble, "There's a customer over there. We'd better go somewhere else."

Alexis finished a cup of coffee that Keith had graciously offered her while they had been talking in the employee lounge. She dropped it into a trashcan and walked toward the lobby.

"Excuse me," said a voice.

Both Alexis and Frank turned to look behind them. A white-bearded man smiled timidly, his left hand in his pocket and a plastic grocery bag in his right. "Yes?" Alexis raised an eyebrow. The man looked familiar to her and she couldn't figure out why.

"I couldn't help but overhear, and I was wondering, were you talking about the man that left the store about thirty minutes ago, perhaps forty minutes?"

Alexis and Frank exchanged a glance. "Maybe," Alexis said. "What did he look like?"

"Oh, a big burly man with a long scar on his arm."

There weren't many people in Whellaby's at night, aside from the night crew. Alexis and Frank exchanged another meaningful look. They both turned back to the customer. "Let's go see if we can borrow the manager's office for a minute, shall we?" Alexis suggested.

Keith was more than willing to allow the private detective and the cop to use his office for a few minutes of privacy. He didn't ask what it was about; he merely left the room and made his rounds to see how the work was coming along.

Alexis sat down behind the manager's desk and crossed her legs, her left ankle resting just above her right knee. She clasped her hands over her stomach and leaned back, her fedora angled slightly over her dark eyes.

Across from her, Adam sat in the armchair. "Hmm, this is comfortable," he said, bouncing slightly. Near the door, Frank yawned.

"What's your name?" Alexis asked the customer.

"Adam Strand," the older man replied.

Alexis made a mental note of the man's name. She and Frank had already introduced themselves. "Tell us more about this guy you saw. What was he wearing?"

"A Whellaby's uniform, actually. He bumped into me. It crossed my mind to report him for being so rude, but I'm not the type to let things bother me."

"I see."

"Is that the man you were looking for?"

"It's likely, since he's the only one of the night crew that left early tonight, and around the *right time*." Alexis looked at Frank.

"It's him, all right," Frank said.

"Did you hear him say anything, Mr. Strand?" Alexis asked.

"Call me Adam." The man smiled. "He did say something, actually. He was on a cell phone. People never pay attention when they're on cell phones."

"What did he say?"

Adam thought for a moment, and then chuckled quietly. "Hang on, I'm thinking."

"Take your time."

All at once, Adam remembered. He waved an index finger in the air. "Rocko!" he exclaimed. "He told some man named Rocko that he was going to meet him at a pub in thirty minutes. He's probably there by now. And, let's see—" Adam appeared to be thinking. "There are only a few bars in Witchfire. There's the Coral Reef Tavern, the Lucky Strike, and the Black Mare." Adam's face glowed. "And there's only one that's open all the time. I have to drive past there to get home at night after I go shopping. The parking lot is usually pretty full."

"The Black Mare," Frank said. "The strip club on Tenth and Broad." Frank looked at his watch. "It's almost happy hour. They serve breakfast during the 'Wild Ponies at Sunrise' show."

"Uh-huh," Alexis said, crossing her arms over her chest. "I see you've been there."

"Once or twice." Frank blushed.

Alexis turned back to Adam again. "Would you mind giving me your phone number?" she asked. "Just in case we have some more questions for you."

"Oh, certainly." Adam found a piece of paper and a pen. "I'm no stranger to this kind of work."

"Oh?" Alexis asked.

"I'm retired now, but I used to be a professor of

Criminology at Temple. I've worked with the cops before, mostly for research for my books."

"Ah-ha! That's where I've seen you! I read a couple of your books. *Studying the Criminal Psyche* and—"

"*Rehabilitation and the Prison System at a Glance*," Adam finished. "Not my best work, but I wrote it for my dissertation."

"No, it was fantastic!" Alexis exclaimed. She took the paper with his number on it, folded it and put it into her pocket.

"Well, I'm glad to meet a fan. I didn't think I had any," Adam said, chuckling again.

When Alexis and Frank left Whellaby's and Adam toddled off to his old van, it was nearly four o' clock. It was a twenty-minute drive to the Black Mare, which was situated far enough away from Witchfire's residential area that the citizens didn't complain too much. Shark Bite might still be there, if the information was accurate. Alexis hoped that it was.

Chapter 13: A Broken Window and a Missing Photo Album

Throughout the remainder of her shift, Naomi's mind was reeling. She couldn't stop thinking about the blue-eyed man and the intruder that had leapt across the path of her Buick days ago. She couldn't help but wonder if those two men were one and the same.

Ramsey seemed to notice her distress and asked if she was okay. She insisted that she was fine. At the end of the night, when the sun was rising, Oliver and Naomi walked out of the store together. Oliver had his arm around the distraught Naomi.

"Don't worry, it'll be all right," Oliver assured her.

"Damn right it will be," Naomi echoed. "Because if anybody messes with me, they'll regret it." Naomi knew she was talking big and that she couldn't really back that up with action, but it didn't matter. A good friend was beside her and the night was over. She could finally go home and sleep.

Naomi and Oliver walked around the side of the building. That was when Naomi saw her car; the driver's side window was smashed in and there was glass everywhere. She was beginning to wonder how she had come to be so unlucky. It seemed that negativity had followed her from Quakertown to Witchfire. It was annoying, like being unable to shake the common cold, but it was also severely detrimental—like finding out that you have three months to live.

Naomi wasn't sure how long she had, but she knew that death was lurking around her like a plague, and she knew that someone was following her. Was it someone who wanted her dead, or was it an admirer who had gone too far? She didn't know the answer to that question. All she knew was that she had to call her father. She would let him call the cops.

The phone rang four times before her father picked up. It was six-forty in the morning, which was when Roy usually rose from his warm bed to face the cars that needed to be worked on. He always had a lot to do and only two employees to help him with it. Naomi's thoughts drifted and she unintentionally zoned out.

"Hello?" Roy repeated.

"Oh, sorry Dad, it's me," Naomi said shakily.

"Hey, kid, are you okay?"

"No. No, I'm not. Oliver is here with me." She leaned against her friend, who in turn held her close and rubbed her back in what he hoped was a reassuring manner.

"What's wrong, Naomi?"

"Somebody busted my car window."

"What?" Roy exclaimed.

"I don't know why or what happened; I guess they were trying to find something to steal." Even as she said this, Naomi was staring into the car windows. The stereo was still there. This struck her as odd, because she had recently installed a brand new system. Even her CD collection remained, which she had left on the passenger seat.

"I'll get the tow truck and be there in a few minutes," Roy said. "Will you be okay?"

"Yeah. Oliver said he would hang out with me until you got here."

"All right. See you soon."

Naomi hung up her cell phone and slipped it into her pocket. "I can't believe this," she mumbled brokenly. "I just got this thing fixed and somebody broke into it. It must have happened when hardly anyone was here. We wouldn't have heard anything from inside. My God—I can't believe nobody heard the window break."

Oliver walked over to the car and peeked in the window. "If you broke into a car, wouldn't you try to steal an expensive stereo system?" he asked, echoing Naomi's thoughts.

She shrugged. "Maybe it was just before the cops got here last night. Maybe whoever it was saw them and freaked out."

"Can you think of anything else you might have taken with you to work?"

Naomi thought for a moment. "I . . . ."

"What?"

"The photo album I was going to show you." The night had been so busy, she had forgotten about it.

"Oh!" Oliver exclaimed. "Your vacation pictures."
Oliver looked into the back seat. "Where's the album?"

Naomi spent the next few minutes looking under some
things in the back seat, searching underneath the seats, and
even checking the trunk, but she didn't find the photo
album. She thought of the man in the blue shirt. She
thought of the date she had made for Saturday night.
Naomi gulped. "Oh my God," she mumbled. "The
album's gone."

"Did you forget to bring it?" Oliver asked nervously.

Naomi slammed the back door. Some pieces of glass
fell from the remains of the driver's side window. "No, I
distinctly remember putting it on the seat next to me when
I got in the car," Naomi stammered. "Whoever broke into
my car must have stolen my photo album! Don't you see
what this means?"

"Oh, shit." Oliver didn't want to say it, but he was
thinking it. *Maybe she really does have a stalker.*

The tow truck was an older Chevy, with *Vogler's Auto
Repair* emblazoned on both sides. The engine rumbled as
Roy climbed out of the driver's seat, his shoulder-length
blond hair tossed around his face by a sudden breeze.

He walked up to Naomi and put a hand on her
shoulder. "You okay, kid?"

Naomi shrugged. "First night out with the Buick and

this happens." She gave Oliver a meaningful glance. She was thinking, *Don't tell him about the photo album, okay? I'll tell him about that.*

Oliver seemed to get the message. "Well, I'd better be getting home," he said. He gave Naomi a hug. "If you need me, call me, okay?"

While Roy was peering into the car, Naomi whispered in Oliver's ear. "I might call out tonight, for obvious reasons."

"Geo's off, just like last night. I'm sure he could come by and keep you company."

"I might ask him to," Naomi mumbled. "I might ask him if he'll sleep on my couch." Naomi stopped talking when her father walked over to the two friends.

"See you later, Mr. Vogler," Oliver said.

"Bye." Roy turned to his daughter. "There's not a lot of glass on the front seat. I'll drive the car onto the tow truck."

"I could have driven it home," Naomi said sheepishly.

"Not on my life, you won't. Hop in the truck, I'll only be a minute."

Naomi was in no mood to argue. She was exhausted, paranoid and dreading Saturday night. It was Friday morning. She had no way to cancel the date because the stranger hadn't given her his number. She began to wonder if he had done that on purpose, or if he had simply been nervous enough to forget. For some reason, he hadn't told her his name, so she couldn't even look him up in the phone book.

"God damn it," she mumbled. "What the hell have I gotten myself into?" She sunk into the passenger seat and closed her eyes. Once her father secured the Buick on the back of the tow truck, he climbed into the driver's seat and the two of them were headed back home.

Chapter 14: Naomi Prepares for Her Date

Naomi's dad parked the Buick in the secondary garage where Naomi did her own work. On the way up to the house, they passed the main garage, which was a large building that could house five vehicles at a time. Because Witchfire was such a small town, there was usually a maximum of three cars in the garage. Roy's two employees were working on a Honda when Roy and Naomi passed by.

"I'll be back out soon, guys," Roy called.

Pedro and Devon waved at Naomi and Roy. Naomi said "hello" and followed her father into the house.

Inside, the air conditioning was on. It was certainly a relief; although it was still early, it was beginning to get hot outside. Naomi went into the living room and sat down on the couch. She felt safe here, especially with her father's company. Sometimes, being alone in the house trailer out back made her a little nervous, even before the recent happenings.

Just as Naomi had suspected, Roy was on the phone with the police before he even opened the fridge to see about breakfast. Once he had made the report, he went in the kitchen. "Want some eggs?" Roy asked.

Naomi followed him. "Have a seat. I'll make us some breakfast."

"All right," Roy said, slumping into a chair.

"Over easy?"

"Sure, why not."

As Naomi picked up the frying pan and set it on the stove, she had a split-second flashback to the day that she had found her mother lying dead on the kitchen floor in Quakertown. Naomi stared distractedly at the eggs without even removing any from the carton.

"You okay, Naomi?" her father asked.

"Yeah. But you know what? I think I'd rather have cereal." She shoved the eggs back into the fridge and retrieved a carton of corn flakes and a bottle of milk. The two of them dished out the cereal, poured the milk, and talked between crunchy bites. Finally, Naomi decided that she had to tell her father about everything that had happened last night.

When she told him that she had something to say, he said, "I'm listening, kiddo."

Naomi barely stopped to breathe as she told him about her adventurous night at work. She told him about Shark Bite throwing Rey Kustafik into the baler and about the cops showing up. Then she told him about the blue-eyed man from the bar and her date for Saturday night.

"He's seen me here before," Naomi said.

"Here? I probably know him then. I bet he's one of my customers."

"He didn't say. He also didn't tell me what his name is."

92

"Hmm." Roy scratched through his mustache. "You don't think he's the one who was outside your trailer, do you?"

"Dad. That could have been a deer or something." Naomi knew that she was only trying to make herself feel better. In truth, she was thinking the worst.

"That was the same night the garage was broken into. Sure, it could have been a deer, but this whole situation gives me the creeps. I think I'm going to go to the pound tomorrow and pick up a big, black kill dog."

"Are you serious? That's what Oliver said you should do."

"And he's probably right. I'm not a big fan of dogs, but we could use a loud, vicious one around here. We do have a junk yard, after all. It fits. What's this guy from the bar look like?"

Naomi thought for a moment. "He's tall and blond and has blue eyes. His hair is short and he has spiked bangs. He also has a mustache and a goatee. He's thin and a little muscular."

Roy raised an eyebrow. "You *noticed* him a lot, didn't you?"

Naomi blushed. "He was looking at me at the bar. I couldn't help it."

"Mmm-hmm. I have a feeling I might know him. Is it okay if I meet him?"

"Sure. If you think you do know him, I'd prefer it that way. I wish I could cancel the date, but I don't have his number."

Roy looked suspicious. "I don't know, Naomi, you look as though you like him a little bit."

"I don't know him!" Naomi retorted. "He disappeared before I could have a full conversation with him."

"Well, if he's the guy I think he might be, then you probably don't have much to fear from him. We'll see."

"Dad, at this point, I *fear* every guy I see, especially if they're wearing a blue shirt," she said sourly.

Naomi went to her trailer home, locked the door and closed all the curtains, even though it was broad daylight. She was a strong woman, but today, she felt weak. Most women her age didn't have muscles like she did. She had been working on cars for a long time, first at her uncle's shop in Quakertown and then with her dad in Witchfire. She could probably throw a pretty hard punch if she had to. Mentally, she had allowed herself to become paranoid and easily frightened and she felt that this didn't match her physique. She felt as though something were wrong with her.

Outside her window, the world continued to turn. As Naomi slept through the morning, people went about their daytime jobs, anxiously awaiting the end of the last workday of the week.

Naomi dreamt that the blue-eyed man came to her trailer and sat down in her little kitchen. She made him breakfast, and then he died. As Naomi stared down at his body on the linoleum, the blue-eyed man transformed into her mother, whose wide and vacant eyes stared accusingly at her daughter, her lips parted as if to say, "It was all your fault. *Everything.*"

Saturday evening arrived more quickly than Naomi would have preferred. She wore a pair of tight blue jeans, her wallet chained to her pants. She wore a Jargon band t-shirt that Geoffrey had given her. She was a little tired, mostly because she had gone to work Friday night, after all. Geo hadn't been able to keep her company that night; he had already made plans. Naomi didn't want to call out from work only to spend a night alone in her trailer.

It was five-thirty. It wouldn't be long before the blue-eyed man arrived. Naomi was worried, but she knew that she could handle herself if the situation took a turn for the worst. For the most part, she was confident that it wouldn't. Despite her suspicions, she didn't think that the blue-eyed man looked especially dangerous. She also didn't think that a man who was stalking her would bother to ask her on a date.

As she walked through the back yard, she heard a loud bark. She bypassed the back door and walked around the front, wondering where the sound had come from. Near the junkyard that stretched along one side of the property, a big black Doberman roamed at the end of a long chain. The animal stared at Naomi and then growled. Naomi hurried inside.

Her father was sitting at the kitchen table, eating pizza. "Hey, kid," he said. "Hungry?"

"I have a date, remember."

Her father finished a slice and nodded. "Right. I almost forgot. When is he getting here?"

"He said he would pick me up at seven." Naomi sat down at the table and crossed her arms in front of her. "I've never really had a date with anyone before," she mused.

"There's a first time for everything." Roy put the remainder of the pizza into the fridge and sat back down. "Are you worried?"

"Extremely. But I don't think this guy is the one that tried to break into your garage," she said. "Besides, something else happened that makes me think that."

"Hmm?"

"Whoever broke into my car—" She paused. "I think it was the guy who was sneaking around here. He took something."

"Why didn't you tell me this before?"

"I don't know. I guess I didn't want to worry you."

"What'd he take?"

"A photo album."

There was a long silence. Naomi could tell that her father was wondering why someone would steal a photo album and not a CD player. "Why would anyone take that?" he asked, echoing what Naomi had been thinking.

"There were a lot of pictures of me in there, from when we went to the mountains."

"You still think you have a stalker?" Roy's brow furrowed.

"Don't you?" Naomi asked.

"I was beginning to hope *not*. Tim Brockman stopped by today to see if anything else suspicious had happened."

"Tim Brockman?"

"He's the cop that always brings his car over here for oil changes."

"Oh."

"I told him things were back to normal, for now. He stopped by because he heard about your car getting broken into. Maybe he can do us a favor, come around more often or something. If there is someone watching you—" Her dad shook his head and sighed. "This is not something that I want to be thinking about. Maybe you should sleep in the house for a while. You'd be safer in here with me and I do have that guest bedroom."

"Maybe, but not right away. Besides, I lock my door and my windows. And I've been closing all the curtains. And I noticed that dog out front."

"Ah, his name is Diesel," Roy said. "I picked him up at the SPCA today. He was the angriest dog there. Nobody else would take him."

"*Great*," Naomi said sarcastically. "So I'll be safe from people, but that thing out there will take my arm off."

"Nah, I think once he gets comfortable, he'll be all right. For some reason, he warmed up to me real fast." Outside, the dog barked. "I'll talk to Tim. I've known him for a long time. Maybe he can do something the other cops can't."

"They won't do anything unless somebody actually gets to me," Naomi pointed out.

"Don't say that. Tim would. I'll give him a call."

He stood up and went into the living room. A moment later, Naomi heard him talking on the phone. At seven-fifteen, just when Naomi thought that her date might not show up, the doorbell rang.

Alexis's office was in an old building in the center of town. Her name was on the door, but she guessed that not many people saw it, because she hardly got any cases. She was sitting in her chair with her feet on her desk, smoking a cigar. Across from her, Frank Gibson sipped a cup of coffee.

"So 'Shark Bite' Carter got arrested, eh?" Alexis exhaled and puffed rings of smoke into the air.

"Yeah, it turns out Rey Kustafik is pressing charges. Shark won't be in jail for long, I'm sure. He's got a good lawyer."

"What about Kustafik?"

"He's got a good lawyer, too. We'll see. I've heard

there might be a settlement. Regardless, Carter lost his job. Whellaby didn't even hesitate to fire him."

Detective Nevid's left eyebrow rose dramatically. "Wasn't old man Whellaby afraid that Shark Bite would throw him in the baler, too?"

"I don't know. Haven't you talked to him recently?"

"No. We had a brief conversation. He's still got me after this so-called killer, the one who apparently talked Timmson into hanging himself. He said right away that he didn't think Carter had anything to do with it."

"I don't know, Alexis. It's not looking good."

"I know. I mean, how do you convince people that somebody snuck into Whellaby's before Timmson had opened for the morning and forced him to hang himself?"

"It's a long shot," Frank agreed. "But on the other hand, stranger things have happened."

"That's true, and that's why I'm stumped. I think I might have to talk to Traci Corin."

"Your friend at the mortuary?"

"Yeah. She may have dealt with his body."

"What would she know?" Frank wondered. "You think there was an autopsy?"

"Why not? He was a suicide. Are you feeling all right, Frank?"

"I'm just a little tired."

"You and me, both." Alexis put out her cigar and sighed, pulling her fedora over her eyes. "I could sleep for seven days."

Chapter 15: A Night in Witchfire

His name was Richard Weston. Roy had a good memory.
Every year, Richard would bring his car to Vogler's Auto
Repair for his inspection. Roy had even seen him in town
once or twice. The tall blue-eyed blond had a
recognizable face and deep eyes that seemed to suggest
that he was thinking about something extremely important
all of the time.

The three of them stood nervously in the kitchen for a
few moments. Then, Richard looked at Naomi and said,
"Shall we?" He opened the door for her and the two of
them walked outside.

Roy watched them depart. Near the junkyard, Diesel
the Doberman snapped his huge jaws, barking after the
black Integra as it left the driveway.

Roy's cat curled around his legs, mewing. "I swear to
God," Roy mumbled. "If anything happens to her, I'm
going to have that guy's head in a basket."

"*Mrow*," the cat said.

For a few moments, the car ride was silent. Finally,
Richard spoke. "Your dad seemed suspicious of me for
some reason."

"Well, let's just say a lot of strange things have been going on lately," Naomi admitted nervously.

"I'm sorry I didn't tell you my name the other day. I was a little nervous." He turned onto Maine Street. "I feel silly about it. What kind of person asks someone out on a date and doesn't even mention their name?"

Naomi shrugged. "It was a little weird."

"How does dinner and a show sound to you?" Richard asked. "I figured we could keep it casual and go the Blue Plate. I know this club in the next town. A jazz band is playing there tonight."

"Sounds fine to me."

The club they went to was farther away than Naomi had expected. It was a forty-five minute drive, but Richard seemed to think it would be worth it. They decided to save dinner for afterwards and ended up at the Blue Plate (or the Night Kitchen) at around ten-thirty. They got a booth in a far corner and ordered their food.

By this time, Naomi had gotten somewhat comfortable around Richard and had nearly forgotten about her recent troubles. They had talked a lot over the course of the evening, discussing cars and Richard's job at Arbour Bookstore off Maine Street.

"What else do you do?" Naomi asked, settling in with a cup of coffee.

"Have you heard of *Dark Times*?"

"What, that magazine about 'supernatural Witchfire?'" Naomi asked, scoffing.

"I'm one of the editors," Richard said.

"Oh. Sorry. I didn't mean to . . . ."

"It's okay. I admit we're a small operation, but we have been gaining readership. That's in partnership with the Witchfire Paranormal Investigations Team, which I co-founded."

"So you're a writer and a ghost-hunter?" Naomi smirked.

"That's about the size of it, although I prefer the term *Paranormal Investigator*. We've had a couple big jobs lately. We investigated the O'Neill homestead a while back, the old farm where, supposedly, 'the witch of Nacre Township' was burned at the stake. And we worked briefly with the guys who publish *Strange New Jersey* when they were doing their book on Pennsylvania. Some very weird things have happened in Witchfire over the years. When I'm not dealing with all of that, I spend a lot of time here, just thinking."

"Interesting."

"You think this is all ridiculous, don't you?"

Naomi almost laughed. "No, I'm intrigued." She paused. "Okay, it does sound a *little* ridiculous, but I do find it interesting."

"You sure?" Richard smiled shyly.

"Yeah, I'm sure. I've just grown up with a more scientific viewpoint. Everything has a part, a place."

"You're a good mechanic."

"Yeah, I am, actually. When I think philosophically, it

103

usually ends in my viewing a current situation as though it were just another machine, something with parts that can be broken or fixed, replaced or ignored."

"Now *that's* interesting," Richard said. "You have a very cold view of the world, don't you?"

"I wouldn't say that. I just try to think logically."

"Me too. There's something we have in common."

Naomi turned and faced him, placing her empty coffee cup on the table. "I'm sure we have more than that in common. Were you worried?"

Richard leaned forward. "I was a little worried that you wouldn't enjoy yourself, but you seem to like my company. Tell me about yourself. Did you grow up around here?"

"No. I was born in Quakertown, unfortunately," Naomi mumbled. "I moved here about a year ago, after my mom died."

"Oh. I'm sorry," Richard said sincerely.

"That's okay; it's been a while."

"I won't ask what happened. We can leave that story for another time."

Naomi thought of the intruder on her father's property and the slavering jaws of Diesel the Doberman. She shivered.

"Are you okay?" Richard asked.

"I will be. But I have to admit, I've got a story for you if you're willing to listen."

"We've got all the time in the world."

"Well, in that case . . . ." Naomi told him *everything,* starting with the man who had run in front of her car and ending with the most recent occurrence, the theft of her photo album. "I don't think that was an animal outside my window that night; I think it was a man," Naomi finished.

"That's pretty scary. Can't the police do anything about it?"

"I doubt it. My dad knows one of the cops, though. He brings his car to us for service. Hopefully, he can help us out a little bit on the side. Then again, I could just be paranoid. It might have been a deer I heard in the bushes. I almost believed it for a while. Then somebody broke into my car and now I don't know what to believe."

"Don't shrug it off as paranoia," Richard advised. "Always trust your instincts. What are you going to do now?"

"I don't know." Naomi shifted in her seat and stared listlessly out the window and into the dark night. "I've never felt completely comfortable in that trailer. I mean, where I live. I always wake up and I think I'm in my old bedroom, at my mom's house."

Richard cocked his head, a sympathetic look on his face. "I know what you mean. I miss my old house sometimes. Back in New York, we had a beautiful old house. My parents still live there. I tried to get as far away from that place as I could. I lived down south for a while."

"I definitely tried to get as far away from Quakertown as I could." Naomi laughed sardonically. "Didn't get very far." She began to fold her paper napkin into a curious shape just as the food arrived. "I didn't have the money to go anywhere else. I didn't think I had anybody to turn to, either. And I was too messed up, anyway."

"What do you mean? Was that because your mom died?" Richard bit into his sandwich.

Naomi nodded. "Mom and I got along really well. But I haven't been able to cook ever since it happened. And I was a really good cook, too. Richard, I could cook *anything*, you name it." Naomi looked up and saw his questioning gaze.

He swallowed his first bite and set down his sandwich, rubbing his hands on his napkin. "Dare I ask?"

Naomi gulped. She always had trouble recounting the tale, even to her closest friends. She had been growing past the incident, but she couldn't help but blame herself. Sometimes, it still felt fresh in her mind. "Mom was allergic to some things," she explained. "I cooked something for myself and I went upstairs. I can't remember what I was doing; I guess I was in the bathroom or listening to music, or something. I blocked most of it out of my mind. I didn't hear her call to me when she got home." Naomi paused.

"Take your time," Richard said. "You don't have to tell me about it if it's painful."

"No, that's okay. It's good to talk about things.

Anyway, I made this dish. I can't even remember what it was. It was just for me, mom wasn't supposed to eat it. She did." Naomi fiddled with her French fries. Suddenly, she didn't feel hungry anymore. "I came downstairs and found her. She had an allergic reaction. They told me that she died almost instantly of anaphylactic shock."

Richard didn't know what to say. He felt as though anything he said wouldn't be good enough, but he tried anyway. "What did you do?"

"I turned myself in."

All around them, the bustle of the world disappeared. The diner may as well have been empty. In the universe of Naomi and Richard, no one else existed.

"What do you mean?"

"I called 911 and told them that I'd killed her." Tears formed in Naomi's eyes. It had been so long since she'd cried about her mother's death; it had been so long since she had allowed herself the privilege.

Richard watched, spellbound. "But it wasn't your fault," he said weakly.

"It *was*." Naomi ate her dinner, but only because she knew that she would feel worse without it. For a while, neither of them spoke.

Finally, Richard felt that he had to break the silence that had risen around them. "It's much too easy to blame yourself, Naomi. It's harder to let go of the past, I know. I didn't have an easy childhood. I know it doesn't compare to what happened to you and so recently, but I can relate in some ways."

Naomi hung her head, somehow afraid to look into his steely blue eyes. "Tell me," she mumbled.

"We moved around a lot when I was a kid. I lost all of the friends I made because of it. My parents tried to force me into a conservative mind-set that I didn't want a part of. I've never had many friends, Naomi, and not many people to turn to. You don't have much either." He reached across the table and took her hand. "Although, we both just made a new friend."

"Thanks, Richard." Naomi smiled nervously and then returned to her dinner.

She wrote his phone number on a diner napkin because she had left her cell at home. She shoved the napkin into her pocket before they left. It was after midnight.

For the first time in her life, being alone made Naomi uncomfortable. It seemed that every little noise frightened her. Her mind felt weak. She felt as though she were in the wrong body. She had always believed that her physical strength would protect her, but the idea of someone watching her without her knowing it was quietly eating away at her subconscious. For some reason, she felt as though she could trust Richard, so she invited him into her trailer for a drink.

Naomi switched on a light. Around the lampshade,

glass beads hung. The curtains were already drawn. The muggy evening had made the living room feel hot and sticky, so she turned on the air conditioner. Richard sat down on the couch and Naomi retrieved two cold beers.

There were empty beer bottles all over the coffee table. There were empty mugs and dirty dishes. The carpeting hadn't been vacuumed in a while.

"Shit. This place is a sty," Naomi said, handing Richard a Yuengling Black and Tan.

"It's okay," Richard said, shrugging.

"No, you don't understand." Naomi took a swig from her beer and then set it down on the table amongst the empty bottles. "I'm usually a pretty clean person, but lately . . . I don't know. I've had so much on my mind."

During the awkward silence, Naomi set about putting the recycling in bags and rinsing the dirty dishes. By the time she was done, the coffee table was clear again and the room looked a little neater.

"I'm sorry I've been so depressing," Naomi said. "I hope I didn't ruin the evening for you."

Richard had to laugh. "Don't apologize. I haven't had such a successful date since I was a teenager."

"How old are you?"

"Twenty-eight. How old are you?"

"I'll be twenty-two next month on the thirteenth," she said sourly. "An unlucky number for an unlucky girl."

"On the contrary, thirteen is a lucky number," Richard said, turning to face her. "Or at least, it's *my* lucky number."

"I wish it were mine." Naomi glanced at her beer and realized that she'd already drunk half of it. "I haven't been feeling very lucky lately." She turned her head and looked at him.

"How about now?" He leaned over and kissed her.

There was a split second in which Naomi didn't know what to think. Then she recoiled, standing somewhat haphazardly from the couch. "I'm still not feeling lucky," she stammered. "Look, I'm not ready for this. It's almost one in the morning. I think you'd better leave."

"But, Naomi, everything was going so well."

"I said, *I think you should leave.*" She spoke firmly and without hesitation.

Richard seemed dejected. As he stood up and walked toward the door, Naomi detected a hint of anger in his expression. It passed fleetingly and was replaced with confusion and hurt. She almost felt badly for him. *But,* she reminded herself; *the night wasn't going* that *well.* At least, not well enough that she was ready to get physical with a man she barely knew.

As soon she heard Richard's car start up in the driveway, Naomi began to regret telling him to leave. Only one lamp cast light across the living room in her trailer home. She didn't even have a house cat to keep her company. Complete silence fell in around her.

"Damn it, Naomi, quit being such a wuss," she cursed herself. "I can't believe how paranoid I am lately!"

She knew that there was only one thing that could calm her. Naomi went into her dark bedroom, retrieved a large flashlight and walked outside.

The heat of the day had long since dissipated, but the air was humid. Naomi realized that she was sweating as she walked toward the garages. The moon was almost full and cast an ethereal glow on the husks of broken down cars that sat beyond the chain link fence.

As she looked out on the graveyard of empty machines, Naomi felt almost comforted by the silence that had once frightened her. She remembered what she had told Richard earlier: "It usually ends in my viewing a current situation as though it were just another machine— something with parts that can be broken or fixed, replaced or ignored."

Naomi had a talent for remembering words, especially in conversation. She felt that she had unwittingly exposed an important part of her psyche to Richard and she hoped that he wouldn't use it against her. She hoped that he would understand why she hadn't wanted to kiss him at that moment and why she had told him to leave.

"I hope he understands it," Naomi mumbled to herself. "*I* sure don't." As she went over the event in her mind, she began to feel silly. She had been on a date with a very attractive man who was also a good listener. Why in the

111

world had she kicked him out? "Stupid, Naomi, stupid," she said aloud. Her voice seemed to get lost in the darkness.

She saw the sleeping form of Diesel the Doberman and snuck quietly past, hoping that he wouldn't wake up and bark. At one point, she thought the dog had lifted its head and seen her, but perhaps Diesel had known that Naomi meant no harm. Naomi walked around the small garage, the one with her name painted on the side, and found her way into the junkyard.

By then, she had gotten used to the dim, bluish light of the moon and no longer needed her flashlight. She switched it off as she walked in between a derelict 70s Nova and an '85 Buick.

For some reason, walking among the broken vehicles calmed her. Some of the cars were nothing more than frames. There were others that had no engines, or whose seats had been torn out. There were still others that barely looked like cars, their parts so rusted and surrounded by tall weeds that it was hard to imagine them being driven down a wide stretch of open road, chrome glimmering.

Naomi found a Trans Am whose doors were missing. She slipped onto the torn driver's seat and leaned back, staring up at the sky through the busted T-top. There were no stars, so she stared at the moon for a while, mentally pinpointing each pock in its surface, each flaw that made it unique.

Her thoughts drifted back to Richard. They'd had fun

at the club outside of town. Dinner had been fine, except
for when Naomi had told him about her mother. She felt a
little embarrassed and sort of regretted opening up to him.
It wasn't often that she became teary-eyed in front of
people she hardly knew. She found it strange that she had
been so quick to tell him so much; Naomi wasn't usually
very talkative and never about her own past. She allowed
herself to think that Richard might be different. He might,
after all, be a man whom Naomi would enjoy spending
more time with.

She had to wonder what would have happened if she
had allowed him to continue kissing her. She thought
about what might have happened if she had kissed him
back. For a long while, Naomi sat in the Trans Am
running through a slew of what-ifs. That was when she
heard something hit the ground somewhere near the
garages. There was a gate over there, right behind Diesel's
new doghouse. Naomi looked up, but she didn't hear any
barking.

For a moment, her heart pounded as she wondered if
someone was out there, hiding in the shadows. She slunk
down in the bucket seat.

"If someone were over there," Naomi whispered,
"Diesel would have started barking." This relaxed her a
bit. Diesel was a big dog with sharp ears. A loud noise
wouldn't have gotten past him, even if he had been
sleeping. It had sounded like a piece of metal, perhaps an
old car part, hitting the dirt. Naomi wasn't sure what to

think, but she knew that no one would have gotten past Diesel.

She decided to head back inside and go to bed.

As Naomi walked around the garages and back toward the house, a dark figure crept through the night. On the ground by his doghouse, Diesel was chewing on a bloody steak. Naomi was none the wiser.

Chapter 16: Alexis Nevid Digs a Little Deeper

Traci Corin wanted to know why her friend, the private eye, wanted to see Marty Timmson's autopsy report.

Traci sat behind her desk in the cramped office and dropped the file on top of the ink blotter. "There's nothing to it," Traci said. "You want the short story? He killed himself." Traci's long blond hair fell around her eyes. She pushed it back behind her ears and shrugged. "Not everybody writes a suicide note. Some people just *go*. Nobody ever expects suicides. They're always the ones that seem to have the happiest lives. You know that, Alexis. You remember my cousin."

"Yeah, I remember Tommy." Alexis sighed. Tommy had left behind a pregnant wife when he had found a desolate clearing near the swamps that cradled Nacre Township and shot himself in the head. Suicides always reminded Traci of her cousin. Alexis sat down across from her friend. "But there's something different about this guy," she said. "I can feel it."

"I will admit; you've always had a good instinct, Alexis. But I know how much you value the truth. Timmson killed himself. There's no way you can get around it." Traci slid the file across the desk. "Take a look for yourself. It was those two wires that killed Timmson. There was no foul play except his own."

Alexis flipped through the file. Traci had been right. "Looks like I'll have to read between the lines." Alexis stood up and turned toward the door. "Thanks for your help, Traci."

"Anytime, sweetheart."

"I can't help but think that Timmson was murdered, though. I'll have to look into this."

"You do that, Alexis." When the detective left, Traci leaned back in her chair and sipped from a bottle of soda. "That woman just doesn't give up," she said to herself.

Naomi woke up at ten-thirty in the morning after a night of fitful sleep. She had dreamt a lot but couldn't remember any of the images that had crossed her mind.

The sky was gray and it looked like it was going to rain. Naomi went across the yard to her father's house. She had to go out to the garage to find him. Roy was working on a Dodge pick-up truck with Devon and Pedro. Naomi said hello to the three of them while thunder rumbled somewhere in the distance.

"A storm's coming." Roy emerged from the garage, his eyes on the sky. "Better make sure your windows are closed."

"They are." There was a slight chill in the air. Naomi was barefoot and wearing a pair of denim shorts. She zipped up her windbreaker.

116

"Would you like to have lunch?" Roy asked.

"Sure." Naomi looked down at the ground as she walked, stepping carefully on the gravel.

"Hey, I'm sorry we haven't gotten to fix that window of yours yet. We've been pretty busy in the shop lately. I think I'll have Devon do it this week."

"Okay."

Roy took a long look at Naomi's face. "What's up, kid? You have a lot on your mind?"

She shrugged. "Nothing much. I just woke up."

"I can tell. Bad dreams?"

"I don't know. Why?"

They reached the front porch and Roy held the door open for Naomi. "You *look* like you had a bad dream."

"I'm not surprised." Naomi walked into the kitchen and sat down at the table.

"If it's any consolation," Roy began, shutting the door behind him, "Tim Brockman's going to make sure that he takes a couple drives out here for the next few nights, just to make sure there aren't any prowlers. And Diesel hasn't been barking at all."

"That's not *just* what I was thinking about, Dad. I was hoping that I had forgotten to bring that photo album to work the other night, but I couldn't find it anywhere. Someone definitely stole it and I do think someone's following me."

"We'll get that taken care of. Don't forget that twenty gauge shotgun I've got in the pantry." Roy got some veggie burgers out of the freezer. "What else is on your mind?" Just as Naomi was about to open her mouth and speak, Roy interrupted her. "Wait, let me guess. It's that date you had last night, isn't it?"

Naomi rolled her eyes. "Yes."

"Did it go well?"

"Mostly. Especially considering it was the first real date I've ever been on with anyone. I guess you always make mistakes when you try something for the first time."

"Uh-oh. What happened?" Roy listened intently as he cooked the burgers in a frying pan on the stove.

Naomi's face fell. "I told him about Mom."

For a moment, Roy almost forgot that he was cooking. "Isn't Oliver the only friend of yours that you willingly told about that? Didn't Geoffrey have to convince you?"

Naomi nodded. "That's why I'm so confused. I never felt so comfortable around anyone before. I almost cried in the diner."

"Well, forgive me for saying so, but what's the problem?"

"Hmm?"

"What's so bad about feeling comfortable around someone? Before, you were worried that Richard was the man who was outside your window in the bushes."

"I wish you hadn't brought that up." Naomi sighed.

"Look, let's face it, Naomi." Roy flipped the burgers. "I can't always be around for you. The more friends you have, the better. And honestly, if you have a boyfriend around, that's one more person looking out for you."

"Dad, I can protect myself." Naomi stood, a little irritated. "I hope you're not suggesting that I can't."

"Not at all, Naomi. In fact, I was a little afraid of you when you first came to live here. Don't you remember?"

She smirked. "I'd almost forgotten about that."

"Mike Jennson, that mechanic who used to work for me. He got *much* too fresh with you and—" Roy shook his head. "I'd never seen a girl shatter a man's nose until that day. I figured if I was ever a bad father, you'd do the same to me."

"It didn't take me very long to find out that you weren't the person I thought you were," Naomi admitted.

"That's good to know." Roy went back to the fridge. The burgers sizzled in the frying pan. "Do you want ketchup or mayonnaise?"

Naomi sighed and leaned tiredly on her right elbow. "Decisions, decisions."

Alexis was struggling with a few very important questions. Did anyone on the night crew of Whellaby's grocery store have anything to do with the death of Marty Timmson? Had anyone on the night crew see Timmson before he had died?

Alexis gathered the names of each of the night crew employees, including some people that had quit the night crew within the past six to twelve months. Mr. Whellaby was able to give her some notable details about some of the members of the night crew, but not all of them; for the most part, he was never there at night.

He told Alexis that Josh 'Shark Bite' Carter had a history of anger management problems. Keith Ryan, the night manager, had known for a long time that Carter was on some kind of medication to calm him down. Ramsey was apparently a quiet man and kept to himself for the most part. He had been arrested once several years back for some kind of drug involvement. When Mr. Whellaby told Alexis that Ramsey had been charged with possession of marijuana, Alexis doubted that Ramsey was the person she was looking for.

"There's a new girl, Naomi Vogler," Mr. Whellaby said. "I met her once, but I wasn't the one who interviewed her for the job. I don't know much about her except that her father owns Vogler's Auto Repair."

Alexis nodded. "Thanks for your help," she said. "I'll interview the crew tonight."

"I hope you find what you're looking for, Ms. Nevid."

"Me, too."

Alexis called Frank Gibson at nine-thirty, a half-hour before the night crew was due to arrive for their shift. The private detective leaned back in the chair behind the manager's desk. She was wishing that she had a cigar.

"Frankie."

"Alexis. What's up? I just sat down to watch Charlie's

Angels."

"You're not having that dream about Farrah Fawcett again, are you, Frankie?"

On the other line, Frank Gibson snickered. "Maybe. What's it to you?"

"You're an animal." Alexis rolled her eyes. "How about coming down to Whellaby's? I thought you might want to help me interview the employees, try to figure out what happened to Marty Timmson."

"I'd rather we discussed the part about me being an animal."

"Figures. Look, are you coming down or not? I just thought you might be interested."

"Cool it, Alexis; I'll be there in fifteen minutes."

Alexis smirked. "Good. See you then." She hung up the phone.

One of the night crew stock associates had called out that night. Severin Windor, a balding, middle-aged man who rode an old motorcycle to work every day, had complained of a stomach virus. On five out of seven nights, Severin normally stocked aisles one through four. Tonight, Ramsey and Naomi were told to do aisle eight and go straight to aisle one.

Naomi was tired. She had been having trouble sleeping. When they first arrived at Whellaby's that night,

Naomi and Ramsey talked for a few minutes about Shark Bite, wondering what had happened to him. Ramsey told Naomi that a detective and a cop were lurking around the store somewhere. He also mentioned that a strange rumor had been circulating.

"What kind of a rumor?" Naomi wanted to know.

"The dairy manager, Stephen, said he heard that some people think that Marty Timmson didn't really kill himself."

"What do you mean?"

Ramsey shrugged. "I guess somebody thinks he was murdered. I don't know why, though."

"Didn't he hang himself?"

"That's what I thought," Ramsey agreed. "But maybe there's more to the story than we've been told. Did you see the newspaper article about it? They said it was suicide, too."

"I don't read the paper." Naomi glanced toward the end of aisle eight. "Look, here comes Keith. Maybe he knows something."

Keith looked especially worn out. They were having a busy night. There were a lot of customers in the store that evening, a lot more than usual. It was only ten-thirty and Keith had already been called up to customer service five times. Naomi had even seen an old lady yelling at Keith about some expired frozen chicken she had purchased two days prior. He looked as though he were regretting his decision to work in retail.

"Hey, Keith," Ramsey said.

"Yo. How's it going?"

"All right. Naomi and I were wondering something."

Keith stopped walking and yawned. "Yeah? What's up?"

Naomi shoved her hands in her pockets. "Ramsey heard there were some cops around somewhere."

"Geo told me he saw them in the lobby," Ramsey explained.

Keith nodded. "There're here to talk to the night crew. They'll tell you what it's all about. I think they're planning on calling everyone into the office one at a time."

"Oh. Why?" Naomi asked.

"I'll let you two find that out for yourselves." Keith left aisle eight and walked toward the back room. Naomi and Ramsey got back to work.

A little while later, Naomi was stocking the cat food when Geoffrey walked over on his way to the candy aisle.

"Hey, Naomi."

"Hi, Geo." She shoved the rest of the cat food onto the shelf and picked up a case of canned fish. "What's up?"

"You don't know?"

"Huh?" Naomi appeared confused. She had been lost in thought and was wondering if she had missed something.

"I thought you would have seen my car at your dad's house," Geo said, sighing. "It died on me again. And your dad's all full up with work, so he won't be able to get to my car until Thursday. But at least he was nice enough to let me drop it off today, even though it's Sunday."

"Oh. That's a bummer," Naomi said, carefully stacking the cans on top of the ones that were already on the shelf. Naomi had to step aside to let a few customers by.

Geo had a depressed look on his face. "It couldn't have happened at a worse time."

"Why?"

"I was supposed to help my grandmother move on Thursday, and my car probably won't be fixed by that afternoon. She's going into assisted living. I'm all she's got, other than my uncle, but he's not around a lot."

Naomi was well aware of the fact that Geo's mother was long-since dead and his father lived in North Carolina. He was also an only child and didn't have many cousins. Naomi frowned. "How are you going to get there?"

"I guess I'll have to take the bus."

"When do you have to be there?"

"I don't know. I was going to go in the early afternoon and probably spend the night and help Gram get settled. It's supposed to be really nice on Wednesday. I was going to go for a walk, too." Geo shook his head. "Damn it."

Naomi knew that what she needed more than anything was some good company. She put the last can on the shelf and dropped the empty box on the floor. "I can drive you," she decided.

"Are you sure? She lives across the swamps in Helsontown. It's about forty minutes away."

"Helsontown's pretty big."

"Yeah, so . . . are you sure?"

Naomi thought for a moment. "Sure, I'm sure." She smiled. "What are friends for? I'll pick you up on Wednesday afternoon."

Naomi stepped aside for another customer. She glanced at him briefly and then picked up another case of cat food.

"Excuse me, sorry," the man said.

"That's okay." Naomi cut open the case and stacked some more cans on the shelf.

About an hour later, Naomi was called into the manager's office. She recognized the detective. She and the tired looking cop had both been there on the night that Shark Bite had thrown Rey Kustafik into the cardboard baler. Naomi sat nervously across from her.

The woman shook hands with Naomi. "I'm Alexis Nevid," she said. "I'm here to ask questions of everyone on the crew about Marty Timmson's death."

Naomi reeled. She hadn't expected that one. "Didn't he kill himself?"

"Yes," Alexis replied. "We're just tying up loose

ends." Somehow, Naomi didn't believe her. "Did you work the night before Timmson died?"

Naomi thought for a moment. "I was here when he was found."

"Did you see anything strange?"

"No."

Alexis rolled her eyes. "That's it, Frankie," she said, looking at the cop. "You can go, Miss Vogler."

The manner in which the detective spoke sounded a little condescending, but Naomi tried to ignore it. Suddenly, a thought struck her. "Um, I can't really help you, but maybe you can help me," she said.

"How so?"

Just then, Keith walked in.

Naomi stood up. "Can we talk in private?"

"Sure. Come on out to my car with me. I could use a cigar."

The moon hung high in the sky. Stars speckled the black expanse. The dim pole lights illuminated the empty parking lot. Alexis's car, a sleek black Ford ZX2, was parked beneath one of the flickering lights. The private eye opened the driver's side door to retrieve a cigar.

"Looks like the place emptied out pretty quickly," Alexis said, gesturing to the empty lot. An old van was parked on the other side of the lot, but beyond that, no other customers were currently in the store.

"It happens that way sometimes," Naomi said sheepishly.

126

"So what do you need help with?" Alexis said. The detective was aloof, but not uncaring.

Still, Naomi could tell that Alexis didn't think she would have much to say. Naomi stood there nervously and scratched her arm. A breeze picked up. Ever since it had last rained, the temperature had been going down more at night. Naomi wished she had worn her jacket. "Someone's been following me, I think," she said quietly.

Alexis puffed on her cigar. "That's a hefty accusation. If you want me to look into something for you, it has to be more than '*I think*.'"

"It is. But, at the same time, it isn't."

Alexis could see that this conversation might take a while. "Hop in my car and we'll talk for a bit."

Naomi told Alexis all about the man who had run in front of her car and about the strange rustling outside her bedroom window. Alexis wanted to know if she had any proof.

"Someone tried to break into dad's garage, but other than that, I just have a gut feeling," Naomi replied weakly. "I know that's not much, but I think I have a pretty good instinct." She turned and looked into the detective's dark eyes. "I just know somebody's following me."

Alexis sighed and leaned back in her seat. She puffed on her cigar and blew the smoke out the window. "This is very strange," she said.

"Hmm?"

"It just seems a little too coincidental for three equally

strange incidents to come from three different people that are in some way related to . . . ." She paused, and then gestured to Whellaby's. "Well, the grocery store."

Naomi nodded. "And it all happened around the same time. First, Timmson's found dead, then I almost hit that guy in my driveway and then Shark Bite throws Rey in the baler." Naomi frowned. "Do you think he meant to kill him? I mean, do you think Shark meant to kill Rey?"

"I don't know. I don't think so," Alexis murmured, scratching behind her ear. "It just seems unlikely. Josh 'Shark Bite' Carter does have an anger management problem, but he doesn't have a criminal history and—" Alexis raised an eyebrow. "Why am I telling you this, anyway?"

Naomi shrugged. "Because I'm curious?" For a moment, neither of them spoke. Finally, Naomi said, "Will you help me?"

"What do you want me to do?"

"I don't know." Suddenly, Naomi felt very silly and unprepared. "I'm not sure. I just . . . I just want this to be over with. I want to feel safe. One of the guys that comes to my dad's shop is a police officer and he said he would check on us more often, but I don't think it's enough. I just have this uncanny feeling that someone's watching me all the time. I know it sounds crazy. And I can't even really pay you, anyway, at least not that much." For a moment, Naomi flashed back to the night that she'd been alone in the junkyard and heard a crash. At the time, she had attributed it to an animal, but—

"I'll do my best," Alexis said, interrupting the young woman's thoughts. The two of them climbed out of the car and started walking back toward the grocery store.

Just then, Naomi caught sight of Oliver's car. There was something on the hood. Naomi's eyes widened. "You want proof?" she exclaimed in a bout of nervous excitement. "There it is!"

On the hood of the car, illuminated by the dim pole lights, was a single red rose. Next to it was a handwritten note. Naomi picked it up and studied it for a moment.

The note read, *Naomi, my love, we will be together soon.*

Alexis leaned forward, slamming her hands on the manager's desk in the office. "Damn it!" she exclaimed. "My car was parked facing the road. We never would have seen anything, and I know there was nothing on that car when we came outside!" The rose and the mysterious note were lying in front of her on the ink blotter. "That means that whoever left that rose for Naomi was in this store with us, and then left."

Frank had never seen Alexis look so agitated. "Lexxy," he said soothingly, "Calm down."

Alexis reeled. Her pinstripe fedora seemed to accent the glimmer of fury that crossed her nearly black eyes.

"Don't call me that, Gibson."

Frank sunk back in his seat. Alexis only called him by his last name if she was angry with him. He had gone too far with the pet name—much too far. "Sorry, Alexis."

Fortunately for Frank, she had already ignored him. She turned to Naomi, who was sitting in front of the manager's desk. Once again, Keith had made himself scarce. "Naomi, you and I went outside at about ten after midnight, correct?"

"That sounds right," Naomi agreed.

"Are you completely positive that there was nothing on Oliver's car when we walked past it the first time?"

"I'm absolutely certain. I would have seen it the first time."

"That means that whoever left that 'gift' had to have walked behind my car while we were talking in order to leave it on Oliver's car. Frank has already taken a look around. There aren't any customers in the store anymore and the only cars in the parking lot belong to the employees."

"What kind of idiot leaves a present for someone they're stalking when the cops are everywhere?" Naomi wondered.

Alexis crossed her arms over her chest. "We are looking at obsession. This man thinks that he loves you. He's completely taken by you. Don't you think that he would *want* you to know who he is?"

Naomi thought for a moment. "I did come pretty close

130

to believing that I didn't have a stalker, but that my dad had a thief."

"This stalker of yours wants you to believe in him. He wants you to remember he's there," Alexis decided. "He is likely very lonely and very fixated on some fantasy that—"

"All right, John Douglas, enough with the profiling," Frank said. "Let's get to the point. Which one of the customers in this store was Naomi's stalker?"

"That will be a difficult question to answer. I'll have to look at the security tapes."

They called Keith into the office and asked him to let them into the security room. Naomi had an extended break while she watched the tape with Detective Nevid and Frank.

The security room was no bigger than a half bathroom, with two small chairs and three video screens. A keyboard and various buttons allowed the operator to search through the cameras in the store. Mr. Whellaby had purchased the new system only recently.

After Keith let them in, Alexis had a seat in front of the screens and picked the precise time and date to play back the videos. She chose the time that she and Naomi had gone outside to the car.

Alexis looked behind her at the night manager. "Are there any cameras in the parking lot?"

Keith thought for a moment and then shook his head. "I don't think so. There's one in front of the door, but you won't know which guy you're looking for. You will see every customer that was in here, though."

"But I can't see anybody crossing the lot to Oliver's car?"

"No." Keith knew about Naomi's stalker. She had reluctantly told him about it moments before in order to explain why they needed to see the videos. He seemed disbelieving, leaning more toward thinking that Naomi had an *admirer*, not a stalker.

"Damn it," Alexis muttered. "There were so many people in here tonight. I guess I'll just have to take a good look at everybody on the tape." She paused, turning to Naomi. "It's almost as if this guy picked the busiest night of the week to leave that note for you, just to increase his chances of not being seen."

"Hiding out in the open, you mean," Frank said.

"Well, make yourselves at home," Keith said, opening the door. "Naomi, try not to be too long in here." Then he walked out.

Naomi made herself comfortable next to Alexis and they watched the tape from the front of the store, studying every face that walked out the automatic doors.

An hour or so later, Alexis and Frank were standing out in front of the store while Alexis enjoyed a cigar.

"Anything in the security tape catch your eye?" Frank

132

asked.

She exhaled, turned toward Frank, and shrugged. "Just a whole lot of faces, Frankie. I printed out a picture of every one of them." She handed him an envelope.

He pulled out a stack of glossy photographs. "How many people were in the store tonight, anyway?"

"I don't know. I lost count after twenty-two. Ryan did say that Sundays are the busiest, even for night shift. I have this funny feeling that Naomi's stalker knows that, too."

"Are you sure it's a stalker?"

"I'm positive. I've seen this kind of thing before. I worked on a similar case once."

"Oh?"

"Yeah. Only, that time the stalker turned out to be a jealous ex-husband. This time, it's some creep following around an innocent young woman." Alexis put out her cigar. "Walk with me?"

"Where to?" Frank asked, stuffing his hands in his pockets.

"I'd like to take a look around, now that I've interviewed all the employees."

Chapter 17: Clues in the Parking Lot

Frank followed Alexis back into the building and through the back room. Keith showed them the door that led to the boiler room where Timmson had hung himself. Actually, the door led to two places. If you went inside and took a right, you would walk down a short flight of stairs and into the back parking lot where the eighteen-wheelers unloaded their freight in the morning. If you took a left, you would walk up a long flight of stairs that led into the boiler room. Alexis decided to take a left.

The closer they got to the room that kept Whellaby's running 24-7, the louder it became. Above them, huge motors groaned, rumbled, and hummed, each one of them keeping a different freezer or refrigerator running smoothly.

The boiler room was about the size of a living room with a concrete floor. There were short aisles in between each of the huge motors. The room was well lit. There was a panel on the wall that was somehow related to the alarm system; if one of the machines went down, an alarm would sound. Alexis and Frank wandered around the room, observing.

"Where did Timmson hang himself?" Alexis asked.

Keith nodded toward one corner of the room. "They found him right over here."

"Frankie, did you get anything on this?"

"I did look at the report."

"Did it say *how* he was found?"

"Oh, I can answer that," Keith interrupted. He seemed excited to be a part of the investigation. "I talked to Mr. Whellaby. He said the body was facing away from the wall." Keith walked over to a large black Ford engine and gestured to the area above it. "Whellaby said the body was here, hanging in front of the duct." There was a silver colored duct leading away from the Ford engine and up toward the ceiling.

Alexis had no idea what these giant motors did, only that they were very loud. "How does Whellaby know so much about how the body was found?" Alexis asked curiously.

The night manager looked a little confused. "Are you serious?"

Alexis looked at Frank Gibson, and then back at Keith. "Yes."

"Whellaby is the one who found the body," Keith said, arms spread. "I thought sure he would have told you."

Alexis was perturbed. She distinctly remembered Mr. Whellaby telling her that an employee had found Timmson's body in the boiler room. After hearing what Keith had to say, she sunk into a silent reverie and wandered downstairs. Keith went into the back room to work on a few things and Frank followed Alexis. At the bottom of the flight of stairs, Alexis pushed open the back door and wandered out into the parking lot.

She suddenly regretted her reluctance to take the case seriously. At first, she had seen it as easy money; like everyone else, she had assumed it was suicide. At some point, she had begun to doubt her own assumptions; after all, a good detective must examine all possibilities. Something about the entire situation made her uncomfortable. She cursed herself for not spotting the patterns earlier—the strange manner in which Timmson had hung himself, and Whellaby's deceptiveness. What was going on in this town?

It was a cool night and it smelled like rain. There had been quite a storm earlier; perhaps more rain would follow. Alexis looked up at the dark sky, and then across the parking lot toward a forest that stretched out behind the store. In this part of the lot, there were no lights.

"Tell me something, Alexis," Frank said.

"Hmm?"

"How is it that you didn't know that Spencer Whellaby found the body?"

"Don't tell me that you knew?" Alexis turned and looked at him.

"I wasn't sure. I haven't been dealing with it directly. Don't worry; you're not the only ignorant one. But why wouldn't Whellaby tell you?"

"I don't know." Alexis scratched her chin. "There's only one thing I can think of." She drifted off for a moment. "Whellaby must know something about

Timmson's death; otherwise, he wouldn't have tried to hide the fact that he discovered the body that morning. Something very strange is going on here. I just wish I had picked up on it sooner."

Alexis walked out into the dark night. Frank had to squint to see her. Even then, her outline was only slightly visible under the cloudy sky. "Where are you going, Alexis?"

She switched on a flashlight she had been carrying. "I'm taking a look around this parking lot," Alexis said. "If Timmson really was murdered, then the killer probably came in through this back door. It would explain why none of the night crew saw anything strange that morning."

"Did anyone see Timmson?"

"None of the morning shift people did. None of the night crew did, either. It's possible that Timmson slipped by them that morning and right into the back room. But it's even more likely that he came in through that back door—" The yellow beam of light flashed across the parking lot and illuminated the door that led into the short hallway and up the stairs into the boiler room. "And I would have to guess that Timmson was accompanied by his killer."

"*If* he was killed," Frank added. "We haven't completely established that yet."

"Well," Alexis said. "We have a store owner who apparently found the body, but failed to tell his hired private detective, and we have a body that mysteriously appeared in the boiler room in such a way that everyone would naturally assume that it was suicide. What we have to ask ourselves is—" Alexis paused. "Why didn't anyone see Timmson come in for his morning shift? Keith informed me that the opening manager would always go right to the manager's office, but not even Keith saw Timmson come in that morning. The second question is why did Whellaby lie to me? Why didn't he just tell me that he was the one who found the body?"

The flashlight darted over the pavement as Alexis walked over to join Frank near the building. Frank shrugged. "Who knows? I can think of a few possible answers, but I'm sure you've already considered them."

"Whellaby knows something, like I said earlier."

"Right. And—"

"Timmson didn't go in the front door."

"And the extremely speculative conclusion, the one that we have absolutely *no* evidence for—"

"Marty Timmson wasn't alone when he walked up those steps."

"So what are you trying to find out here?"

"Don't ask stupid questions, Frank." Alexis flashed the light in his face. "I'm looking for . . . ."

"Clues?"

"You said it, I didn't. I wouldn't have used that word. I would have used 'evidence.'"

"No matter what you call it, you're not going to get it,"

139

Frank said. "It's been raining, for one thing. Anything someone might have dropped in this parking lot has either been run over, washed out, or both."

"Even so." Alexis disappeared into the darkness again.

Frank stood by the building waiting for her. About twenty minutes later, while Alexis still roamed the pavement, Keith came outside to find them. He nodded in the direction of the detective's flashlight. "What's she doing out here?" he asked.

"God only knows," Frank said. "Looking for something she won't find."

"What if she does find something?" Keith wondered.

"It would be luck. Pure luck."

Alexis disappeared for forty-five minutes. It was a dark night and Frank knew that she was a strong woman, so he wasn't worried. He went inside and read a newspaper. Meanwhile, Alexis was venturing into the forest behind Whellaby's grocery store. On a hunch, she had walked back and forth along the tree line, examining the ground with her flashlight. Just as it began to drizzle slightly, she found a narrow path that led into the woods.

As the rain pattered off the brim of her fedora, Alexis crept in between tall trees and shrubs. This path was clearly meant for deer, not humans. She wasn't able to go very far. She walked for perhaps a half a mile before larger tree branches that would have forced her to bend down or push through bushes deterred her. It would have been fine for a deer, but it wasn't for her.

She didn't make a sound. The flashlight reflected off tiny droplets of water on leaves. She glanced amongst the shadows of the forest. She was looking for something; she told herself that she wouldn't stop until she found it. Finally, she reached down and scooped something up, shoving it into her jacket pocket.

From where she stood, Alexis could see the outlines of houses against the sky. The woodsy area wasn't very deep. There was a development beyond it. She presumed that she could reach it by taking a right out of Whellaby's and driving a minute or two in search of a small neighborhood.

For the last time, she examined the parts of the path that were most difficult to traverse. She noted her own careful footprints in the mud. On the morning that Timmson had died, the ground had been dry. The rain hadn't come until yesterday. There wasn't much ground cover in the forest and it was only natural that when it rained, the area would become a tad muddy. Alexis knew that if someone had walked down this path in order to reach Whellaby's on the morning of Timmson's death, he or she wouldn't have made any footprints in the mud, because there wouldn't have *been* any mud.

Alexis examined any withered plants that grew on or near the pathway. There was plenty of grass that still grew here, just not enough to keep the area from getting messy when it rained. She even saw a few signs that animals had been here recently, perhaps right before she had arrived. Alexis recoiled when she saw the dung.

"*Yuck.*"

Just as she had hoped, there were weeds along the path. Some of them had been broken in patches that measured about six to eight inches, which was just about the length of a shoe. She had no proof that the damage to these plants had occurred on the morning of the alleged suicide, but she figured that it was a good guess. The path didn't extend very far into the woods before it became very difficult to travel on, so it didn't seem likely to Alexis that someone would have come through here on a 'pleasure walk.'

She examined the weaker tree branches that crossed the path in some places. There were numerous broken twigs and it was clear to Alexis that someone—or something—had come down this path and purposely broken branches in order to get by. If it hadn't been for that, she would have had a harder time walking through.

In the area of the woods where it became even harder for a person to walk, she could see how someone who was short enough or small enough could duck under branches or squeeze past bushes. She didn't have a lot of bulk, but she was tall and not at all wiry.

As she emerged into the parking lot once again, finally able to stand up straight without bumping into something,

she turned and looked behind her. She had come to her
conclusion—and she didn't like it one bit.

Chapter 18: Running to the Night Kitchen

As the sun rose over Vogler's Auto Repair, Roy walked out to the shop with his hands in his pockets. Devon and Pedro had arrived at their usual time and were already hard at work. Geoffrey's car was proving to be more of a difficult job than they had expected, but Devon had to install a new window in Naomi's car that day. Pedro would have to work on Geo's car by himself.

Roy said he would be right back; he had to go into town and do some food shopping. That was when Devon got a call on his cell phone. He stepped outside to answer it.

"Yeah, this is Devon."

By the chain link fence, Diesel slept with one eye open.

"Actually, I hadn't gotten to it yet." Devon turned and looked back at Naomi's car, parked in the garage. "We've been pretty busy lately." He turned away. A confused expression crossed his face as he puffed on a Marlboro. He looked up toward Roy's house as though worried that his boss would catch him talking on the phone.

"That's a pretty strange request. I guess I shouldn't ask why you want it done," Devon said into the phone. "No, I can do it. But it'll cost you." The mechanic stepped around the garage. Pedro was too far away to hear him. "A lot, man. It'll cost you a lot. Think *higher*." There was a pause. "Yeah, that's more like it. I ain't cheap, not for a job like that."

Devon stood there listening for a moment. Finally, he said, "I'll do it," and hung up the phone. As he turned to walk back to the garage, the dog growled.

Alexis and Frank sat in the detective's cramped office. Frank had just arrived at her behest, and she had yet to share what she had discovered in the woods behind Whellaby's grocery store.

Frank was drinking a cup of coffee. It was nine p.m. and he was off-duty for the night. Lately, though, he had found himself spending his off-duty nights with Alexis, sitting in her office and drinking coffee until his hands shook.

If only, he thought to himself, *we could meet in my bedroom instead.* He quickly banished these thoughts because she had just turned and looked at him. He wouldn't have been surprised if that sharp brain of hers could read his thoughts.

Her fedora was sitting beside her on top of a pile of law books. She opened one of the top desk drawers and retrieved something from inside. She dropped two wrappers on the desktop.

"There you are, Frankie," she said matter-of-factly.

"I don't get it. You took up chewing gum?"

"What kind of a cop are you? Take a look at what it says on the wrapper."

Frank peered downward. "Okay. They're wrappers for nicotine gum, the kind you chew to quit smoking. I didn't realize you'd given up cigars."

Frank knew where she was going with this, but he always had a lot of fun playing mind games. Alexis knew this; her eyebrow raised characteristically and she leaned back in her chair.

"Quit fucking around, Frankie. I found these in the woods."

"Yeah, I figured. So what? Lots of people chew gum and lots of people try to quit smoking."

"I showed you that path, remember?"

"You're right. It was narrow and I can't see a lot of people trying to walk down it unless they lived right at the end of it."

"There is a house right at the end of that path. I just didn't feel like ducking, crawling, and climbing around all those branches and bushes just to get to it. But there were a lot of broken branches out there. *Somebody* decided to climb through all that, probably because they knew they'd be less likely to be seen." She paused, seemingly for effect. "Whoever used that path was thin, small, possibly short, and wiry, and is trying to quit smoking." She dropped the wrappers on the desk again. "Those wrappers were caught in the grass by a tree."

147

"So we've got a guy who probably chews two pieces at once to get more nicotine. Still, you can't take a giant leap like that and assume that this person is the same person who—hypothetically—went in the back door of Whellaby's with Marty Timmson."

"I think it's a safe bet," Alexis said firmly. "Nobody was seen. There weren't even any customers in that morning. And none of the morning shift people remember seeing any cars except their own."

"You're still making a pretty big leap, Alexis."

"You watch." Alexis tapped a fingernail on the desk. "I'm going to bet ten to one that the guy who knows the most about what went on that morning lives in that development. And I'm going to take one more leap, Frankie."

"What's that?"

"Spencer Whellaby knows who that skinny gum-chewer is." Alexis looked almost triumphant. "I'm going to get to the bottom of this. You'll see."

"I certainly hope so," Frank Gibson said. "If anything strange went on, you're the only one who's looking into it. As far as the guys at the station are concerned, Timmson killed himself—and that's that."

Naomi woke up on Wednesday night in a cold sweat. She'd had another bad dream. This time, she had been cooking a meal for her father *and* Richard. The entire time, she was trying to stop herself. She tried to tell herself that it would only end badly, but the dream continued despite her protestations. In the end, her father and Richard were both dead, their bodies sprawled on the floor and radically decomposing in front of her eyes.

She got out of bed and turned on all the lights. It was after dark and everything was quiet. She knew that her father was probably asleep by now. Naomi almost wished that she had to go to work. At least, then, she wouldn't be alone.

When she was finished with her shower, she went back into her bedroom wrapped in a towel. When she dropped the towel and pulled on her underwear and a pair of jeans, she thought she heard something outside her window.

Naomi froze. Goosebumps rose on her flesh. She grappled in the closet for a shirt, anything to cover her breasts, and then pulled it on over her body without bothering to put on a bra. It was a band T-shirt with 'Led Zeppelin' emblazoned across the front. Naomi wouldn't have cared if it were inside out. The sudden and unidentifiable noise had sent her reeling.

She turned and stared toward the window. Meanwhile, she picked up her jacket and put it on. She grabbed her steel-toed boots and slipped them on over her socks. She doubted that it was chilly outside, but she wanted to be able to run if she had to. She didn't own sneakers.

As she stood near the door of her bedroom, she

realized that she had to look out the window. If it were only an animal, then she could comfort herself by verifying that nothing dangerous lurked beyond the glass. If it *weren't* an animal—

Naomi put this thought out of her mind and stepped toward the window.

Outside, something moved. Naomi froze again, resisting the urge to hide. "No," she told herself. "Look out the window. It's probably just a deer."

The curtains were already half-open. As she stood beside the window, Naomi reached over and gently pulled the curtain aside. Then she screamed.

There was a face pressed up against the glass, eyes wide and leering. Naomi threw herself back, stumbling. She caught her balance and looked back at the window. The face had disappeared, but she could see the bushes rustling, as though whoever lurked out there was withdrawing quickly.

The only thought that crossed her mind was the thought of escape. She threw herself out of her bedroom and ran for the front door. She didn't have any sort of weapon, not even a pipe or a baseball bat. She decided that she would run to her father's house.

Naomi quieted herself for long enough to open the door and step outside. It was warm, but a slight breeze set all of the hairs on her neck standing on end. Then she ran for the back door of her father's house. The journey through the yard, across the porch, and up to the door had

150

never seemed so long. She tried the knob, but it was locked. Glancing back toward the trailer, Naomi caught sight of a dark figure advancing on her. She yelped and tried to get the door open, but it wouldn't budge. The house was old, and although the lock had been broken at one time, Naomi supposed that her father had fixed it recently.

Realizing that she had no other choice (because she had no time to pound on the door), Naomi vaulted over the side of the porch and caught herself before she fell. Then she shot up and ran around the side of the house, toward the garages.

She felt in her pocket for her car key and realized that she had forgotten it back in the trailer. "Damn it!" she cursed. She ducked around the side of the garage and came to a second realization—her car was still locked in the main garage. She didn't even have access to it.

Suddenly, a sharp sound broke across the silence of the night. Diesel was on his feet, barking. Naomi ran to his side. "It's okay, boy," Naomi said shakily. She extended her hand, frightened. The dog sniffed her and seemed to realize that she wasn't a threat. Naomi unhooked the lead from the fence. Normally, she wouldn't have felt so safe near the dog, but tonight, she felt that Diesel's presence might help her a great deal.

"Come on, Diesel," Naomi whimpered. "Let's go!"

Suddenly, the young woman and the dog were running down the driveway, the dog at the human's behest. The leash tugged at her hand as Naomi ran, glancing behind her every so often. She heard footsteps behind her. She heard someone running after her. Her heart pounded in her chest. When she reached the end of the driveway, the dark figure was brazen enough to call out her name.

"Shit!" Naomi shouted. She stumbled and then caught herself, running as fast she could, the dog beside her. Diesel would turn his head every so often, reeling at the intruder, his jaws snapping open and shut as he barked; Naomi urged him onward.

The best she could do was run until she reached the heart of town, which was only about a mile down the road. "Run, Diesel, run!" The words came out as more of a mumble than a yell. Whoever was behind Naomi had strong legs; he was gaining on her.

They reached the end of the lane that led to Vogler's Auto Repair. Naomi shot out across Maine Street, Diesel close on her heels. A driver slammed hard on their horn as Naomi's long legs took her across the road in several bounds. She swung around and looked behind her. She and Diesel were standing on a well-lit street, surrounded by houses. The tree line along the winding road that led to Naomi's home was dark and shadowed. Whoever had been following her was gone, disappeared into the trees.

Naomi could hear her heartbeat in her ears and could feel the sweat beading on her face. Without a second look back, she and Diesel turned and hurried toward the Night Kitchen.

It was twenty minutes to ten o' clock. The man stood in front of the Night Kitchen strumming his guitar. He was leaning against the wall and whistling a tune, trying to recall the notes to a song that he had heard years ago as a child. The sound of pounding feet interrupted his thoughts. A dog barked in the night.

Just then, a figure shot out of the darkness. It was a woman. She nearly fell as she reached him. The guitar player set aside his instrument and caught her before she toppled to the ground. A Doberman growled at him. The woman leaned on him, gasping for air.

"Calm down!" the man urged. "You're safe now. What happened? Come inside, I'll get you a glass of water."

Naomi wasn't sure how she did it, but she managed to tie Diesel's leash to the railing near the door. Then she allowed the stranger to guide her into the diner, which was well lit and smelled of fresh coffee and pastries.

Naomi had never looked so haggard. She slumped into the booth across from the stranger, still gasping. Her hair was sticking out in all directions, her eyes were wide and bloodshot and her face was wet with sweat. The waitress asked if she was okay, but she didn't answer. The man said something to the waitress, after which the woman brought them both a glass of water.

"My name's Brian," the man said. He dipped a clean napkin into his water and wiped the sweat from Naomi's forehead. "I've seen you here before. What's your name?"

"Naomi," she mumbled. She allowed Brian to wet the napkin several more times and gently dab her face. Then she slipped out of her jacket. She was finally beginning to cool down.

She remembered seeing Brian outside the diner numerous times. His guitar was sitting next to him in the booth. His curly hair was pulled back in a ponytail.

"What happened, Naomi?" he asked. His voice was soft and comforting.

Naomi was grateful that he was there, even though she didn't really know him. "There was someone . . . ." Naomi paused and cleared her throat. "There was someone chasing me. He was outside my bedroom, watching me. I saw his face in the window. I got Diesel—" She gestured out the window, where the dog waited. "And I ran."

"We should call the police."

"No, no, I'm not ready," Naomi mumbled. She thought of Alexis Nevid. "Besides, I hired a private detective. I can call her."

"What's her number?"

"I don't know. Her name's Alexis Nevid. Is there a phone book?"

"Hang on, I bet they have one up at the front desk."

While Naomi sat at the table waiting for Brian to return, she thought about the face she had seen in the window and wondered who it had been. The only person that she could think of was Richard. A little voice in the back of her head was trying to convince her that Richard had been after her all along. He had found where she worked without much trouble. He had known where she lived. *Put the pieces together, Naomi, your date from the other night is also your stalker—*

Naomi nearly hit the ceiling when someone tapped on her shoulder. She turned and gasped. It was Richard.

"Naomi, are you okay? You look like hell." He slipped into the booth beside her.

For a moment, Naomi studied his face. He was wearing a black T-shirt and jeans. Naomi caught a whiff of shampoo and guessed that he had showered recently. His hair was neat and his blond bangs jutted out in short spikes. His goatee was neatly trimmed and his head was cocked as he looked at her with an expression of sincere worry.

Naomi had to note that this man *did not* look like he had just run a mile in the middle of the night. "Um," she managed.

"Naomi? Are you okay?" He turned so that he was facing her completely and he took her hand. "You look scared to death."

"I'm okay."

Before she could say anything else, Brian returned.

155

"Hi. You are?"

Richard released Naomi's hand. "Oh, sorry, my name's Richard."

The two men shook hands. "Brian."

"I've seen you around before. You're the guy that plays the guitar out front, aren't you?"

"Yeah, that's me." Brian sat down across from Naomi and slid a piece of paper across the table. He looked over at her, tapping the paper with his index finger. "I looked up Alexis Nevid and found her office number in the phone book. I doubt she's still there, but you can give it a shot on my cell phone." Then Brian looked back at Richard. "Are you a friend of hers?" When Richard nodded, Brian continued. "She's just had a hell of a shock. You might want to keep an eye on her for a while." Brian handed Naomi his cell phone. "I'll be out front. You can use that as long as you like." He picked up his guitar and stepped outside.

Naomi dialed the number and listened. The phone rang several times. Then: *"Hello. You've reached the voice mail of Alexis Nevid. I'm not in the office, but if you leave your name and number, I'll get back to you as soon as I can. Thanks a lot."*

Chapter 19: A Brief Escape

Richard sat with Naomi for a long time. He had been at
the diner with friends, but he urged them to leave without
him. He wanted to make sure that Naomi was all right.
After a time, Naomi finally explained the recent
developments, including the gift that had been left for her
on Oliver's car.

"So you really do have a stalker," Richard said,
remembering what Naomi had told him on their first date.

"Yeah." Naomi stared down at her empty plate.
Richard had insisted on buying her something to eat.
Although she had been hesitant at first, she was very
grateful.

"So who's this Alexis Nevid person?" Richard asked.
He was still sitting beside her, even though the other side
of the booth was vacant. Brian hadn't come back for his
cell phone yet, but they could both hear him strumming
his guitar out front.

"Alexis is a private detective," Naomi explained. "She
was at Whellaby's investigating Marty Timmson's death
and when I got to talk to her, I asked if she would help
me."

"I thought Marty Timmson killed himself? I read about
it in the paper," Richard said curiously.

"Apparently, Mr. Whellaby thinks he was murdered. I

157

don't know. I just wish I could talk to Alexis right now."

"I'm so glad you're okay," Richard said, taking her hand again. "Don't worry, Naomi. I'm not going to let anything happen to you."

Naomi was a big girl; she could take care of herself. But somehow, she believed Richard. For the first time that night, she smiled weakly. That was when the phone rang. Naomi recognized the number; it was Detective Nevid.

"Naomi, I got your message. Is everything all right?"

"No." Naomi spent the next minute or so explaining the events of the evening to Alexis.

"Why didn't you call the police?"

"I didn't think of it. The first thing I thought of was to go wake up my dad, but his door was locked and I didn't have the key. So I got Diesel and ran."

"Did you call your father?"

"I tried." Naomi really *had* tried; the problem was, her father was a deep sleeper. The phone never woke him up.

Without thinking, Richard began to rub Naomi's back while he listened to her end of the phone call. Her eyes fluttered. She seemed to be enjoying the massage, so he didn't stop.

"Yeah," Naomi said, and then listened. "Well, I'm not sure that the cops would do anything, anyway. I haven't been hurt by this guy yet." Naomi paused. "You're right. I know. He did chase me." Richard continued to listen. "Yeah, I suppose he was threatening to harm me, in a way.

But what good does that do when I don't know who he is yet?" Naomi fiddled with her empty coffee mug. "You're going to check *where* about the rose? Oh. Yeah, I see. Okay. Thanks, Alexis."

A moment later, Naomi hung up the phone. Richard felt a little awkward all of a sudden and stopped touching her. She looked at him briefly, blushing.

"What's the news?" Richard asked nervously.

"Alexis said she's going to spend the next few days watching Whellaby's. She already has pictures of all the evening regulars that she took from the video surveillance. She said it's likely that one of the regular customers at Whellaby's is my stalker."

"What was that you said about the rose?"

"She's going to take some of the pictures to the local florist shops and see if any of the cashiers recognize anyone. She said maybe she could find the guy if she can find out who bought the rose."

"What if it's not a guy?"

Naomi looked a little confused for a moment. "I hadn't thought of that. But the person outside my bedroom window was *definitely* a man."

Naomi and Richard lapsed into a moment of silence. Outside, Brian played his guitar.

It began to drizzle and the town of Witchfire smelled like rain. Brian didn't want his guitar to get wet. He walked back into the diner and sat down across from Naomi. He didn't know the blue-eyed man very well, but he had seen him in the Night Kitchen various times. In fact, the guy came into the diner a lot with his friends. Brian had just never spoken with him, until tonight.

"Are you going to be okay?" he asked Naomi.

She had been staring down at the surface of the table. Now, she looked up at Brian. "I guess so," she said. Even she knew that the statement wasn't all that convincing.

"You should call the police," Brian advised.

"I already tried to talk her into it," Richard said, shaking his head.

Naomi looked at Brian. "Can I use your phone again?"

First, Naomi called her dad. She left a voice message, got nervous, called again and kept calling until he picked up. She had lost count as to how many times she called her father, but she knew it was well over ten. He wasn't easy to wake up.

When he answered the phone, he sounded groggy. Naomi explained the situation to him. He wanted to come get her, but she insisted that she would get a ride home. After a while, she was able to calm him down; she hung up the phone and handed it back to Brian.

Then Richard offered to drive Naomi back to her father's house, with Diesel in the back seat.

Chapter 20: Red and Blue Lights in the Driveway

As they entered the driveway, Naomi peered out the passenger side window, wondering if she would be able to see her muddy tracks in the grass or on the side of the driveway. She saw nothing but darkness and the shadowy silhouettes of the trees lining the road.

"Are you okay?"

Naomi turned to look at Richard. In between the two front seats, Diesel was panting and enjoying the ride. Naomi shrugged. Then she shook her head. "No, I'm not. I'm scared."

"Well, at least you won't be alone tonight."

In a split second, Naomi wondered what he had meant and fleetingly imagined spending time with Richard in her bedroom. The thought dissipated when she saw the flashing red and blue lights in the driveway, up by the garages. "Oh, I see what you mean," she mumbled dumbly.

They pulled in next to Naomi's garage. She could see the colorfully painted wall, a mural that she had completed on a happier day. After all that had happened recently, she wasn't sure that she could ever be comfortable here again. After her mother had died, she had assumed she had already seen the worst. Quickly enough, Naomi had realized that she was mistaken. Her birthday was coming up. Would she even live to see it?

"Naomi!"

As she climbed out of the car, her father rushed over to greet her. He threw his arms around her. "Hi, Dad."

Roy stepped back and surveyed his daughter. "Are you okay?"

"I'm fine."

"Are you sure? After what just happened?"

His blue eyes watered, his brow crinkled, and Naomi could have sworn that her father had been crying. He hugged her again, holding her as if he were afraid to let her go, and then stepped back reluctantly.

Behind Naomi, Diesel jumped out of Richard's two-door Integra and roamed over to his doghouse, his nose to the ground.

"Hello, Richard," Roy said. "Come on, you two. Let's go up to the house."

In the shadowy night, Naomi caught sight of several police officers talking amongst themselves.

Tim Brockman was a tall middle-aged man with a thick figure. Naomi thought that he looked pretty tired. She wondered if he had been off-duty when Roy had called him. The other cops milled around outside while Roy, Richard, Naomi and Tim talked in Roy's living room.

Officer Brockman scratched his head through his salt

and pepper hair. He had already listened to Naomi
describe her first and second encounter with the apparent
stalker. "So you didn't see all of his face?" Brockman
asked.

"No, I didn't," Naomi replied nervously. "Not enough
to identify him, anyway." She paused, suddenly aware
that she was shivering. "I saw his eyes."

"Do you remember anything specific about him?"

"Not really. Only that he had this terrible look on his
face. I don't know how to describe it." Naomi knew what
she had seen in his face, but she wasn't going to say it out
loud. She couldn't get the word past her lips. It froze in
between her teeth and if it had been food, she would have
choked on it. She had seen lust in those eyes, the worst
kind of lust imaginable: the *possessive* kind.

An unimaginable terror was rising through her and
making her feel nauseous. She recalled a smirk on that
face beyond the glass. It was the kind of expression she
remembered from the faces of children she had played
hide-and-go seek with in elementary school. It was the 'I-
found-you-and-I'm-going-to-get-you' look.

There's only one thing to do, Naomi thought. *I have to
go on with my life. I* cannot *let him win.*

Brockman and a couple of the other cops wandered the
field near the house, hoping to find something that the

intruder had dropped. Outside Naomi's bedroom window, they found crushed plants in the flowerbed where someone had walked and half a footprint in the soft loam. Although there was evidence that someone had been there, there was no evidence as to *who* it had been. It was getting late in the night and the cops had no choice but to leave. Brockman promised that he would watch the area more carefully, and the flashing lights soon flickered off and disappeared.

Inside Naomi's trailer, Richard sat down on the couch with a beer. Naomi joined him, her limbs still shuddering from nervousness. She covered a mental checklist in her mind. She had secured the locks on all of the windows, drawn the curtains and—

She turned and looked at the front door. It was locked. She sighed heavily. Beside her, Richard sipped his beer.

"I wasn't sure I'd ever be back in here again," he commented.

"Don't take it personally," Naomi said, shaking her head. "I . . . I don't know."

"*I* do. You've been scared. You weren't sure if you could trust me."

"You just said a mouthful." Naomi leaned back and took a long gulp from her Yuengling. She turned and looked at him. "To be honest, I wasn't sure for a little while if you were . . . ."

"You can say it. I understand. But as much as I would enjoy that," Richard began, a smirk crossing his lips, "I would never spy on you through your bedroom window."

Naomi almost laughed. Then she thought of the night that Richard had asked her out at Whellaby's Grocer. "How did you know I worked at Whellaby's? And how did you know that I lived here?"

"I was wondering when you were going to ask me that." He took another swig from his beer. "I hang out at the Night Kitchen a lot and I also like to spend my Friday nights at the local bars when bands are playing. There's one band I've been following for quite some time now."

"Let me guess—Jargon?"

"Exactly. After a while, I got to know Geo Harp pretty well. I'll admit, I found out that you two hung out together and I asked him about you. I told him not to mention it, though. I didn't want you to get the wrong idea."

Naomi nodded. "That makes sense."

"The Jargon show at the Coral Reef Tavern was the second show of theirs that I'd been to at that bar." He turned to her, a curious look on his face. "That night, you were the only girl in that entire bar that . . . *well* . . . You were the only one that looked like a human being, someone I could relate to. All the other girls were so *fake*." He blushed. "I couldn't take my eyes off you."

"You didn't answer my second question."

Richard looked suddenly defeated. He fidgeted where he sat. Naomi could tell that it had taken a lot for him to express himself so honestly. She almost felt badly for making him uncomfortable. At the same time, it was fun, and it was distracting her from her recent troubles.

"Um, I've seen you here before," he said, stumbling briefly on his words. "I asked some people in town and found out you were Roy's daughter."

"This *is* a pretty small town. Everybody knows everybody," Naomi admitted.

For a while, the two of them sat there holding their beers. Naomi wasn't certain, but she thought she might have put a damper on the conversation. After a while, Richard suggested they watch a movie. After looking through a collection of DVDs on one of Naomi's bookcases, they chose *Ladyhawke*. As Naomi popped open a second beer, she was finally able to relax, at least for a little while.

Chapter 21: The Jester and the Riddler

Right after Alexis had spoken with Naomi on the phone,
the detective had gone to Whellaby's and sat outside the
store until sunup, photographing almost anyone who
walked through the front doors. She limited the picture
taking to men that appeared agile or at least strong enough
to run a long distance. Naomi had described the man who
had run in front of her car as being relatively slim,
although she hadn't been able to see too much because he
had been running so fast. Alexis supposed that the man
she was looking for was between the ages of twenty and
forty. If he was an older man, it was likely that he had
victimized more than one woman, so she asked Frank to
check the police reports for anything that suggested a local
'peeping tom.'

So far, he hadn't called her, and she was more tired
than she'd been in a long time. Unfortunately, she
couldn't sleep yet. That morning, once all the local
businesses had opened for the day, Alexis got in her car
and drove down Maine Street. She had one major goal for
the day. She started at Summer Flower Shop on the
corner of Maine and Oak. At around 9:30 that morning,
Alexis walked up to the cashier at the flower shop. She
asked for the manager and showed him her badge.
Without further hesitation, Alexis brandished a small stack

of Polaroid photographs.

As she handed the photos to the manager, she said, "I need to know if any of these men came in here and bought a rose recently."

Naomi had a vague memory of a flickering clock, perhaps the one on the VCR beneath her television. She remembered the numbers 2:43 and recalled soft sounds beside her, like whispering. Naomi wasn't sure if it had been a dream or not, but she remembered her eyes opening briefly, just long enough to see Richard bend forward and kiss her on the forehead. When she woke up, he was gone.

It was noon. Her cell phone was vibrating on the coffee table. She picked it up.

"Hello?"

"Naomi, it's Geo. Are you still up for driving me?"

"Driving?" Naomi trailed off. She suddenly remembered her promise to Geo. She had told him that she would drive him to his grandmother's house on Thursday. "Is it Thursday?" she asked tiredly.

"It is. I can still catch the bus if you'd rather not drive. It's up to you."

Naomi looked around at the empty room. She suddenly felt very nervous. "No, it's okay. I'd like the company. Can I pick you up at one? I just need to jump in the shower real quick."

"Take your time," Geo said.

"All right. Thanks. I'll see you soon."

"Sounds good, Naomi."

She didn't bother to tell him about what had happened the night before; that could wait. Naomi clutched her stomach as she went into the bathroom. She must have drunk her beer too quickly. The hot water woke her up. She blinked into the steam as the water cascaded off her body. She tried not to think about the man who had chased her away from her own house. Today, she would have company and she would be able to escape, at least for a little while. Maybe by the time she got home, Alexis would have discovered the identity of the mysterious lurker.

The old Buick was waiting for Naomi in the driveway, parked by her garage and flanked by the chain link fence that surrounded the junkyard. The sun reflected brightly off the hood and the windshield. Naomi squinted as she walked through the driveway, passing the shop. She said hello to Devon and Pedro, then climbed into her car. It was almost two in the afternoon.

Despite the heat, Naomi was comfortable in her shorts and T-shirt. She rolled down the driver's side window and the passenger side window with a push of a button

and started down the driveway. Her broken window had
been fixed, it was a beautiful day and Naomi would be
able to spend her time with a friend. She was still shaken
after the night before, but there wasn't much she could do
about it except hope that the police and Tim Brockman
found some useful information soon.

"Naomi!"

She hit the brake and turned, leaning her head out the
window. Her father had emerged from the garage and was
walking steadily down the driveway. She merely looked
up at him as he reached her car. "Hey, kid. Where're you
headed?"

"I'm driving Geo to Helsontown." Naomi turned down
the stereo and tried to relax on the blue velour seat.

Roy crossed his arms over his chest. "I'm surprised to
see you out and about so soon, after what happened last
night. I wish you wouldn't go."

A wave of anger suddenly overshadowed every other
emotion that Naomi was experiencing. She clenched her
fists. "I won't let this control me," she said decidedly.
"Nobody, no matter who he is, is going to keep me from
living my life."

To Naomi's surprise, her father smiled. "Good," he
said. "You've got your cell phone on you, right?"

"Yes."

"Call me if you need anything. I'll try not to worry
about you too much." He reached in the window and
patted her gently on the shoulder.

As Naomi drove away, she laughed inwardly at what her father had said. It had been a joke, and the punch line was simple. Roy had been playing the protective parent ever since he had driven to Quakertown to retrieve his traumatized daughter. The thought of him 'trying not to worry' was absolutely preposterous. Naomi felt badly for him because she knew that he would be overwrought with paranoia until she piloted the Buick back into the driveway later that evening.

Still, she had promised Geoffrey that she would drive him to Helsontown, and that was what she was going to do. Despite the fact that she was alone, she felt better and better the farther she got from her father's house and her trailer. After last night, she wasn't comfortable at home anymore.

When Naomi got to Geo's house, he was waiting out front. A few cars passed her by as she pulled over by the sidewalk. Geo hopped in the front seat and Naomi merged with traffic once more.

Geoffrey leaned forward, pressing buttons on the CD player. "Nice set-up," he said. He turned up the volume and a Modest Mouse song began to play. "You do it yourself?"

"Yeah," Naomi said proudly. "I'm not good with electrical stuff, though. It was a hassle." She fiddled with the volume a bit more and enjoyed the feeling of the breeze against her face as they drove down Maine Street.

Naomi pressed her foot on the gas and felt the Buick

171

glide along the pavement. In front of them, a little green Mazda sped up as the road turned into a highway. Behind them, a rusted blue Chevy shambled along, picking up speed.

Alexis spent the entire morning making a list of possible suspects. Each man or woman was a person who may have had some kind of motive in exacting revenge on Marty Timmson. She was certain that it had been a murder. First, she would interview suspects. Then, she would follow up on her instincts. She would use the solid information as her first lead. Her instincts remained unsupported by concrete evidence; they would have to wait.

Whellaby had dug through the employee history to retrieve the names and addresses she now held in her hand. She was sitting in her ZX2 in the grocery store parking lot with the window down. She looked at the first name: Cory Pleco, the former meat department manager. Whellaby had told Alexis that some of the women in the store had taken to calling him 'meat creep,' due to his lecherous nature and inability to control his wandering eyes. He had been fired two months prior after being seen switching tags from a pound of roast beef to an extremely expensive filet. The act had been caught on camera and Pleco had been told to leave. Alexis doubted that he had anything to do with Timmson's death; Pleco lived on the other side of town, seven miles away, and Alexis was looking for someone who lived close enough that he could have arrived on foot.

No one had seen anyone suspicious in the parking lot, so she supposed that whoever had killed Timmson had walked there rather than driven. It was likely that whoever she was looking for lived within a three-mile radius.

Behind Whellaby's was a stretch of forest and then a development. Meadow Lane Road ran alongside the store, and across the road was another patch of woods and a smaller development for retired folks. Those two developments were the only two in Witchfire. The town was mostly made up of old houses and some trailer homes.

She also had to consider the possibility that the murderer had an accomplice; someone who would have been willing to drive the killer to the store and do a quick fade while nasty business was carried out in the boiler room. No one would have seen a vehicle drive up in the back. Perhaps the killer had met his or her driver up the road a bit. In which case, it would be even harder to support the murder theory because the supposed killer could have come from anywhere.

Alexis sighed and leaned her forehead against the steering wheel. She had only considered one name so far and already, she was at a loss for ideas. The boiler room hadn't been treated as a crime scene in the first place. Any evidence would be long gone. She almost had to hope that the gum wrappers and the broken twigs in the woods would be helpful in her investigation. Otherwise, someone would get away with murder and Alexis would go home without a paycheck.

I can't let that happen, she thought to herself. She wasn't sure if she was thinking of the killer getting away with it or of the lack of money in her pocket. Either way, she had to solve the case—whatever it took.

Cory Pleco wasn't much help. Alexis drank stale coffee with him in a dingy living room and just before she left, he asked her out on a date. She politely rejected him. According to Pleco, the loss of his job had nothing to do with Marty Timmson. It was a younger man in the meat department that had reported him, and an assistant manager that had decided to check the cameras. Alexis wondered if that manager had been Rey Kustafik.

She left Pleco's house feeling as though she needed to take a shower. Next on the list was Piers Murphy, who had been fired from his cashiering job because he had screamed at a customer. Apparently, the man had been in the army, suffered serious injuries and was on medication for his post-traumatic stress disorder. He had only lasted a few weeks at Whellaby's, but Alexis decided to talk to him anyway.

Murphy turned out to be just as unhelpful as Pleco, although he was very polite and did *not* ask the detective out for a drink. Murphy had been on good terms with Timmson. In fact, the ex-cashier confessed that he had wept upon reading the notice in the paper. Alexis wondered if his medication had made him overly emotional.

Most of the people on the list proved unhelpful, only mildly suspicious or they had very good alibis. At about two-thirty, Alexis parked her car in the parking lot of a drugstore on Maine Street. She dialed Spencer Whellaby's number and waited while it rang. Then someone picked up the phone and spoke tiredly. "Hello?"

"Mr. Whellaby, this is Detective Nevid. Listen, I've gone through the entire list you gave me and turned up nothing."

"All ten of them?"

"All ten." The company had let ten people go over the past year; Alexis thought that seemed like a lot. Then again, she had never worked in retail. Perhaps that was normal.

"Hmm." Whellaby thought for a moment. "There are a couple more you could try."

There were a couple of questions Alexis wanted to ask Mr. Whellaby, but those would have to wait. For now, she would just listen. "Who?"

"Two young men, actually. They used to work

overnight in the dairy department. Jesse Donahue—
everyone called him the Jester. And then there was his
friend, Gerry Howard."

"And what'd they call him? The Riddler?" Alexis
asked jokingly.

"Hmm? Oh, no. They called him Gerry."

Figures, Alexis thought. "What'd they get fired for?"

"They didn't get fired. They both quit on the same
day."

"What happened?"

"There were rumors going around about them. You
see, we had this overnight cashier who was getting
forcibly transferred to my other store."

"Your other store?"

"Yes, I own a department store in Helsontown called
Spencer's. They wanted to get rid of Jules—that was the
cashier—so I decided to send him to work in Helsontown.
He didn't like it one bit. Actually, he and Timmson had a
bit of a falling out the month before Jules left."

"Maybe Jules had something to do with it. What's his
last name?"

"Oh, no, not Jules," Whellaby said. "It wasn't him."

"What makes you so sure?"

There was an awkward pause on the other line.
"Instinct."

"Right. So what about these two overnight workers,
Jester and Riddler?"

"Jesse and Gerry."

"Whatever."

"Well, Jules started spreading rumors about them. He didn't get along with them. Jesse supposedly came in one night and got in a fight with Jules. Ever since then, Jules had it in for Jesse and his friend. So as I understand it, he started telling everyone at Customer Service that Jesse and Gerry were lovers. Some of the people who work in Customer Service are real gossipers, so it spread pretty quickly."

"And these two were publicly humiliated?"

"Pretty much."

Alexis thought that sounded like a pretty good motive for murder. What she couldn't figure out was why they would have gone after Timmson and not this Jules character. So Alexis asked Whellaby.

"I don't know," Whellaby said. "I personally doubt they had anything to do with it, but I do remember that Jesse blamed Timmson for not trying to stop the whole mess. I didn't get involved, but I heard a lot about it from Timmson."

"It seems as though you're not placing any real suspicion on anyone, Mr. Whellaby," Alexis commented. "Who do *you* think did it?"

"I don't know, Ms. Nevid, but I'm sure you can figure it out."

Mr. Whellaby hurriedly ended the conversation. Alexis thought that he had seemed rather desperate to leave it all up to her and she had to wonder why.

She was certain that there was something Mr.
Whellaby wasn't telling her. She doubted that he had had
anything to do with Timmson's death, but she was
beginning to think that he knew who did. Alexis still
hadn't spoken with him about the original discovery of the
body. Why hadn't he told her outright that he had been
the one to find Timmson? Something very strange was
going on.

Whellaby had given her Jesse Donahue's address. She
left the parking lot of the drug store and headed down the
street. When she pulled into Jesse's driveway, Alexis
said, "Hmmph." The house was situated conveniently in
the development behind Whellaby's Grocer.

When she rang the doorbell, she didn't have to wait
very long before a young man opened the door.

"Jesse Donahue?" Alexis asked.

"That's me. Can I help you with something?" He was
tall and well built, with short black hair, deep brown eyes
and a confused expression on his face. He looked as
though he'd just gotten out of the shower. He was
wearing a bathrobe and smoking a cigarette.

"I'm Detective Alexis Nevid." She showed him her
badge. "I have a few questions to ask you. May I come
in?"

"What's this in relation to?" Jesse seemed very
reluctant to let her inside.

"Just a couple of things that have happened at
Whellaby's grocery store. You haven't been implicated in

178

anything, don't worry; I just want to ask you some questions."

"All right."

Jesse stepped aside. When Alexis walked into the narrow front hall, he closed the door and led her into the living room. She sat down on an olive green armchair and he slumped onto a couch across from her. The room was muggy and humid. One fan pointlessly circulated the hot hair.

"What'd you want to ask me?" Jesse asked. He put out his cigarette in an ashtray nearby and leaned back on the couch.

"I'm sure you've heard about the suicide of Marty Timmson."

"What about it?"

"Did you know him well?" Alexis asked carefully.

Jesse shrugged. "No, not really. He hired me. He was an asshole. That's all there is to it."

"Why didn't you like him?"

"Nobody liked him," Jesse replied firmly. "Oh, there were a couple people, I guess, but none of the regular associates liked him. There was always something."

"Like what?"

Jesse scoffed. "He never *did* anything. He was a typical manager. I can't understand why Whellaby ever hired him. I guess he got Timmson on the payroll so that he wouldn't have to be there everyday watching the store. Whellaby's rich enough that he can hire as many people as

179

he wants and not have to worry too much."

"I see. What else did Timmson do? Or, not do?" Alexis added.

Jesse got a curious look on his face. "Why do you want to know? What's all this about?"

Alexis had been waiting for that one. "Call it curiosity on Whellaby's part. He wants to know what made Timmson kill himself, so he's got me on the job." Alexis thought that sounded like a pretty good excuse.

Jesse seemed skeptical. "That doesn't make sense to me."

"I can't tell you much; Mr. Whellaby's reasons are confidential. Would you please answer my question?" Alexis was quick to add this inquiry because she could tell that Jesse's interest in her presence was waning.

"You mean, about why nobody liked Timmson?"

"Yes."

"All he did was sit in his office, complain, walk around the store, eat something, and complain some more. That's what I heard from the people in the deli. Supposedly, he had a good family life, but I can't figure out why any woman would want Timmson."

It occurred to Alexis that she had never actually seen Marty Timmson, alive or dead. "Why's that?"

"He was pretty ugly—one of those guys who ages badly. Skinny, wrinkly. Big nose." It was obvious that Jesse would have said something much more derogatory about Timmson if he had felt completely comfortable

180

doing so. There was an unmistakable glint in his eye. He nervously lit another cigarette and mumbled something under his breath.

"I heard that Timmson had something to do with you losing your job," Alexis said.

"Whellaby tell you that?"

Alexis nodded and said that he had.

"There was this cashier that spread rumors about my friend Gerry and I. He got everybody in the store believing that Gerry and I were . . . ."

"Were what?" Alexis knew what he was talking about, but she wanted to hear the whole story from him, personally.

Jesse looked embarrassed. "Gay."

"Why did you blame Timmson?"

"He never tried to stop anything!" Jesse exclaimed. "He knew what was going on, he heard Jules—that was the cashier—insult us, screw with us all the time, but he never told the guy to stop or did anything about it."

"That's a shame," Alexis said sincerely.

"We walked out one day. We'd had enough."

"I can understand that."

Jesse took a long drag from his cigarette. "Between you and me," he said, "I was so pissed. I could have *killed* him."

Chapter 22: Dark Summer Night

The swamps that flanked the town of Witchfire didn't
look like much; they were really just flood planes,
surrounded by avenues of water that overflowed whenever
it rained. The area was chock full of foliage and trees,
forests that a person could get lost in. Witchfire was the
kind of place where eccentric men and women went to
search out solitude. Naomi had heard of a few such
people, wealthy, quiet individuals whose gorgeous old
estates were surrounded by trees and hidden amidst all
those thick leaves and branches.

They passed by several fields outside of Witchfire,
where it was said that one day a year in fall, the Devil
would appear amidst the cornhusks. Supposedly, one
could run races with him in the darkness at midnight. The
runner would know if the Devil had won by the direction
in which the wind was blowing. Naomi didn't see the
point of the story and failed to understand what one could
possibly gain by running through cornfields at night, but
she was aware of the fact that Witchfire had numerous
legends tucked away in its rich history.

It was a hot day, just like many of the days that had
come before it, and Naomi was glad to be out and about.
She and Geoffrey stopped at a little cafe for lunch and
continued on to Geo's grandmother's house, where she

had already begun piling boxes of clothes by the front door. They got to work, and the next few hours passed quickly as they packed and moved furniture.

In front of the little house, Naomi stood with Geoffrey. She stared for a moment at an iridescent glass globe in the middle of a quaint garden. She was distracted from her reverie when Geo laid a comforting hand on her shoulder.

"Are you okay?" he asked.

Naomi thought for a moment. This had to have been the fifth or sixth time that Geo had asked her this, and she didn't blame him. She had gone into detail concerning her late-night run from the unknown creeper, and she had told him all about Alexis Nevid's involvement and the stacks of photos she had printed from the surveillance cameras at Whellaby's.

Geo had been shocked to learn how persistent this stalker was, and remarked that he would have never guessed that such a thing would happen in the quiet little town of Witchfire. Nacre Township itself was almost completely crime free. It was less crime and more of a supernatural shadow that hung over Witchfire, rife with legends and tales that could make a person's flesh crawl. The thought of something truly scary happening in Witchfire was enough to make Geoffrey want to move back to North Carolina, where his belligerent father owned a small farm.

For a moment, the two friends remained silent. A truck had arrived to carry all of Geo's grandmother's heavy furniture to her new abode. Most of the smaller stuff was already there, thanks to Naomi and her Buick. She had only taken three short trips. The kindly old woman didn't own that much.

"Want to go for a walk?" Geo asked. "There's a park down the street."

Naomi, lost in her own thoughts, was startled. "Huh? Oh, sure." She turned and walked down the garden path. "Don't we have to drive your grandma to her new house?"

"You don't have to. It turns out my uncle is arriving from Virginia today. He couldn't make it earlier," Geo explained.

"Oh." Naomi stopped at the end of the sidewalk. She was standing in front of her Buick. "Which way?"

"Right. It's just down the street." Geo pointed.

Naomi saw a line of trees that led from the side yard of an old Victorian. She could just make out a playground a short distance away. The park wasn't very big, but it was a lovely day out. She figured that any kind of a sojourn into the summer heat would help to cheer her, especially with Geo keeping her company.

The two friends started across the street, then stopped so that an old Chevy pick-up truck could pass by. As they walked into the park, a soft breeze shook the tree leaves and the birds chirped musically from their perches.

"You haven't told me whether or not you're okay," Geo said. He spoke quickly and matter-of-factly, as though it were something he had been pondering for quite

185

some time.

"I'm fine, really." Naomi stepped carefully across some rocks in a shallow stream. Geo jumped over and joined her. "Of course, it's not easy," she continued. "I've been having nightmares and I'm always afraid to go home."

For a moment, the two of them stared into the trickling water. "I have a second bedroom at my apartment," Geo said. "You're welcome to stay with me for a little while."

"Really?"

"Certainly. I even have a futon."

The idea was very attractive to Naomi. She knew that Geoffrey lived in a second floor apartment in an old house on the South side of Witchfire. Who could possibly peek in at her if she wasn't on the ground floor? "Geo, that sounds great. Could I really spend a couple nights at your place?"

Geo echoed what Naomi had told him the other night at Whellaby's. "What are friends for?"

Naomi smiled warmly and gave Geo a big hug. After their walk, they helped Geo's grandmother arrange her furniture at her new place. Geo's uncle was a college professor; they chatted for a little while about various things. As the afternoon wound down, Geo decided to spend the night at his grandmother's new house so that he could help her with various chores on the following morning and spend time with his uncle. Naomi hadn't wanted to leave by herself, but she did. At around eight-thirty that evening, Geo gave her a hug and told her to be careful. He also asked her to call him when she got home, no matter how late it was, just so that he knew she would be all right.

"I'll be fine, Geo, really," Naomi insisted. But even as she climbed into her Buick, she knew that she wasn't entirely certain. As she drove back onto the highway and headed toward Witchfire, she began to feel a little uncomfortable.

Naomi turned up the stereo and listened to the Grateful Dead. A good distance behind her, a Chevy truck rumbled along; Naomi never noticed it.

After talking to Jesse Donahue, Alexis drove back to her office downtown. She sat in her car for a moment watching the sun set. Then she went upstairs, opened a window and lit a cigar. The warm evening breeze flicked at a stack of papers. She weighted them down with a heavy conch shell that she had found in North Carolina. She stared at the shell, exhaled a puff of smoke and stared at the shell some more. That was when the phone rang. Alexis picked it up.

"Detective Nevid here."

"Hi, Alexis. It's Frank. What are you up to?"

The papers on the desk fluttered in the breeze again. "Just thinking," Alexis said. "What do you want?"

"You find the missing link in the suicide case yet?"

"No, not yet. Is that all you called about?"

"Actually, no. I called to tell you that I looked through all the police reports to see if there had been any reports of peeking toms, stalkers, things like that."

"Anything?"

"Not a thing, Alexis. Not recently, and nothing of any consequence. I'm sorry."

"Damn it." Alexis leaned forward and put out her cigar in a nearby ashtray.

"I'm guessing that means you haven't made any headway at all, huh?"

"Actually, I have. Sort of." She told him about Jesse Donahue, but she didn't tell him a lot. She had a habit of being paranoid about the security of the phone lines. "I feel like Whellaby knows something he's not telling me. I'm going to call him tonight."

"I won't ask."

"Not on the phone, Frankie. I'll tell you later. I just have this hunch."

"You were always good with hunches, Alexis. Let me know how it turns out, okay?"

"Sure thing, Frankie."

Naomi had been driving for about ten minutes before she realized that the same truck that had followed her out of

Helsontown was still behind her. She tried to put it out of her mind. First, she turned up the CD player. For a little while, she focused on the music.

As it got darker, the headlights of the other vehicle became more distracting. It was still a good distance away from her, but the lights were piercing through her back window and hitting her rearview mirror. She flipped the mirror up and continued to listen to her music.

After a couple of minutes, Naomi turned the stereo down and picked up her cell phone. She found Oliver's number and pressed the call button. When Oliver picked up the phone, he sounded groggy. Naomi asked if she had woken him up.

"No, it's okay. I was just trying to take a nap," Oliver hazarded.

"I'm sorry," Naomi said. She squinted as a car passed by with its high beams on. "I just wanted to see if you were up for hanging out tonight."

"You have off, too?" Oliver asked.

"Yeah."

"I don't think I'm doing anything."

"It's Thursday," Naomi said.

"Then I'm definitely not doing anything." Oliver sounded happy about it. "Why don't you come on over? We can figure out what to do from there?"

"Okay!" Naomi breathed a sigh of relief. "That's awesome; I really didn't want to be alone tonight."

"Is everything okay?" Oliver asked.

"It could be better. I'll give you an update when I get there."

"Where are you?"

"Oh, about twenty-five minutes away." Naomi glanced out the window. "I'm headed through the swamps. No-man's land, so speak."

"Right. Well, you'd better get off the phone. You should be home before it starts storming, though."

"Storming?"

"Yeah, it's supposed to rain. I think we're supposed to get some thunder and lighting, too. There's a flood watch."

"Ugh," Naomi mumbled. "Well, I'll see . . . Oh, shit."

"What's wrong?"

The old Buick's lights had suddenly dimmed. The car began to slow down. Naomi hit the gas, but nothing happened. She quickly veered the Buick to the side of the road, nearly dropping her cell phone in the process. "Damn it!" she cursed. "Oliver, something's wrong with my car. Oliver? Oliver, are you there?"

As the car came to a complete stop, Naomi looked at her phone. The signal was fluctuating. She knew that there was a certain point on this road where most cell phones lost their signal; she figured that she had reached that point. Behind her, headlights flashed while someone else parked behind her. Tiny drops of water began to splatter against the windshield.

She had a small flashlight on her key chain. When she

190

popped the hood, the light cast eerie shadows around the engine. Naomi was aware of footsteps hitting the pavement, drawing nearer and nearer. She was cognizant of the fact that she was alone and in the middle of nowhere. She began to wish that she had a tire iron in her hand, but it was already too late. A man turned the corner, a wide smile on his face.

"Hi. Need some help?" Droplets of water dotted his wire-framed glasses. There was stubble on his chin and he looked as though he was straining to see her. The strange man was wearing a purple and green blazer, an unusual contrast to his gray and white camouflage pants. Naomi guessed that he was in his mid-thirties.

An SUV passed by, headed for Helsontown, and Naomi wished that it had stopped. "I, uh . . . I can take care of it," she said nervously. "I'll just walk down the road and bit and see if I can get a hold of a friend of mine." She took her cell phone out of her pocket and was about to dial her father's phone number when the stranger interrupted.

"Oh, there's no need for that." In any other situation, Naomi might have thought that his voice sounded soothing. She couldn't help but detect an overabundance of kindness, as though the stranger would have done *anything* to ensure that Naomi was safe.

"Don't I know you from somewhere?" Naomi asked. "You look kind of familiar."

The man shrugged. "Most flowers look much like

other flowers. Although, some are more unique than others."

"Right," Naomi mumbled. She looked at her phone, which had no signal. She put her phone back in her pocket, looked back at the strange man and sighed. He was the only person within miles. It was dark outside and her phone wasn't working. He was a little odd, but perhaps he could help her. "I don't understand what's wrong," she said, standing in front of her car.

"What happened?"

"It just turned off. I'm thinking it might be an electrical problem." Naomi remembered telling Geoffrey that she wasn't that good with electrical systems; it was true. When it came to engines, body work, tires, brakes and exhaust systems, Naomi was almost a genius. Electronics were not her strong point by any means. "I'm a mechanic," she explained. "I've never had this problem before."

"Did you run out of gas?"

"No. I would have known if that had happened." She ran the flashlight over the engine again. Naomi allowed the light to linger on the battery. "Maybe there's—wait a minute. What's—"

There was something attached to the positive battery cable and Naomi didn't know what it was. It was something she had never seen before. She had worked on this Buick numerous times. The idea that she could have missed something was almost preposterous, yet here it was—a connection, a wire, but leading to where?

"Would you like a ride somewhere?" the stranger asked. "I can take you anywhere you'd like to go."

Fortunately for Naomi, she had already figured it out. "*You*," she mumbled, almost breathless.

As he reached out for her, a devilish grin on his face, Naomi shot down the street, tripped on a fallen branch, and tumbled headlong into the woods.

Chapter 23: Taking a Leap

Alexis called Spencer Whellaby and asked him if she could come over to his house and discuss the case. She told him that she had a few leads, which was true, but she didn't tell him that her leads involved questioning him.

The detective had briefly entertained the idea that Whellaby might have killed Marty Timmson, but that wouldn't have made any sense. A man of Whellaby's age and social standing in the community had no reason to murder an underling. Alexis had wondered what would drive a man like Whellaby to kill, and there was only one reason that she could think of. Whellaby had something to hide. Nevertheless, Alexis didn't think that he had killed Timmson, not even to conceal his secrets. There was something else. Tonight, she was determined to find out what it was.

Whellaby's house was on the desolate side of town. An abandoned high school and a museum of Witchfire's odd history stood side-by-side, one occupied with people and artifacts, the other occupied by shadows and cobwebs. A sign by the old high school read: 'Future home of the Witchfire Public Library.'

Alexis had been to the museum before. A little old lady who claimed to be the descendent of the only witch ever burned in Pennsylvania ran it, and it was nothing special, certainly not if you had lived in Nacre Township for most of your life.

The abandoned high school was a different story. There were so few kids left in Witchfire that the majority of them took buses to neighboring towns for their education. The Witchfire high school was too big, and the entire East wing of it had burned to the ground two years prior. Nobody had ever figured out why it had happened. Alexis thought they might as well blame the Devil, since the majority of Witchfire's population seemed overly preoccupied with the occult.

Even Whellaby himself dabbled in the supernatural history of the town by donating funds to the local historical society. Alexis thought that he probably donated money to the little old lady who owned the museum, as well.

Spencer Whellaby's house was down the line from the old high school. He had a long gravel driveway that led in between two ominous looking statues of lions. Alexis knew that Whellaby hadn't put them there; the big cats had come with the property and had deteriorated a good bit over the years. Alexis drove her ZX2 past the lions and down the narrow driveway, which was about a half a mile long. She parked in front of a big old farmhouse and got out of her car.

Alexis had only been to this place once before, but she loved the house. Whellaby took good care of it. Behind the house was a small barn that had been recently painted.

In the night, Alexis could only make out the dark shape that she presumed was the barn. She went up to the front door and rang the doorbell.

Just as Mr. Whellaby stepped aside and invited Alexis into his home, it began to rain. The rain was very light, but Alexis could tell that a downpour was coming. Thankfully, Whellaby had a cozy home; Alexis told him so.

"Well, thank you, Detective Nevid. It's not often I have company. Come on into the living room." They stepped through a small foyer. The soft lighting, the dark carpeting over the wood floors and the tapestries on the walls combined to make a very quaint, comfortable atmosphere. There was no television in sight, only tall wooden bookcases. Whellaby had been reading a book before Alexis had arrived; the paperback was sitting on an end table, overturned to mark where the old man had left off.

Whellaby was wearing a T-shirt and a pair of slacks. Slippers sat in front of his armchair. He sunk into the soft material and offered Alexis a seat on the couch. The room was cool and comfortable. An old dog was curled up on the carpeting. When a crack of thunder shattered the silence of the night, the dog's ear twitched, but he remained asleep.

"What was it you wanted to talk about, Miss Nevid? Have you discovered anything new?"

"Actually, yes." Alexis took off her fedora and set it

on the coffee table.

"Would you like anything to drink?" Whellaby had started to get up, but Alexis shook her head.

"Don't worry about it. Just relax. I only came here for information."

The old man's brow furrowed. "Is something wrong? You sound upset."

"I'm fine. I'd like to know about *you*. I think you have something you should tell me."

Mr. Whellaby was a sharp-minded intellectual. Alexis appreciated that in a person. She knew that she wouldn't have to explain much in order to make her point.

Whellaby leaned forward, frowning. "Exactly *what* are you insinuating?"

The old dog lifted its head tiredly, and Alexis smirked. "Mr. Whellaby, Jesse Donahue has a motive and a location that would have been perfect for sneaking into your store and sneaking out unnoticed." Alexis folded her hands in her lap. "This *Jester*, as you called him, lives right behind your store in a development. I could probably have the cops after him in seconds as a prime suspect, if I had enough evidence. But Jesse Donahue didn't do it. And do you know how I know?" There was a glint in her dark eyes and a look on her face that dared the old man to say anything she didn't like.

"I . . . I don't know," he said softly.

Alexis leaned back. "You, Spencer Whellaby, don't *think* that Donahue did it, isn't that right?"

"That's true."

"But it's not just that. You *know* he didn't do it."

"Excuse me?"

"You hired a detective, Whellaby. You got one. I've got news for you; I'm on to you." Before Whellaby could respond, Alexis continued. "You're the only one that suspected that Timmson's death was a murder, not a suicide. You're the only one that *frantically* came to me, insisting that it wasn't an accident. You could have just as easily told the cops that, but you knew they would think you were crazy, or they would ask for proof you didn't have. You made a fool of me by not telling me that *you* were the one who found the body. The reason you hired me was because you were hoping that I would find out what you already knew."

"You're not making any sense." Although he had spoken firmly, Whellaby appeared nervous and uncertain. He kept glancing at the windows as though somebody was watching him.

"Who are you looking for out there, Whellaby?" Alexis glanced at one of the windows. "Whoever it is that's keeping your mouth shut?"

"I wasn't looking for anybody." Now he sounded angry. "I don't like where you're going with this and I won't stand for it."

Her expression softened. "Listen to me. Nothing's going to change unless you tell me the truth. I could find out for myself, but it'll be a lot easier if you just come clean."

Whellaby leaned forward and rubbed his eyes, then his temples. "I . . . I wasn't supposed to tell you. You were supposed to find out on your own."

"Find out what?"

Whellaby looked up. "I didn't want to tell you that I was the one who found him, but I knew you would find out eventually."

"And you saw the killer, didn't you?" Alexis asked calmly.

"Yes. I know who killed Marty Timmson." Whellaby sighed and clutched the paperback he had been reading before Alexis arrived. "I gave you all of the recent termination reports," he said. "All of the people you talked to were fired recently."

"But there was somebody else who was fired, more than a year ago," Alexis presumed.

Whellaby nodded. "He insisted that it had been a mistake. He was accused of stealing."

Alexis was beginning to get annoyed with Whellaby's tendency to lead her on and not tell her the whole truth. "How do you know he killed Timmson? And *who* is he?"

For a moment, everything was a blur. Fat raindrops splattered against Naomi's face and she found herself scrambling on a bed of moist leaves and pine needles. Her head was throbbing and she suddenly became aware of the fact that she had fallen down a short hill and hit her head on a branch. She wasn't sure what was going on, but she knew that she had to think fast. She could hear someone advancing on her, someone with a heavy step.

In the darkness, Naomi got to her feet and felt in her pocket for her cell phone. She couldn't use it now, certainly not without reception—and especially because she could see a dark figure coming toward her. There was no time. Naomi turned and ran into the woods. She had no idea in which direction she was headed, only that she had to get away from the madman who was following her.

Naomi thought of the face she had seen in her bedroom window. She thought of the man who had chased her across her father's property and into town. The stranger who had stopped behind her on the highway was clearly the same person. He had finally caught up with her. She knew she had seen him somewhere before, but she couldn't place him.

With only the will to survive prevalent in her mind, she jumped over rocks and tree roots as the rain pounded on her head. Behind her, she heard a man's voice calling out.

"Naomi! Where are you going?"

There was an eerie tinge of disappointment in his voice, like a child whose dog had run away from home. It began to rain harder. Naomi's heart was pounding. She ducked under branches and ran past young trees, almost falling several times. In the back of her mind, she was thinking; *this is it, I'm going to die.*

And that was when she remembered where she had seen him before; the man who was chasing her was a customer from Whellaby's grocery store. Lightning flashed across the sky and for a split second, Naomi could see gnarled tree branches, wet leaves dancing in the breeze and twisted shrubs ahead. Whoever was following her, he didn't give up. His voice, like warm oozing oil, resonated through the night.

"Naomi, didn't you like the rose I left you? Didn't you like my note? I'm very upset that you're being so rude to me, Naomi." His loud voice, edged with hurt, seeped through the thin film of Naomi's clothing much like the cold rainwater that was soaking her to the bone. "I love you, don't you understand?" He called out to her. "I was so shy at first. Whenever I saw you, I froze up." His words were labored as he moved faster.

Naomi saw a slope ahead. A crevasse in the earth appeared like a Godsend and Naomi jumped into its grasp, spotting a hole or cave just big enough for her to hide in. There were caves like this all through the woods of Witchfire and it was just her luck that she should find one. Brambles ripped at her clothes and her skin. She jumped and shoved her body into the rocky hole in the ground, hoping that it was dark enough that her stalker wouldn't be able to see her.

As Naomi cowered in her hiding place, she realized her mistake. There was no way out except to expose herself.

What if he didn't look any further for her? What if he waited for her, expecting her eventual emergence?

From somewhere above her, Naomi heard his voice. "Naomi, you must understand. I've watched you for so long." In his effort to catch his breath, the man's voice was almost raspy. "I loved you the first moment I saw you. You were so beautiful. You were working at Whellaby's. I asked you where something was, and when I heard your voice, I was . . . I was stunned into silence. You're so perfect. I want you. I must have you."

Naomi thought it was a wonder that he could say so much after running as much as he had. She was still catching her breath—and she was terrified. She must have sat there, crouched in the dirt and sitting on rough, pointy rocks, for over five minutes. Those five minutes felt like an hour. After a time, she heard footsteps—and then she heard nothing.

She began to wonder if the man had gone to look for her somewhere else. Perhaps he thought that she'd run farther away. Perhaps he thought Naomi was headed back to the road. Maybe he would look for her closer to the tree line. She felt as though she was about to fall apart, break down, or worse—admit defeat.

I can't give up, she thought to herself. *I said I wasn't going to give up, I said I wasn't going to let him win. I'm not going to let him win now, either.*

If she got away, Naomi could send the cops after him. She had to depend on the need to carry out justice. She

203

had to believe that the best thing, at all costs, was for her to escape so that she could make sure that this stranger was punished for what he had done. Naomi glanced around for something that could be used as a weapon. She saw a branch, but it was too flimsy. There were many rocks around her, so she picked one that had a blunt point on it. It fit comfortably in her hand.

And then she climbed from the tiny cave and out into the open.

Chapter 24: Running Through the Woods

Richard lived in a spacious apartment above Witchfire Bookstore. The building and the bookstore were both owned by an elderly couple that didn't seem to know what the going rate for apartments was. As a result, Richard only paid five hundred dollars a month, utilities included. Going to work was as simple as walking down the stairs and into the book store.

The smaller second bedroom in the apartment was where Richard kept his computer and most of his books. There were a couple of posters on the walls and a bulletin board devoted to some of Richard's favorite photos that he had taken on ghost hunting expeditions.

One of the windows that overlooked the street was open. Richard watched as a fat fly bounced pointlessly against the screen in an attempt to escape the rain, and then buzzed away. There was the occasional flash of headlights, but for the most part, the only light beyond the windows emanated from street lamps.

Richard turned back to his computer and was about to type another sentence in a new story he was writing, when he was suddenly overcome with an intense anxiety. He wouldn't have been able to explain it if he had tried.

That was when the phone rang.

Naomi wished that she knew what his name was. She had
run through the woods after climbing out of her hiding
place and somehow managed to dial 911 along the way.
She told the dispatcher something about her Buick parked
on the side of the road, what road it had been and how she
had ended up in the woods, but then she had lost
connection. It was a wonder she'd had enough signal
strength in the first place.

"I know you're hiding from me, Naomi." The man's
voice snapped around the trees like a boomerang looking
for a target. It was pouring rain and Naomi was soaked to
the skin. She kept moving, skirting around tree trunks and
slipping behind shrubs when she thought that the man
might see her.

He was tall and lithe, but not very quick. Naomi was
small and muscular from working on cars all of her life.
She had noticed that the stalker wore glasses. It was likely
that his eyesight wouldn't help him in the dark, and it was
also likely that the rain made it worse for him.

At periodic intervals, she would duck behind
something and peek at her phone, ensuring that the light
was low so that it wouldn't be seen by the man who was
following her through the trees. She didn't know where
she was. She would have been panicking if it weren't for
the adrenalin that was pumping through her veins, forcing
her onward.

For only a second, a bright flash of lightning turned the dark forest into a collection of stark whites and grays as Naomi crouched behind a tree, panting. She slipped down a short hill and hid behind another tree. Her hands shook as she dug in the pocket of her jacket. Somewhere behind her, she heard a branch break. The sound of the rain hitting the ground was deafening. She pulled a piece of paper out of her pocket and glanced around her. In the distance, she could see the silhouette of an old derelict mill, long since abandoned and left to rot in the midst of the forest by a stream. She read the number by the faint glow of her cell phone and dialed.

After two rings, Richard picked up the phone. Naomi had just enough time to tell him where she was before the signal disappeared and the phone died.

Frank called Detective Nevid's private cell phone and told her that there had been an emergency call from some girl who was being chased through the woods by a maniac. Alexis wanted to know what the girl's name was and Frank told her that it was Naomi Vogler.

As the rain slapped against the windowpanes and the wind began to attack the humid air with a seemingly purposeful intent, Alexis left Whellaby's house and ran for her car. She had gotten all of the information that she needed from the old man. Right now, none of it mattered.

She had to reach Naomi. Up until now, the cops hadn't been able to do anything to help her. There had been no evidence of a stalker until the note and the rose had been left on the hood of Oliver's car.

Alexis hadn't been able to track down the stalker through the little evidence that existed. She had checked both of the florists in town and none of the staff of either store remembered seeing any of the men in the photos that Alexis provided.

For three nights in a row, Alexis had watched Whellaby's grocery store, carefully noting each person that came and went and memorizing the faces of the regular customers. Despite her efforts, there was no suspect, only a shadow that drifted through Witchfire like a ghost. Whoever the stalker was, he was smart.

The only physical reminder that someone had intruded on Roy Vogler's land had been the markings on the door of the garage where a prowler had tried to break in. But nothing had been stolen and no one had been hurt. Naomi had been left to wait until the inevitable moment when the nameless man took his chance to strike, when his inherent shyness erupted in a sudden burst of courage. That courage was all that it would take for the unknown lurker to take hold of his obsession.

As she drove, Alexis got back on the phone with Frank. "Okay, Frankie, I'm headed down Maine. Where'd you say I'm supposed to go?" Two cop cars with flashing lights passed her by. Two more followed.

"Head out toward the highway. I'm right behind you. The girl didn't know where she was, Brockman told me, but she described some paths that could be the township hiking trails near the swamps. Sounds like she ran downhill toward the low-lands. Have you been there?"

"I've done some camping in that area."

"Look for some parked cars on the side of the road. We got a hold of Naomi's father and he says Naomi drives an '86 Buick."

"Oh, shit . . . Is Roy okay?" A lot of people knew Roy; he was the best mechanic in town. Even Alexis had taken her ZX2 to Vogler's Auto Repair in the past.

"He's holding up. Probably pacing back and forth like a crazy man, though."

"Can't blame him." Alexis glanced to her left, and then sped around a corner through a red light. She was grateful that there was hardly any traffic. "See you there, Frankie."

"Right." Frank hung up his phone. Alexis sped up, following the flashing lights. They switched off a moment later; the detective knew that the cops were trying to be discreet. They didn't want the madman to know they were there.

Naomi wasn't sure how long it had been. She only knew that she had been running for quite some time. Her body

209

ached and the rain was slicing through the leaves above her and cascading relentlessly down her face and chilling her to the bone. Then again, perhaps she was cold because she was terrified.

She could hear his voice behind her, tinged with a lilting determination; it was the voice of a man who was nowhere near giving up.

Had it been a half an hour or an hour? Or had it only been twenty minutes? Naomi couldn't gauge the time. Somewhere along the way, she had dropped her cell phone in the wet leaves.

"Naomi, stop playing games with me." The voice was beginning to sound disappointed, like a parent who feels that they must punish their errant child. "Everyone must follow in the path of natural destiny," he continued. "Just as flowers and weeds must grow, you are fated to be with me."

Naomi tripped on a root and fell to her knees on a steep incline. Another gash in the earth stretched out before her. When a flash of lightning lit the forest, she saw blood on her hands and wondered where it had come from. She felt something warm on her head and tried to ignore it. Her eyes were brimming with tears that wanted to fall, but she held them back. She had to keep going. If she stopped for any length of time, he would surely catch up to her. Naomi glanced behind her and caught sight of a shadow.

"There you are," a voice said.

Naomi gasped and fell forward, dodging the hand that

reached for her. She grappled with the earth and clambered to her feet. Something grabbed at her shirt. "No! Let go of me!" Naomi's voice emerged sounding like a raspy, weak imitation of her normal self, shocking her.

"Come back here!" This time, the man's voice sounded angry. She managed to pull away from him. She heard her shirt rip. Naomi stumbled through the trees as the stalker followed her, first slowly and then quicker as his feet got used to the rougher terrain. The old mill was off to Naomi's left. She veered to the right, hoping to avoid getting trapped in a dead end.

He was close behind, but she heard him curse. He had tripped, or gotten caught on something. Naomi didn't look back to find out what had slowed him down. She hurried onward, despite the fact that her body had nearly had enough.

Naomi shrieked when she saw a dark figure looming ahead of her. A light shone in the distance. How had he gotten ahead of her so quickly? She stumbled and fell again. The man darted forward and caught her. She heard a voice say, "Hang on, Naomi," but it wasn't the voice of the man who was following her. It was someone else.

There was a yell and the ear-shattering sound of a gun going off. Branches snapped. Naomi's eyes fluttered. Just as a clap of thunder shook the ground, she fainted.

Chapter 25: Waking From a Dark Dream

Alexis turned and peered into the dark forest. A gunshot had shaken the humid air and sent a group of tiny bats fluttering up from the trees, somewhere in the distance. Only the lightning had allowed her to see the nocturnal creatures. The rain was beginning to let up, but the water was still dribbling off the edges of Detective Nevid's fedora.

Tim Brockman and several other police officers, clad in raincoats, descended upon the forest like wolves on a hunt. They had called for backup. Sheriff Bardnt was already there, talking with someone through the radio in one of the county cars.

Alexis played a flashlight over the two abandoned vehicles sitting by the side of the road. She walked briskly over to the Buick. The car's headlights were still on and the hood was up, so she opened the car door, found the switch and turned off the lights. Then she went to the front of the car and shined the flashlight onto the engine.

"Hey, Rogers!" She called to one of the cops, who came over with his flashlight.

"Yeah, Nevid."

"Look at this." She pointed the beam toward the positive battery cable. Something was attached to the car that didn't look like it belonged there. "What do you suppose that is?"

Rogers shrugged. "Hell if I know. I don't know a car from a bicycle."

"Have somebody look into it. I'm going into the woods." Alexis didn't bother to listen to the man's reply. She went toward the line of dark trees and slid down a muddy embankment. Then she walked off into the darkness.

Several miles beyond the road, two people were alone in the rain. Richard, a .22 in his right hand, was holding the limp Naomi in the crook of his left arm as though she were a rag doll. A few minutes had passed since he had fired the gun. Someone had been following Naomi; he had seen the silhouette of a man. The gun had done the trick. Richard wouldn't have killed anyone unless he absolutely had to, but shooting the pistol into the trees had presumably scared off the attacker.

As the rain turned to a mild drizzle and the thunder and lightning began to move farther away, Richard yelled out into the darkness. "If you're out there, you'd better not try anything, you son of a bitch, or I'll fill you full of lead!" Richard had a talent for sounding threatening when he wanted to. It came from a childhood of having to stand up to bullies in his native New York.

After a while, he decided that he had scared the man

214

off. Richard turned his attention to Naomi. He slipped
the gun into a holster and swiftly lifted Naomi into his
arms. Just as he was trying to remember which direction
he had come from, a host of white lights burned his retinas
and voices sounded out through the dense woods.

Alexis had somehow gotten ahead of the cops that were
combing the forest. She was the first to spot the man
standing in a tiny clearing with a woman in his arms. Her
head was hanging back, her eyes were shut and her short
black hair, soaked and disheveled, was hanging down over
the man's arm. There was blood on her head, seeping
from a wound that was hidden under her hair. The man
turned toward them, blinking.

All the flashlights illuminated him. All the cops stood
on guard. They were all assuming the same thing—that
the man who was holding Naomi was the same maniac
that had chased her to this very location.

"Hold on," Sheriff Bardnt said, raising an arm.
"Whoever you are, put her down and step back." The
only sound for several seconds was that of the safety
latches on the officers' guns being released.

The man in the clearing shifted Naomi in his arms and
held her closer. "I'm not putting her down. My name is
Richard Weston. I'm not the one you're after." He
blinked. "Would you mind lowering those lights, I can't

see a damn thing."

Sheriff Bardnt said something, and then the lights lowered. Alexis stepped down into the clearing. When the blotches in his eyes disappeared, Richard could see the woman clearly. She was wearing a water-resistant trench coat and a pinstripe fedora. She flashed a badge at him. "If you're not the one we're after, who are you?"

Sheriff Bardnt stepped up, an expression on his face that told Richard that this detective, whoever she was, wasn't well liked. "You'll have to come with us, Mr. Weston. You're the only one in the middle of a forest with a girl who just made a 911 call. Put two and two together and you get four."

"Bullshit," Richard snapped, continuing to clutch Naomi to his chest. "I saw the guy who was chasing her. He got away. I scared him off."

"You were the one that shot that gun."

"Yeah, I brought it with me because Naomi called me and told me she was in trouble. Who the hell are you, anyway?"

The Sheriff told him. "You'll have to excuse my gruffness," he said, not unkindly. "But you do have to come with us so we can get this settled."

"My car's on the other side of the woods," Richard said, nodding his head in what he assumed was the correct direction. "I parked it on Dark Hollow Road."

"That's fine. Somebody will bring you back there to get it." The Sheriff stepped aside. "Come on, let's go.

And don't forget the girl," he added sardonically.

"How could I?" Richard followed the cops and the detective through the woods and back to the road.

In Naomi's dreams, she was still running through those woods. The only difference was, when her attacker grabbed her by the back of her shirt, he actually caught her and pulled her down onto the muddy leaves and the slick rocks. The ensuing nightmare was a barrage of bloody violence so vivid that Naomi awoke in a cold sweat. A shriek erupted from between her lips and she startled. Someone grabbed a hold of her and when she turned to see who it was, she was staring at Richard, his pale face illuminated by the dim street lamps of Witchfire. They were in the back of a car and they were moving.

Naomi gasped for breath and leaned back. She was suddenly aware of the fact that her entire body was in pain.

"Naomi, calm down. You're safe now." Richard pulled her close to him. "We're taking you to the hospital. Then I have to go back to the police station with Detective Nevid."

"Detec . . . . " Naomi began. She peered into the front of the vehicle. A woman glanced back at her. "Alexis," Naomi mumbled.

"You okay back there, kid? You had me pretty

worried."

Naomi looked down and saw what a mess she was. Her shirt was ripped along the side where the man had grabbed at her. She was covered in dirt. Wet leaves were stuck to her pant legs. She was aware of an intense throbbing on her head. She reached up slowly.

"No, no, don't touch it," Richard said, taking her hand. "You bled a lot, but head wounds will do that. Did he hit you?"

"He . . . . " Naomi tried hard to think. She usually had a good memory, but it didn't feel that way today. She guessed that she had a concussion. It suddenly occurred to her that she had run into something in the woods, that one of her falls had been the result of hitting her head on something, probably a branch. She told Richard this.

"Well, it'll be okay," he said. "We're almost to the hospital. They'll fix you up."

"Officer Brockman will stay with you until we can get back," Alexis told her. "It shouldn't be too long."

Naomi found herself wishing that Richard could stay with her instead. He and Detective Nevid left her with Brockman at the hospital, where her father was waiting for her.

Two days later, it was a Saturday. It was sunny and the wind had been replaced by placid, still air that made Roy

sweat while he stood in the garage in front of Naomi's
Buick. Across the driveway, the flowers in the garden
were bright and standing tall, refreshed by yesterday's
storm. Roy had spent the morning mowing the lawn, so
everything looked pristine.

That afternoon, he had brought Naomi home from the
hospital. He was considering going inside and checking
on her for a fifth time, but he stopped himself. She was
taking a nap on the couch in his living room and wouldn't
want to be disturbed. Roy was trying to suppress his
paranoia, but he couldn't help himself. It wasn't as
though he had much to distract him from his thoughts;
Pedro and Devon were both on their lunch break. They
had gone to the Blue Plate Diner.

Detective Nevid had spoken with Roy at the hospital
and advised him to take a look at Naomi's car. She
suspected that the stalker was an intelligent man, capable
of trapping his prey in a most creative way. She had
informed Roy that she had seen something strange
attached to the battery. Alexis's theory was that Naomi
had discovered this just as the man had approached her,
causing her to run into the woods in an attempt to escape.
As Roy stood there staring at the engine, he caught sight
of what Alexis had been talking about.

The detective wouldn't have known what she was
looking at, but Roy did; someone had purposely sabotaged
Naomi's car.

When Richard left work that evening, he went straight to Naomi's house in the hopes that she would be well enough to see him. When he arrived, he found Roy, Oliver, and Geoffrey sitting together on the front porch of Roy's house. Roy stood anxiously from his seat when he saw Richard advancing up the sidewalk.

"I'm glad you're here," Roy said. "We've been discussing things."

Richard glanced over at Geo and Oliver, who both looked very forlorn as they each sipped a beer. "What things?" Richard asked. "Where's Naomi?"

"She's inside napping. She's been on that couch ever since she got back from the hospital this afternoon." Roy sat back down. "Have a seat."

There was an empty picnic bench nearby, so Richard sunk reluctantly onto the painted wood. "How is she?"

"She's fine," Roy said, though he didn't sound convinced.

Geo shook his head. "This is going to blow you away," he interrupted.

"I'm listening." Richard waited.

Roy told him everything. "I took a look at Naomi's car because Detective Nevid said that she thought someone might have messed with it. Well, somebody did. He knew that Naomi is a mechanic, otherwise he would have used something simpler to cause her to break down." Roy

220

paused, as though he didn't want to believe what he was saying. "Somebody put a remote controlled kill-switch on that Buick."

"I'm not sure I understand," Richard said, who wasn't much of a car person.

"I'll explain it the best I can," Roy told him. "See, there's a switch on the car's computer that's normally turned on. If there's a collision, the switch automatically turns off the fuel pump to prevent any fires if the gas line is ruptured. There's a way of messing with this switch so that a person can control the car by remote, which is what happened to Naomi's car. I haven't discussed this with her yet, but by the looks of it, her car died at the side of the road because somebody who was driving behind her pressed a button on a remote and basically shut the car off."

"That's the craziest thing I've ever heard," Richard said.

"It's true. I pulled all the wiring off today. Brockman came over it to pick it up; the police are holding onto it. Somebody went to great lengths to plan this."

Geo chimed in. "Somebody knew that Naomi planned to drive me to Helsontown yesterday. She and I had talked about it at work, and there were a lot of customers in the store that night. This guy must have been right near us, listening. I don't know how else he would have found out."

There was a moment of uncomfortable silence as

everyone present considered the dreaded facts. If the stalker had been there to hear Naomi and Geo talking about their plans, he had been one step ahead of Naomi from the very beginning. He had probably watched her on a regular basis and memorized her schedule.

"He's clever," Roy said. "Without the remote control, a car set up with this kind of wiring can't be started by normal means."

Oliver stared at the cement porch and thought to himself: *I wonder why this guy has so much free time on his hands?*

"Wait a minute," Richard interjected. "If that's true, then how did Naomi leave the house in the first place? And how could this stalker have installed a kill switch without being noticed? That doesn't make sense."

"That's where it gets worse. Someone else had to have turned on Naomi's car for her without her realizing it. Which means that somebody was close enough to watch her ever since she left the driveway on her way to pick up Geo." Roy looked past Richard toward the garage. Pedro and Devon had recently returned from their lunch break, and they were hard at work on a VW Beetle in the garage. "Devon replaced Naomi's window the other day, after it got broken into at Whellaby's. Devon's an expert when it comes to the electrical systems in a car."

"One of your mechanics did it?" Richard asked incredulously.

"There's more going on here than we can see," Oliver

said nervously. "That mechanic probably knows the stalker somehow."

"I bet he paid him real well to install that switch," Roy said, grinding his teeth nervously. "But I can't fire him until I know for sure that it was him."

"How could it be otherwise?" Richard wondered.

"I don't know. I really want to go out there and kick his ass, but I have a feeling Detective Nevid and my buddy Brockman will have a better idea."

"You mean, you think we should sneak around to catch the sneak?"

"*Exactly.*"

The curtains were drawn in the living room. Roy's cat jumped up onto the blanketed young woman lying on the couch and curled up on top of her legs. Naomi peeked over the top of *The Western Lands* by William S. Burroughs and said, "Hello, Tammy." Then she angled the book again so that she could read easier and sunk into a long silence. Aside from the ticking of the clock, there were no other sounds. Then, the front door in the kitchen opened.

"Hi, Naomi."

She recognized Richard's voice and pulled herself into a sitting position, marking the place in her book and setting it on the coffee table. Richard sat down beside her.

"Hi," Naomi said. She didn't feel like talking. She blinked as a shot of pain went through her head. She had on a bandage, but every time she sat or stood up too quickly, she would get a strange sort of rush and feel as though she were about to fall over.

Richard noticed, leaned forward and put a hand on her shoulder as though to steady her. "Are you all right?"

"Sure," she mumbled unconvincingly. "Terrified, in pain, only mildly distracted by *that* . . . . " She nodded toward *The Western Lands*. "Other than that, I'm terrific."

"I tried to call you this morning. I talked to your dad for a bit." Richard leaned back, clasping his hands in his lap. "He can't stop thanking me. There were tears in his eyes."

"I don't know what to say, Richard." Naomi lied back down and curled up, pulling the blanket up to her chin. The air conditioning was on full-blast and the room was chilly. She looked at Richard, once again taking note of his deep blue eyes. "You could have been killed."

He shook his head. "I really don't think so. And tell me the truth—if you had really thought that he would kill me, would you have called me?"

"No."

"You're lucky that call even came through, and even luckier that you had just enough time to tell me that you were near that old mill." He shivered. "I don't want to think about what might have happened if I hadn't showed up."

224

Naomi didn't, either. "How come you know so many of those little back roads?"

"There are hiking trails all through there. And I did some ghost hunting at the old mill. Dark Hollow Road seems to be the central theme to a lot of creepy ghost stories."

"So I've heard."

There was something about a woman killing herself in the woods off Dark Hollow, but no one knew if it was true or not because it conflicted with another old wives' tale about a young mother taking her small children to the forest to slaughter them. Naomi had heard the bloodier version from the owner of the Gourmet Cafe, a little coffee shop in town. She remembered the man's excited expression as he had told Naomi "you can still hear the children crying on real quiet nights."

Naomi sighed. "I don't think any of that is true."

"Maybe not," Richard said, shrugging.

"The truth is worse than the fiction."

Richard slipped off the couch and sat on the floor in front of Naomi, who was resting her head on a pillow. He leaned against the couch and looked straight into her eyes. "I think you should spend a few days at a friend's house. I'm worried about you."

"So is everybody else." Naomi paused. "I'm sorry that sounded mean, I didn't intend it to."

"That's okay."

"It's just, my dad said the same thing. And the police

want me to go to a women's shelter for a little while."

"What do you think?"

"I think I need to talk to Alexis."

"You should give her a call." Richard leaned back. "Do you need to sleep?"

Naomi's eyes fluttered. "Yeah. I have a headache."

"Did they give you anything for the pain at the hospital?"

"Yeah, but . . . I just feel terrible." Naomi's eyes were closed.

Richard leaned forward, hugged her and kissed her on the forehead. "I'm a phone call away, remember that."

"I will. And—Richard?"

"Yeah, Naomi?"

"Thanks for saving me."

Richard smiled. For a moment, he thought he might blush. "Anytime."

Chapter 26: Alexis and Frank Think it Over

"Frankie, I need to talk to you." Alexis puffed on another cigar. A stinkbug flew awkwardly through the air and rammed its shell-like body against the table-lamp.

On the other line, Frank groaned. "I just had a beer and I just climbed into bed, *just now*."

"What's that I hear in the background?" Alexis smirked. She knew what it was, but she wanted Frank to tell her because it amused her.

"It's Farrah Fawcett talking to Bosley," he said grumpily. "I'm not coming over to your office now, I'll miss the show. And I don't know why you always want to hang out in that stuffy little room, anyway."

Alexis frowned. "You have a night off, huh?"

"Yeah, finally. Unless something happens, I'm staying right here, glued to the TV. Got that?"

"I got it, Frankie. How about this." She paused. "How about I come over to your house?"

"I thought you'd never ask. Shall I chill the wine?"

"Frankie, for Christ's sake, be serious for once." Alexis put out her cigar. "I got some very important ideas and I'd like to discuss them with you."

"Do these ideas involve you, me, and a hot tub?"

"No, Frankie."

He sighed. "All right. Come on over. I'll get

227

dressed."

It was ten-thirty at night when Alexis pulled into Frank's driveway. Frank had a cozy little bungalow that his father, a real-estate agent, had left him in his will. The seventy-three year old had passed away last year, and Frank had moved from his dingy little apartment to this quaint house that was set back from the road and surrounded by trees and shrubs.

Frank didn't seem to have any ambitions to move out of Witchfire. He had lived there for nearly ten years and was completely content with it. Then again, there weren't many towns like Witchfire.

Alexis parked her ZX2 next to Frank's Oldsmobile. She went up the front walk and rang the doorbell. The lights were on and Alexis thought she could hear a television. A moment later, Frank opened the door.

"Come on in," he said. The cop stepped aside, ushering Alexis into the front room.

The house was dimly lit and there wasn't much furniture. The scent of patchouli made the place feel comfortable. That was one of Frank's little quirks; he liked to burn incense. Frank was a tough looking guy from Chicago, a laid-back cop with a lazy attitude and a predilection for old detective movies. He had unwittingly gone most of his life without realizing that he fit almost perfectly into a common 'bad cop' stereotype. But when people found out that he enjoyed burning incense, the stereotype tended to collapse.   Alexis knew another thing about Frank that most people didn't know; he had an unusual hobby. During the spring and summer months, he enjoyed pressing flowers. Some of these fragile specimens were framed and hanging on the walls of the foyer.

Alexis followed Frank into the tiny living room, where the private eye sat down on a plush sofa. The living room was at the back of the house, and there was a sliding glass door that Frank had installed a year or so prior. It had replaced an old rotting wooden door that Frank had gotten sick of looking at. During the day, the sliding glass door provided a nice view of a spacious back yard. Now, she could see fireflies blinking in the inky darkness.

"Would you like something to drink?" Frank asked. He was in the kitchen, peering into the refrigerator.

"No thanks." Her favorite drink was whiskey on ice, but she knew that Frank didn't drink liquor.

The cop came back into the room holding a Guinness. He sat down in an armchair and yawned. He was wearing a pair of pajama pants and a T-shirt. He was still thinking about how much he wished he could go back to bed. "How's the girl?" Frank asked.

"Naomi?"

"Yeah."

"She's okay. Shaken up, but okay," Alexis said. "I

went to talk to her this evening. I invited her to stay at my apartment for a little while. She's spending tonight at her dad's house, and tomorrow night she's going to my place."

"Really?"

Alexis nodded. "You sound surprised."

"I've never seen you get so personally involved in a case before," Frank said.

"I feel like I need to help her. She's a tough girl, but something tells me she's been through a lot. I can see it when I look at her." Alexis leaned back, staring thoughtfully at the fireflies beyond the sliding glass door. "She reminds me of me when I was younger. Something bad happened to her. I feel like she needs a friend, an older woman to look up to."

"You're probably right about that," Frank said, sipping his beer. "You're usually right."

"It's just a feeling I get."

"Did you figure out who the stalker is yet? You seem to be one step ahead of the cops."

"I haven't told anyone about my progress," Alexis said. "Those assholes would be pissed if they knew how close I was."

"So you don't know yet?"

"No." Her reply was bitter. "Naomi did see his face, though. I want to have her look at the photos from the store surveillance again and see if she recognizes anyone, but I want to wait until she's feeling a little bit better."

"Well, once you get him, we can arrest him and charge him for harassment and trespassing," Frank said, thinking of the numerous times that the stalker had invaded Naomi's privacy on her father's land.

"He did attack her in the woods. We can get him for that. It's a shame we don't have more proof; we could also get him for attempted breaking and entering," Alexis pointed out. When her statement met with Frank's confused expression, she asked, "What, don't you remember?"

"No." Frank sipped his beer again.

"Somebody tried to break into Roy Vogler's garage on the first night that Naomi heard the stalker outside her window. What I'm wondering is, why would this guy want to break into the garage, assuming it was him?"

"Easy—kill two birds with one stone. He could spy on the object of his obsession and make a little money at the same time. I'm sure Roy has a lot of expensive stuff in that garage of his."

"You're right about that," Alexis agreed.

"One thing I'm wondering, though . . . . " Frank yawned again. "What happened in the time leading up to the chase through the woods? What happened to allow Naomi to expose herself and become vulnerable to this guy? And why was he okay with her seeing his face? She might have known who he was and told us. He could have been arrested by now."

Alexis shook her head. "He's too obsessed with her to

care if anyone finds out who he is. He's smart, too. He tricked her somehow. Their vehicles were parked right near each other on the road. Naomi's hood was up. He knew she was going to have to stop for something. And that brings me to the thing that I saw connected to the battery. I showed it to Officer Rogers, but he didn't know what to make of it."

"You didn't tell me about it that night."

"Well, that's part of the reason I wanted to talk to you now. Somebody tampered with that car, but it couldn't have been the stalker. The car is always at Roy Vogler's house, and Roy told me that the vehicle was locked in the garage for a few days."

"Why?"

"The window was broken. Somebody busted it while Naomi was at work and stole a photo album. There's another thing we can get him on, when we find this guy. A *definite* breaking and entering charge."

"Where's your proof?"

"That's easy, Frankie." Alexis looked smug.

"Oh, yeah? How? You could find that album, but you're not going to."

"I will find it, Frankie. You'll see."

"How are you going to do that? You don't even know who the guy is yet. And when you do find out who he is, if he's so clever, he'll get rid of that album before you can get to it."

"I've thought of that. I don't think he will."

"Why?"

"He's getting overconfident. If he thinks that Naomi can't identify him, which he probably does because nobody's caught him yet, he'll get even more confident. If he doesn't think he'll get caught, why should he throw out those photos? They're from Naomi's vacation, which means they have pictures of her in them. I think he's too obsessed with her to get rid of them. And that's not the worst part." She paused. "He thinks he's in love with her."

"What?"

"Mind if I light up a cigar? It helps get my brain going." Alexis tapped the side of her head.

"Your brain never stops," Frank commented, almost sarcastically.

She took that as a 'yes' and pulled out a cigar and her lighter. After she had taken a long drag and exhaled, Alexis was even more certain that she was right. "Yes, yes . . . I think I know what to do," she said firmly. "We have to wait. The cops are probably catching on a little bit. Keep me posted, Frankie. I bet they'll start watching Whellaby's too, figuring the stalker might be connected to the store. They'll probably take photos from the surveillance, just like I did, but for them, it'll be too late. This guy is smart. He won't go to that grocery store as much anymore, if he can help it. He'll start shopping at the general store, or he'll go out of town."

"So you're just going to sit back and do nothing?"

"Not exactly. Naomi will stay with me for a few days, but then she'll have to go home. Otherwise, he'll suspect that someone's on to him. Yes, I know what I'll do." Alexis grinned. "I'll catch him just like a hunter would catch any other animal." She turned and looked at Frank, her white teeth gleaming. "I'll dangle a fresh piece of bait in front of him and wait for him to come runnin'."

Chapter 27: Brian Worries about Naomi

The town of Witchfire never went to sleep. At sunset, groups of insomniac teenagers stood outside the Night Kitchen. Smoldering cigarettes lit up the dark corners of the parking lot. Someone rode by on a bicycle, a front-mounted light peering forth into the night like the one good eye of a lame electric eel in the most foreboding depths of the ocean. Bats swam fluidly through the air, an owl hooted, and somewhere in the distance, a dog barked.

Brian began to strum his guitar. Car doors slammed and two young men approached the diner. Geoffrey went in first, followed by Oliver. A moment later, Brian recognized the two guys as friends of Naomi's and went inside after them. He was wondering how she was doing. His interest was simply friendly concern; at the time, he had no inkling of the events that had recently transpired.

At around midnight, Brian was sitting in a booth in the Night Kitchen, clutching his guitar, which was halfway under the table and leaning up against the seat. He had just listened to Geo and Oliver as they had told him what had happened the night before and how Richard had rescued Naomi. They had also told him about Alexis driving Naomi to the hospital.

Brian had asked them if she was okay, to which they replied that she had been spending most of her time sleeping off a concussion.

Brian spent a lot of time staring off into the distance, open-mouthed and wide-eyed. Finally, he turned and looked at Geoffrey. "Did they catch this guy? I mean, the stalker? I should have known the police wouldn't do a damn thing."

"They haven't caught him," Geo said. "And, how can you blame the cops? They don't have any leads. Nobody saw where he ran. He could still be lost in the swampland for all we know."

"He's smarter than that. I wonder if he had somewhere to go? I mean, I wonder if he knew of a place he could hide out at on the other side of the woods."

"I never thought of that." Oliver's brow furrowed. "I should have called somebody. I feel so horrible. She was on the phone with me, and then I heard her yell about something, and then the phone cut off. I should have known something was wrong," Oliver said bitterly, clenching his fists.

"It's not your fault," Geo said forlornly. "It's mine. I should have insisted that she stay with me at my grandma's new place. There was plenty of room for her, but she wanted to drive back in the dark. She kept talking about how she wasn't going to let this guy scare her."

"Maybe her bravery made her a little bit stupid." Brian shrugged.

Geo and Oliver both glared at him.

"Hey, it could happen to anyone," Brian retaliated.

"The point I'm trying to make is that it's not your fault." He looked at Geo and Oliver both in turn. "How could it be? You can't always be with Naomi in case something happens."

Geo and Oliver exchanged glances. "I bet if she had never gotten that job at Whellaby's, Naomi would have never had a stalker in the first place," Oliver pointed out.

"You think that's definitely where he first saw her?" Brian asked.

"Probably."

"Her father offered her a job at the shop, but she told me she turned it down," Geoffrey said.

"Why?" Brian poked at the remainder of his dinner with a fork.

Geo shrugged. "I think she was just a little uncomfortable with it. She has a lot of pride. I think she wanted to make it on her own, and didn't quite know how."

"I've never heard of a decision backfiring so badly," Brian commented.

"Yeah," Oliver agreed. "Whoever this guy is, he's completely obsessed with her."

'Love' at first sight, Brian thought to himself.

Two days later, Naomi was standing in Alexis's living room, staring through a wide window and across Maine Street. The little apartment was sparsely furnished and there were no pictures on the walls. Most people had photographs of family or friends in their houses, but not Alexis. Naomi wasn't sure if it was because Alexis had no family or friends, or because she simply didn't feel the need to keep pictures of them.

It was about one-thirty in the afternoon and the little town was experiencing another day of record-high temperatures in Pennsylvania. Naomi hadn't left the apartment since she had gotten there yesterday; she was too frightened. Officer Brockman had come to check on her that morning, and her father had stopped by.

Naomi watched the cars drive by as heat simmered over the blacktop and weary looking civilians wandered the sidewalks. From the little kitchen adjacent to the living room in the tiny one bedroom apartment came the sound of metal clinking against metal.

"Lunch is almost ready. I hope you like noodles and burgers," Alexis called. "I have to admit, I'm not a very good cook. I don't really like doing it."

"Better you than me," Naomi mumbled, remembering her nightmares.

"What was that?" Alexis asked, as she peeked around the corner.

"Nothing."

Alexis went back to the stove. "The only thing I'm

really good at making is egg salad, but that's not exactly difficult."

The detective said a few more things, but Naomi wasn't really listening. She was watching the sidewalk in front of the building, her nose almost touching the window. She saw a man with curly brown hair walking toward the apartment complex. Naomi had only recently gotten off the phone with Brian. He had been thinking of her, he said, and wanted to stop by.

Moments later, someone knocked on the door.

Brian was an outgoing, creative young man with a taste for adventure. He was inexorably drawn to other people, wondered what they were thinking, and he was extremely intrigued by Naomi.

When he entered the bland-looking apartment, a tall woman of Native American descent confronted him. "And you are?" she asked. She hadn't bothered to hide the hint of suspicion, and Brian didn't blame her. This was clearly the private detective that Geo and Oliver had mentioned.

"Are you Detective Nevid?"

"That's me."

The young musician couldn't help but notice that the woman's dark eyes were penetrating his, not unlike a determined carpenter bee boring through a thick piece of wood. He couldn't handle her gaze, and found himself glancing past her and into the next room, hoping to see Naomi.

"My name's Brian. Is Naomi here?"

"Yes. She's in the living room. Come on in." Alexis ushered Brian into the foyer and shut the door behind him. He walked tentatively into the living room while Alexis went into the kitchen and tended to something that was cooking over a high flame.

"Naomi?"

When she heard his voice, she turned away from the window and smiled weakly. "Hi, Brian. I didn't think you were coming until later."

"Honestly, I was just desperate to get somewhere that had air conditioning," he said, indicating his Allman Brothers T-shirt, soaked with sweat. "Just kidding. I hope I didn't come at a bad time."

"No, you didn't." Naomi returned her gaze to the street below. "I haven't been outside since I got here."

"I don't blame you. Are you okay? How's your head?"

Naomi turned and parted her hair slightly. "Getting better, see? I don't need the bandage anymore. The cut really wasn't that bad. It just *looked* bad. Head wounds bleed a lot. I'm still not sure how I did it; though I'm pretty sure I hit my head on a branch and was too busy running to think about it." She stood by a bookcase and fiddled with a copy of Dante's *Inferno*. "I'm going back to work tomorrow night." Naomi paged through the book

240

and then put it back on the shelf.

"Naomi . . . ."

There was a long silence. Naomi turned and looked at Brian. "What?"

"Don't you think you should quit?"

Naomi's eyes narrowed. For a moment, it looked as though she were about to cry. She stalked to the sofa and sat down, crossing one leg over the other. "I've been through a lot in my lifetime, Brian. More than anybody my age should ever have to go through. The last goddamn thing I'm going to do is let him beat me." She turned and looked at him, eyes ablaze. "I'm going to beat him, Brian. I'm going to *win*."

Brian sat down next to her. "Nobody wins at a game like this, Naomi. Though I must say, I have to admire your courage."

"And?"

"And what?"

"I can tell there's something else you'd like to say. After all, you didn't sound too sure of yourself," Naomi pointed out.

Brian smiled warmly. "You're an astute judge of character. And you're right. I can't help but think that you're being a little hasty. Naomi, there's such a thing as being too courageous. I mean, if something were to happen to you . . . ."

"Yeah? What?"

"Well, all this courage would be for nothing. I think in

a situation like this, there's really no shame in running."

An image flashed fleetingly across her mind, the same image that plagued her whenever she thought of turning her back on a situation—turning and running. In her mind's eye, Naomi's mother lay on her back on the kitchen floor. Her eyes were wide and white like cow's eyes, her mouth slack and her head sideways on the linoleum.

Naomi turned away, not wanting Brian to see the tears that were beginning to well up in her eyes. "I have reasons for not running, Brian. You just don't understand."

The words hit him like a punch in the face. He suddenly felt very out of place and realized rather awkwardly that he was a mere acquaintance with no more knowledge of Naomi's life or past than a stranger walking by her on the street. He fiddled briefly with an errant thread on his jean shorts and then stood up to leave. "I can see you'd rather be alone. I'll go. I just wanted to make sure you were okay."

"I'm sorry. I didn't intend to sound mean. I just . . . ."

"That's okay," Brian said, shrugging. "Don't worry about it."

"No, it's not okay." Naomi paused. "I mean, there's a lot that I could explain to you, but I just don't have the energy right now. Will you call me later? I have a new cell phone, but the number is the same. I lost the old one in the woods."

"Sure, I'll call you."

Naomi stood up. "Then I guess I'll talk to you later."

"Yeah. I guess."

Brian left, feeling a good deal more uncomfortable than he had when he had arrived, and Alexis walked into the living room with two plates of food. "Hungry?" she asked.

Naomi could tell that Alexis was pretending that she hadn't heard their entire conversation. The two of them ate their lunch in silence, Naomi avoiding the burgers, too nervous to explain to Alexis that she didn't like beef.

Chapter 28: Thurston Davis

Naomi had worked four nights in a row and Alexis had spoken with Keith, asking him to look out for suspicious customers. Naomi's boss knew about her recent troubles and he took it upon himself to look out for her. He often checked on her, peeking down the aisle in which she was working, or asking her if she was all right. After a while, he tried to leave her alone; he was worried that he was annoying her.

Meanwhile, Alexis spent several of those nights parked out front, watching every man who walked into the store. She periodically looked through her stack of photographs. She had numbered each one and wrote in a small notebook every customer that she saw, noting the time beside the entry.

Number 19, fat man with limp and chef's uniform, 2:03 A.M.

A week had gone by and it was a Wednesday. Naomi had worked the night before and she was sleeping soundly on the couch in Alexis' living room. She didn't get up all day. At nine o' clock that night, she was still asleep. By the bookcase, Alexis sat in an armchair, looking through her stack of photographs. At around nine-thirty, she picked out three photographs and set them down on the coffee table in front of the couch.

Alexis wrote a note that said, '*Call my cell phone when you wake up*,' and set it down on top of the photographs. Then, she walked out the door. She had a job to do.

The development behind Whellaby's was made up of five short streets, one of which looped around to meet up with the intersection of two of the five. All of the houses looked the same and it was easy to get confused, especially at night.

On one side of the development, closest to the path that led through the woods and into the back parking lot of the grocery store, was Jesse Donahue's house. On the opposite side of the development was a squat yellow house that looked much like all of the others, except that someone had installed white fencing and planted a lot of shrubs and a garden.

About a quarter of a mile down the street from the yellow house, an unmarked police car was parked under a street lamp. There were several other units positioned somewhere nearby and they were all keeping in close contact.

The two cops in the unmarked Dodge Charger were sipping coffees. One of the cops was Frank. He finished his coffee and reached into the back of the car, depositing his empty cup in a trash bag. Frank's partner pointed across the street. "There, look," he said.

Frank peered into the darkness. A black car had parked some distance away. Farther down the street, hidden by a cluster of trees, was a small white van. The headlights of the little car turned off. Detective Nevid climbed out of the driver's seat. She was wearing jeans and a black button-up shirt, but no jacket. The cuffs of her jeans rested on a pair of black boots, and it was clear that she wasn't hiding a weapon anywhere on her person.

"Is she crazy?" Officer Hager turned to Frank. "She's going in there unarmed!"

"She knows what she's doing," Frank said.

As a few errant fireflies flitted across the windshield, Frank watched Alexis. The private eye turned briefly, sending a pointed look toward the car that held Frank and his partner, and then proceeded across the street toward the yellow house.

The man who answered the door did so with a bemused expression on his face. Alexis guessed that he was in his mid to late twenties. He had a buzzed haircut and was wearing pajama pants and a T-shirt.

"Can I help you?" The man seemed annoyed that there was somebody at his front door and Alexis wondered if he had been trying to sleep.

"Mmm-hmm." Alexis smiled warmly and pulled her identification out of her back pocket. She showed it to the tired-looking man. "My name is Alexis Nevid, I'm a private detective. I was wondering if I could ask you a few questions?"

The man shrugged and stepped aside. "Come on in, I guess. But I was just about to go to bed."

"That's fine, I won't keep you long. I assume you're Thurston Davis."

"How'd you know that?"

"A friend of mine told me what you looked like."

Thurston got a drink of water and padded into the living room in a pair of slippers. He stared at Alexis with the indignation of a cat that had just been kicked. "Oh, yeah? Who?"

Alexis made it appear as though she were thinking deeply. "I think it was Spencer Whellaby," she said, sinking into one corner of a wicker couch.

"He sent you over here? I bet he told you a bunch of lies, too."

Alexis had expected Thurston to have some kind of negative reaction to the news. From what she knew about Thurston's recent dealings, he should have been fidgeting in his seat. On the contrary, he looked as calm a preacher on Easter Sunday.

Wide windows in the living room showed off a beautiful backyard garden. Tiki torches burned brightly along a stony walkway. Photographs of friends or family hung by one side of the door, and three pairs of shoes sat on one side of a dirty rug—one pair of sandals and two pairs of sneakers.

"Do you have a roommate, Mr. Davis?" Alexis asked.

"No. Why?"

Alexis shrugged. "This is a pretty big house."

"I have a girlfriend that visits a lot."

"Oh, I see. Do a lot of gardening?" Alexis caught sight of some beautiful flowers that were visible by the light of the torches. "Those are some lovely roses. My father grew a lot of roses."

Thurston shrugged. "Yeah, a little bit. What were you going to ask me? I'd really like to get to bed."

"It's not too much trouble, then? I mean, you don't mind?" Alexis was trying to play the part of the innocent female. If she could make this man believe that he was smarter than her, she would have him just where she wanted him.

"No, it's no trouble." Thurston sighed. "Go ahead and ask me."

"Mr. Whellaby wanted me to look into your connection with another associate. It has nothing to do with you."

"I find that hard to believe."

"Why were you fired, Mr. Davis?" Alexis spoke tentatively, as though she were stepping on a rotting staircase that was about to snap.

"Why do you want to know that?" Thurston took a few gulps from his water glass, and then popped a piece of gum into his mouth.

"Mr. Whellaby wanted to find out if you knew

anything personal about the man who accused you of stealing. That was what happened, wasn't it?"

"Yes," Thurston grumbled. "A guy I was working with told the manager that I was walking out with grocery items at the end of my shifts. He was part-time and he worked in the deli, Min Rhodson." Thurston leaned forward, brandishing an index finger. "I know for a fact that he reported me in order to cover his own ass. I caught him once. He took a box full of stuff from the deli, headed out the back of the store and loaded it into his car. I told him I was going to report him and he said I couldn't prove anything."

"Didn't they check the cameras?"

"They would have, if I hadn't screwed up," Thurston said angrily. "Rhodson and I got in a fight the next day, and I hit him in front of some customers. He was humiliated, but they kicked me out of the store and I couldn't get anybody to look at the cameras. They sided with Rhodson. He gave the manager a sympathy act after I gave Rhodson a black eye."

"The manager?"

"Timmson."

"Wasn't he the man who hung himself recently?" Alexis asked curiously.

"Yeah, I saw that in the paper."

Alexis took note of the irritated expression on Thurston's face. "You didn't like Timmson, did you?"

Thurston laughed. "Nobody did. Timmson was a

paper pusher who never did a day's work in his life. I don't understand why Whellaby hired him. He treated me like shit. He gave me the dirtiest look the day I walked out of that place." Thurston shook his head. "I never want to go back there again. I shop in the next town. What's all this about, anyway?"

Alexis smirked. "I guess I should come clean, Mr. Davis. I'm not really here on account of an old coworker of yours. In fact, Mr. Whellaby didn't hire me at all."

Thurston rose from his seat, his face reddening. "What?"

"I know something about you, Mr. Davis, something that you don't want other people to know. And I'll keep it quiet for you, too—as long as there's something in it for me."

"What exactly are you trying to do?" Thurston's voice was low, scratchy, and edged with defiance. He spat his gum into a nearby trash basket.

Alexis decided to take a gamble. Even though she was alone with this man, she trusted the fact that the cops were outside, and *hoped* that she was well protected. She had entered the uncertain phase of her plan, the part where she would have to rely on her instincts to guide her. She stood from the couch and faced him.

"I saw you," she said firmly. "I was at Whellaby's in the parking lot on the morning of Timmson's death. I saw you come through the woods and surprise him in the parking lot with a gun. As you can see, I don't have a weapon. I just want to do business."

Alexis tried not to panic when Thurston took a step toward her. "Nobody blackmails me," he snapped.

"After I heard about what happened, I had to assume that you forced Timmson into the boiler room. I bet you tied him up first and made him watch while you got the bale wires ready. You probably gagged him, but you made sure not to leave any marks on him. And then you threatened to shoot him if he didn't put the wires around his neck." Alexis laughed. "Mr. Davis," she said sweetly, "Did you tell him you might consider letting him go if he did *exactly* what you told him to do? I bet that's what you did. After all, a man doesn't have much of a choice when a gun's being pointed at his head. Did you kick him off the duct he was standing on, make him choke to death?"

Alexis's cell phone slipped out of her pocket when Thurston threw her to the ground. The ensuing struggle was one that Alexis hadn't expected. Thurston pinned her down and punched her in the face. She thought she heard something snap and she tasted blood. At some point, she thought she heard her cell phone ring and knew instinctively that it would be Naomi trying to reach her.

The next few minutes became a blur. Alexis fought against her assailant, trying to push him off of her, but despite her own strength, Thurston had managed to catch her off guard. Alexis was sprawled across the floor on her side, her head crushed against the carpeting and her eyes wide and staring desperately toward the glass door and the garden. The flare of torches brightened in her vision, blurring and coalescing, as Thurston's hands wrapped around her neck.

She was aware of only one thought; *is he really trying to choke me?*

She felt his body crushing against hers and she felt his fingers tighten around her throat. She heard him proclaim, "Nobody blackmails me!" Then she heard her own rasping attempts to catch a shred of oxygen, and she felt her body thrashing, shaking and trying to fight against her attacker.

Alexis saw a shadow dart across the yard. The cell phone stopped ringing.

"I killed him, all right! But you're not going to tell anybody about it!" Thurston growled. Alexis nearly passed out, but she managed to bring herself back. With all of her might, she threw her right leg up and into Thurston, catching his groin with her knee. She heard him grunt and curse, and when he had loosened his grip on her neck, she took the opportunity to viciously shove him away as she clawed, punched and flailed.

Then she heard shouts and stomping footsteps. Someone grabbed her up from the floor. Orange lights flickered, and Alexis resisted the urge to black out.

Chapter 29: Alexis Goes to Frank's House

Sheriff Bardnt helped Alexis out onto the front porch. Red and blue lights flickered in the darkness as Thurston was led to a police car in handcuffs. A few of his neighbors stood watching from beyond the fence.

"Are you okay?" the Sheriff asked.

His hand had been on her arm, but she gently shoved him away. "I'm fine. Just a little scuffle." Alexis rubbed her neck.

"I shouldn't have let Whellaby talk me into having you question Davis before anybody else."

"Whellaby is a friend of the Mayor's. He can do anything he wants." Alexis coughed. She spat into the grass.

"Are you still bleeding? We should call an ambulance."

"You call an ambulance and *you'll* be bleeding." Alexis walked off into the darkness, the lights flashing off her torn blouse. As she walked, she tore the wire off of her body and threw it on the ground. It was a good thing she had been wearing it; otherwise, the cops might not have come in when they did.

She walked up to the two middle-aged women who were standing in the street. One of the women offered Alexis a cigarette. Alexis nodded and the woman lit it for

255

her.

"He got you good, didn't he?" one of the women asked, nodding toward the police car that held Thurston.

Alexis shrugged and puffed gratefully on the cigarette. "I guess he did."

The other woman was wearing a bright pink silky robe over pajamas and a pair of untied Nike sneakers. Her blond hair was pulled back in a messy ponytail. She took a cigarette from her friend and lit it. "I heard some noises and came right outside, didn't have a chance to get dressed," she said. "Saw those cop cars, knew it had something to do with Thurston."

"You did?" Alexis asked.

The other woman shook her head. "Honey, you ought to see yourself. I wouldn't be surprised if he broke your jaw."

Alexis was aware of the pain, but she had always been adept at pretending it wasn't there. So she kept on pretending and puffed away at her cigarette, which seemed to be helping. "How'd you know Thurston was trouble?" Alexis asked, speaking carefully to avoid hurting herself more.

"He has a temper," the blond in the pink robe replied. "He yells at people for no reason, all of the time. Why'd they arrest him, for hittin' you?"

"Yeah. Assault and battery," Alexis said. That wasn't the main reason, but they didn't need to know that. Thurston Davis would be charged with attacking Alexis,

256

but only after he was charged with the murder of Marty Timmson. "Tell me something," Alexis began, "Did Thurston have a roommate?"

The two women exchanged a glance, and then looked at Alexis. "Yes."

The woman in the pink robe dropped her cigarette butt and crushed it with the toe of her sneaker. "Don't know his name, though. He's only been in the area for a few months."

Alexis turned and saw Frank open Thurston's mailbox. "Excuse me, ladies. Thanks for your help." The two women walked away and Alexis approached Frank. She tapped him on the shoulder. "What are you doing?"

"Well, to be honest, I was wondering if Thurston was the only resident," Frank said. "Ah-ha." He pulled a piece of mail out of the box. Alexis sidled up and the two of them read the name on the envelope under the flicker of a lighter.

"I bet you won't find out unless you look inside the house. This is a phone bill for Thurston Davis," Alexis said, pointing at the name. "I guess he won't be paying it on time."

"Alexis, you've got blood all over your shirt." Frank shoved the mail back in the box. "You look like hell. How many times did he punch you?"

"You think I remember, Frankie?" Alexis leaned on the mailbox. "I got the best of him, and you know that."

"Yes, you kicked him in the groin."

257

"He won't piss right for a week, Frankie." When Alexis grinned, she looked like a corpse from Night of the Living Dead. A couple of her teeth were missing, and Alexis had no doubt that the cops would find them on Thurston's living room floor during the investigation. Alexis clapped a hand on Frank's shoulder. "I got him pretty hard. I think he'll have to wait for his balls to descend again. That is, if they ever did in the first place."

"All right, Lexxy," Frank said, cringing. "I was wondering if you saw what I saw."

Alexis opened her mouth to demand that Frank address her by her full name, but then she closed her mouth again. She spoke hesitantly. "You saw somebody else, didn't you, Frankie?"

"I did."

"In the back yard, running away?"

"He ran toward the woods." Frank beckoned to his partner, who was waiting by the car. "Hey, go on without me, okay?"

A few minutes later, Alexis and Frank were alone. Thurston's house had been locked up and no one was to enter it except the police. They were hoping to find evidence that Thurston had killed Timmson. They were rather confident in the taped confession that Alexis had obtained while wearing the wire, but they needed more.

"Come on, Alexis. I'll drive." Frank walked toward the detective's ZX2. "Hop in. We'll head back to my place and get you cleaned up."

"Then what?"

"Well." Frank climbed into the front seat and Alexis climbed into the passenger side. They shut the doors and Frank turned the key in the ignition. "There's a Charlie's Angels marathon on right now."

"Just drive, Charlie."

Frank smirked. "Are you saying that you're one of my angels?"

Alexis turned and stared him down, blood drying on her chin, a cut on her forehead beginning to fester. "You say that again and you'll regret it, Frank Gibson."

"Not another word, then," Frank promised.

"I got something to tell you, Frankie."

"What's that?"

"Thurston Davis was chewing nicotine gum."

Frank wasn't surprised. "You're always right, Alexis."

"I know."

The headlights on the ZX2 penetrated the darkness and Frank turned the car around and drove out of the development. That was when Alexis realized that she had left her cell phone on the floor of the living room.

Chapter 30: Charlie's Angels

She had already popped her jaw back into place. It hadn't been broken, and she wasn't quite sure what had happened, but she knew it was in the right spot again. Frank had watched her do it, and he had been thoroughly disgusted.

At Frank's house, in a well-lit bathroom, Alexis tended to her wounds. She wasn't sure how she had gotten the cut on her forehead, but it had bled more than she would have expected it to. Once she had wiped off all of the dried blood with a moist rag, she looked a good deal better. She washed out her mouth and touched her tender bruises. Alexis knew that it would hurt even more tomorrow.

She went into the living room where Frank was reclining in his easy chair. He was wearing a black T-shirt and a pair of pajama pants that had a lot of half-naked women on them. Alexis cocked her head to get a better look.

"Where in the world do you get pajamas like that?" she asked. "What's that one doing?" She pointed at the cartoon of a young lady on Frank's calf.

"Can't you tell?" Frank glanced down. "She's bending over a giant martini." He gestured to the couch. "Have a seat."

"Right." Alexis slumped onto the cushions. Her entire body ached.

"How are you feeling?"

"Horrible, but I'm okay."

"That doesn't make any sense. Are you sure you don't have a head injury?"

"I'm sure, Frankie. Then again, I might be somewhat damaged. I'd have to be, to willingly hang out with you."

"You know you don't feel well enough to drive, Alexis. I know you would have never let me behind the wheel of your car in any other situation."

"That's true," Alexis admitted. She clutched her stomach. "Ever since that fight, I've felt sick. He didn't punch me in the stomach, though. He went straight for the face."

"Do you want some pain killers?"

"I would love some."

Frank started to stand up, and then he stopped. "I'll only give them to you if you watch the Charlie's Angels marathon with me," he decided, grinning.

"All right, but I've got something to tell you." Alexis grabbed a pillow, leaned it against the arm of the couch and stretched out. From there, she watched Frank as he walked into the kitchen and opened the cabinet.

"What's up?" Frank searched through a number of medicine bottles before pulling one out, retrieving a couple of thick pills and putting the bottle away.

"Well, I told you earlier what Whellaby admitted to—

that he *did* see Thurston holding Timmson at gunpoint."

"Yeah." Frank got a glass of water for Alexis and brought her the pills. "What else?"

"You're not going to believe this." She dropped the pills in her mouth and swallowed them with the water, and then she set the glass on an end table. She rested wearily on the pillow once more. "Spencer Whellaby hired me because he wanted me to find out what he *already* knew."

"Huh?"

"He knew that Thurston Davis killed Marty Timmson. By the way, none of this is to be brought up in court. The police know that Davis killed Timmson and that's all they need to know. If anyone found out about why Whellaby was so afraid of Davis, Whellaby would be ruined."

"I don't get it. What don't the cops know? Me included," Frank added sourly. He slumped into his easy chair and turned on the TV. A commercial was on, so he muted it.

"Since before Davis got fired, he's been blackmailing Whellaby. Whellaby told me everything when I went to visit him the other day. He said he figured he owed it to me because he felt like he was sending me on a wild goose chase. He admitted everything—you know he has a wife, right?"

"Yeah, she keeps to herself most of the time. She's had a lot of serious health problems recently."

"Yeah, well, before she ever had health problems, Whellaby was running around with prostitutes and younger women and she never found out. Nobody ever knew. He would go out of town, or go on 'business trips,' and when he went on these trips, he would go to escort services and spend hundreds of dollars on gorgeous whores." Alexis shook her head. "Davis caught him."

Frank's mouth was hanging open. "Whellaby was featured on the front page of the church newsletter last week. Sheriff Bardnt had a copy on his desk."

"Are you saying you don't believe it?"

"No. I'm not saying that. My dad used to hit my mom, but everybody at the church we went to when I was a kid thought he was a saint. All I'm saying is, I mean . . . Spencer Whellaby? He's the last person I would have expected to do something like that."

"I'm sure everyone feels that way. That's why it can't get out. He would be completely destroyed."

"So that's what Thurston Davis had against him?"

"Yeah. So when Whellaby saw Davis holding Marty Timmson at gunpoint, what could he do? Davis told him that if he said anything, everybody in town would see the pictures that Davis took of Whellaby with some half-naked stripper in his arms." Alexis shrugged. "He had no options."

"You sound like you're sticking up for him."

"I'm not saying that what he did was right, I'm just saying that it's easy to be terrified of a man with a gun who has dirt on you."

"That's true. So he must have known what a good

detective you are and figured that if he put you on the scent, you would figure it out, and he would never have to say anything."

"Exactly. Everybody would know I was on the case, Davis would get caught and no one would ever have to find out about the incriminating information that Davis had on Whellaby. Of course, he had to suggest things to me, he had to make it seem like he didn't know by supplying other names and information. I got suspicious. He was the only one who was totally certain that Timmson didn't kill himself. I didn't confront him because I wanted to see where it would go. And some of the people he mentioned, he told me he was certain they hadn't done it—"

Frank nodded. "He was smart about it."

"He wanted justice for Marty Timmson, but he didn't want to expose himself in the process. He didn't want to be publicly humiliated."

"Doesn't he have two grown kids?"

"Yeah, imagine how embarrassed they would be." Alexis rubbed her eyes.

"Are you okay?"

"Yeah, my head just hurts."

"Charlie's Angels is on," Frank said excitedly.

"All right. I'll watch a little bit. But then I think I'd like to fall asleep on this couch of yours."

"Certainly," Frank said.

Alexis turned and focused on the television screen. As

the show went on, Alexis thought about Whellaby and the blackmail. Then she remembered the dark shadowy figure she had seen dart across the back yard at Thurston's house. It could have been her imagination, but Frank had seen it, too. She hadn't asked him where he had been standing, but there were patches of woods on either side of the Davis house, so the unidentified prowler could have gone anywhere.

If Thurston did have a roommate, who was he? Would he willingly tell the cops about the roommate? Why was the roommate in hiding? Perhaps it was inconsequential, but Alexis was worried.

She knew she should call Naomi, but she couldn't remember her cell phone number. The number had been stored in Alexis's own cell phone, which she had dropped at Thurston's house. Her head hurt and her body ached. The medicine that Frank had given her was making her drowsy. She could hear the television in the background, but the sound slowly began to dissipate as Alexis drifted into a deep sleep.

In the morning, Alexis woke up with a thick blanket tucked around her body, and Frank later admitted that he had covered her with it when he had noticed her shivering in her sleep.

Chapter 31: Devon the Dirty Mechanic

Naomi awoke in a strange place. She was lying on a
tattered couch, cuddled up under an old patchwork quilt.
It was a small den, with posters on the walls that depicted
music festivals or bands—M.O.E., JAB, The Beatles, and
Led Zeppelin. There was a guitar on a stand in the corner.
Naomi remembered that Brian had offered her a place to
sleep the previous night, when she had called him in a
frantic panic.

Naomi had found a note from Alexis on the coffee
table in the detective's apartment. Beneath the note were
several photographs. One of them had terrified Naomi. It
was a picture of a man in his early to mid thirties, walking
toward the front doors of Whellaby's grocery store. He
was wearing glasses and had brown hair and a goatee.
Khaki pants and a white T-shirt completed the image of a
seemingly drab character on his way to buy groceries.

Naomi had recognized him immediately. She had tried
to call Alexis, but the phone had kept ringing and had
gone to voicemail. After that, Naomi had been too upset
to be alone. She had called several people and Brian had
been the first to answer the phone. They had gone to the
Night Kitchen and Naomi had shown him the photograph.

"I'd know his face anywhere," Naomi said worriedly.
"He's the man who chased me through the woods, the one

267

that pretended that he was there to help."

"Are you sure?"

"More than I've ever been about anything. I saw his truck several times; I'm certain he followed me the whole day, waiting for me to break down. He knew something was up with my car. He did *something*."

Brian told Naomi that if she ever needed anything, he would be there. At the end of July, Brian and one of his closest friends were leaving Witchfire on a long road trip.

"When will you be back?" Naomi wanted to know.

Brian shrugged, a glint in his eye. "Who knows?" At that point, he had leaned forward on the table and asked, "Would you like to come?"

Beneath the patchwork quilt, Naomi closed her eyes again. She didn't want to wake up yet; sleep was an easy escape from her waking nightmares.

Pretty soon, the newspaper headlines said things like, 'Timmson Suicide Turned Murder' and 'Suspect Confesses to Faking Timmson Suicide.' It became clear that things had played out just as Spencer Whellaby had claimed, when he had admitted to Alexis that he had seen Thurston accosting the manager with a gun.

Thurston admitted to everything, but told the police that he was innocent due to insanity. He had been going to anger management therapy for years and his psychiatrist was ready to plead his case before the court. His lawyer came at a high price and was a thin man with an oily smile and a smooth tongue.

It was almost as if Thurston had been preparing his argument for months, which to some of the cops on the case, seemed to suggest premeditation. A sudden insane outburst would be hard to prove, especially considering the way in which Thurston had carried out the murder. Uncontrollable insanity, if there is such a thing, does not take part in creative schemes to fake the victim's suicide. Thurston's lawyer had a lot of work ahead of him, but he seemed determined to win.

Meanwhile, several weeks before Naomi's twenty-second birthday, Roy was working on a car with Devon. Pedro was out for the day. Officer Brockman had advised Roy not to say anything to Devon. The police were afraid he would run if they accused him of aiding a violent stalker. They still didn't have enough proof to arrest him.

Roy was extremely frustrated that the cops weren't willing to do anything yet. Devon was an innocent looking young man with a handsome physique and laborer's muscles. He had a thick body, but he wasn't fat, and he had a round, clean-shaven baby face with wide brown eyes—it was a combination that seemed positively mouth-watering to most girls. Naomi wasn't one of them. For the most part, she ignored men. Roy knew this. He had seen a lot of women drool over Devon in the past, but his daughter had never been one of them. He had always

269

been glad of that, even more so now.

The two men were standing under a car that was up on the lift. They had checked the exhaust and the catalytic converter for leaks.

"All right, I'll get the car down now," Devon said.

"Hang on a minute." Roy wiped his hands on a rag and tossed the rag aside. "I'd like to have a talk with you."

"What about?"

"My daughter."

Above them, the car's engine rumbled. Roy stepped closer to Devon. The two men stood face to face. For a moment, a heavy silence descended between them. Devon looked confused, and also worried. Roy thought he knew why.

"What about Naomi?" Devon asked.

"You know she has a stalker."

"Yeah. There was a little piece in the newspaper about a girl getting chased through the woods. They said her name was withheld, but everyone knew it was Naomi."

"But nobody knows who the stalker is. Except you."

Devon glanced toward the garage door, clearly uncomfortable. "What did you say?"

"I said that you know who he is. He paid you to install that kill switch in Naomi's car, didn't he? You were the only one anywhere near that car. You did a little more than fix the window."

Devon opened his mouth, closed it and reopened it

270

numerous times, unsure of how to respond. Roy had caught him totally off-guard. "I didn't . . . ."

"Don't bullshit me," Roy snapped.

That order seemed to throw Devon overboard. He threw a hard punch at Roy, but Roy was ready for him. He ducked and then sent a heavy right cross flying at Devon's jaw. His knuckles hit with a sickening crack and Devon was knocked sideways. He scrambled up, his hand on his face. His mouth was bleeding.

"You're crazy!" he screamed shakily.

"You put my daughter in danger," Roy growled. "I'd be more than happy to snap your neck."

Devon walked backwards out of the garage. "I'm out of here," he stammered. "You can't prove a damn thing! I quit!"

Roy stood on the gravel in front of the garage, massaging his fist. He watched Devon's car race down the driveway, bouncing against potholes, with a certain degree of disappointment. It had felt good to punch Devon, but Roy was solemnly aware of the fact that the cops could no longer prove anything, even if they tried. Devon would be gone by morning and would probably never return to Witchfire. The man wasn't a murderer, a con artist, or a stalker—he was just a skilled laborer who was easily tempted by cold, hard cash.

"Shit," Roy mumbled. Then he walked back into the garage.

Chapter 32: Naomi Heads Home

Alexis completely forgot about her cell phone for a week or so. It was a personal phone, she didn't use it often, and most people called her office number.

As she stood in Thurston's living room, Alexis looked through the sliding glass doors and into the back yard. She stared intently at an immense rose bush, its flowers brightening the yard, reaching for the sky.

"Is this it?" An older police officer who was beginning to lose his hair held up a small Nokia so that Alexis could see it.

"Where'd you find it? I dropped it right here." She pointed to a spot on the floor.

"It was over here." The officer pointed at a spot on the opposite side of the room.

"That's impossible," Alexis countered. "I dropped it here, and I know it wasn't kicked over there."

"It could have been."

Alexis frowned. "I guess so." She took the phone from him. It had run out of battery life and died. "I'll have to take it home and charge it. Thanks for letting me in." She headed for the foyer.

"Anytime."

Although the house had been treated like a crime scene one or two weeks before, it wasn't being watched very

273

closely now. Thurston's gun had been found. A residue
had been discovered on the handle, the same black powder
that was on the metal bale wires at Whellaby's grocery
store. The eyewitness account, the confession and the
residue had almost completely sealed the investigation.
The last piece of evidence, a key to the back door of
Whellaby's that Thurston had apparently stolen from
Timmson, put the final touches on the case.

When Alexis drove back to her apartment, she found
Naomi reading a book on the couch. The photograph was
on the coffee table, but she had turned it upside down.
Alexis sat beside her.

"Look, I know I said I was worried about you when
you went out with Brian, but I was glad you called."

"I know, I'm being a hermit," Naomi admitted. "But
it's been two weeks and there's no sign of this guy
anywhere. Why can't they identify him with that
photograph?"

"All we can do is run that photo through the police
records and ask the FBI to check it, Naomi. That's it.
There's no guarantee of success. It's unlikely that he's
been law-abiding up until now, but he's clever, so he
probably gets away with things."

"That's real encouraging."

"You know what I mean. It's going to take a little bit
more ingenuity to make sure that you're safe, and that we
catch this guy."

"How much more?" Naomi dropped her book on the

coffee table and stared indignantly at the upside-down photo.

Alexis remembered the idea that she had posed to Frank; she could bait the stalker and hope that he fell for it. "I have a plan. I would have mentioned it earlier, but I wasn't certain until now." Alexis plugged her cell phone into the charger by the couch and leaned back, her hands on her thighs. "You drive me to your house, and we'll both stay in the trailer together."

"What good would that do?"

Alexis turned to face her. "Well, he's obsessed with you, isn't he? All we have to do is wait. He'll come back. And when he does, I'll be there."

"What makes you so sure of that?" Naomi asked, yawning.

"He didn't hurt you yet. He wants to see if you'll return his affection. If you love him back, he has no reason to hurt you. He could have harmed you when he chased you through the woods."

"He got close. He ripped my shirt."

"But he didn't *quite* catch you."

"You're not saying it's going to get worse before it gets better, are you?" Naomi sighed, running a hand through her hair.

Alexis nodded. "It has to. I'm not sure how far he wants to take this, but he thinks he's in love with you. If he wanted to hurt you, he would have rigged your brakes, but he didn't want you to crash."

"That's another thing—If he's so smart that he had somebody install a remote controlled kill-switch in my car, then why should I go home? I would probably be walking right into a trap. And who could have installed that thing, anyway?"

"That's the question your father's been asking. And when you go back, I'll be there. Then, we wait. This guy will show up. He won't be able to give up; he's too much *in love* with you."

Naomi had nothing to say. She was far too disgusted.

Despite the heat, Naomi wore a pair of baggy jeans. The bottoms of the jeans dragged under her sandals; the tank top she wore failed to keep her cool. She hadn't been home in a few weeks, ever since Alexis had suggested that she stay with her until they figured out what to do. Now, the solution had arrived, but to Naomi, it didn't seem very bright.

There wasn't much they could do. The police couldn't prosecute a man who didn't have a name; they couldn't go after a vague face that could be easily lost in a crowd. They could question those who fit the description, they could put up posters and request the help of the public, but they couldn't stop him from striking again.

As soon as Naomi had identified the photo of the man in the khakis and glasses, the picture was everywhere.

The citizens of Witchfire and surrounding towns were asked to call the police, should they happen to see the man in the photograph. A warrant was released for the arrest of the nameless man, and the neighborhood watch was asked to be extremely vigilant. Most of the townsfolk knew Roy, and they all sympathized. In fact, it seemed that Naomi was more protected than she had ever been. The daughter of an upstanding citizen was under the wing of the entire town, yet—

Naomi still felt exposed, weak and helpless. She knew she wasn't, but there was something about a man coming after a woman—trying to touch a woman, being *obsessed* with a woman—that made the woman in question feel less like a woman and more like a *girl*. The helplessness was followed by fury as Naomi considered the fact that her privacy was being violated. The fact that someone had watched her dress on at least two separate occasions, perhaps more, disgusted her. Her mood continuously flip-flopped from scared to angry, and she often found herself experiencing both emotions at the same time.

She parked her Buick next to her garage. She said hello to Diesel when she climbed out of the car. The dog barked; it took him a few moments to realize that Naomi wasn't a stranger.

"Hush, boy," Naomi told him. The dog whimpered and curled up in front of his doghouse, resting his snout in the grass. Naomi walked around the corner and checked the main garage. No one was around. She went to her car and opened the back door. "No one's here," she said aloud. "They're probably on lunch hour."

Alexis didn't look very threatening when she was lying down in the back seat of a Buick, her knees bent and her fedora obscuring her dark eyes. She flipped the hat up and grinned. "Oh, good. My plan is working."

"If you can call it a plan," Naomi commented.

Alexis sat up. "It would be an even better plan if I had a man back here with me." Alexis glanced around, touching the soft velour. "This is a fantastic back seat; I hope you plan on making use of it." The detective climbed out.

Naomi shut the door. "You're a piece of work," she said coldly. "Come on, my dad should be home."

When they walked into the front yard, Roy was standing on the porch, his hands on his hips. "You haven't been home in ages, kid! If I hadn't known you were at her house, I'd have been frantic."

"I'm fine, Dad."

Naomi and Alexis walked up onto the porch. Roy gave his daughter a big hug. "Come on in, ladies, we'll have some cold drinks. Anybody want a beer?"

"Dad, for the last time, I'm not a lady!"

Alexis laughed. The three of them walked in the house and the screen door shut behind them.

Chapter 33: Living on the Edge

Alexis hated beer, and that's what she told Roy.

"I'm pretty picky, myself," Roy reminded her.

For a little while, they sat in the living room, Roy and Naomi sipping micro-brewed beer, and Alexis enjoying an iced tea. She made mention of the fact that she only drank whiskey on ice, but Roy didn't have any around.

Tammy the cat curled around their legs, enjoying the coolest part of the room, right in front of the air conditioner. The radio was on; the DJ announced Aerosmith. For a long time, they sat there just listening, until Roy finally spoke.

"Alexis called me before you two came over," he said.

This was news to Naomi; she glanced at both of them in turn. "What'd you tell him?" she asked.

"What we'd been talking about," Alexis said.

"She was brave to mention the idea to me," Roy began, "knowing that I would disagree." He took another swig of his beer. "Using you as bait? I think it's a terrible idea."

"Well . . . ." Naomi faltered.

Roy's eyes widened. "You aren't considering it?"

"Dad, there doesn't seem to be any other option, unless somebody accidentally runs into him somewhere."

"I don't think that's likely to happen," Alexis said. "This man is clever."

"You're telling me. By the way, I fired Devon," Roy added.

Alexis nodded knowingly. "The remote controlled kill-switch."

"He *did* install it?" Naomi exclaimed incredulously.

"No one else could have done it," Roy explained. "He fixed your window, he must know this stalker."

"I hope you realize what you did." Alexis was frustrated. "The cops might have gotten it out of him."

Roy hung his head, appearing defeated. "I couldn't stand the sight of him on my property any longer."

"It's okay, Dad, I understand," Naomi said. "I'm glad you kicked him out."

"I didn't exactly kick him out," Roy admitted. "I punched him in the face."

Alexis winced. She'd had enough of that kind of thing lately. "We'll get him. We don't need Devon. This guy isn't going to give up. And when he comes back, we'll have him right where we want him. He won't even know I'm here."

"What makes you so sure?" Roy wondered.

"Instinct." Alexis tapped her temple with her right index finger. "Pure instinct."

Chapter 34: Naomi, My Love

"Naomi, how are you?"

"Richard, that's the fifth time this week that you've asked me that, and still with that tone in your voice like you think I'm going to fall apart or something."

Naomi was standing in the door of her trailer. She could feel the air conditioning hitting her from behind, a freezing cloud of air meeting the heat and humidity that hung in a heavy haze over the yard. She had just gotten home that day, and she was still getting used to it.

Richard mopped his brow with the back of his hand. He could hear music playing in the living room, and he knew it was Aerosmith, one of Naomi's favorite bands. Richard climbed the two small steps and walked into Naomi's living room. "I'm sorry; I've just been worried about you."

"No need to apologize." She shut the door behind him. "I'm just a little on edge. Have a seat. Alexis and I are getting settled."

Richard slumped onto the couch. "Alexis? The detective?"

"Yeah. She's taking a shower." Naomi stepped into the kitchen and poured herself a glass of water. "This is all part of her plan."

"What, the shower?"

"No, staying here." Naomi rolled her eyes. "She thinks we can catch the stalker by luring him back, and she says she'll be here to *personally* corner him. She thinks he won't be able to resist paying me another visit. I hope he's given up."

"That's not likely," Richard said forlornly. "You don't mess with a girl's car and chase her through a forest in the rain just to give up."

"I thought that's what you would say." Naomi sat down next to Richard. "I'm not looking forward to it. And even worse, I think my dad's planning a surprise birthday party." The 'even worse' was spoken in the most sarcastic way possible.

Richard suddenly looked shifty. "What makes you think that?"

"Well, I caught him on the phone earlier and he was acting strangely. He hung up really fast. And—*wait*. You know something, don't you?"

"Me? No way." Richard knew something, but he had been told not to say anything. Naomi's twenty-second birthday was coming up in a week and a half. Roy was planning a big party, and Richard suddenly felt guilty. He had a bad feeling that he was blushing.

"Uh-huh," Naomi said, eyeing him suspiciously.

There was something about the way she looked at him that made him fold. "All right, he's throwing a party, but don't let him know that I told you, okay?"

"Don't worry. I won't," Naomi said, smiling slightly.

"Honestly, I'm disappointed. I figured this would happen, but I don't like parties very much."

"He's just trying to make things easier on you."

"I know, but . . . *still*." Naomi glanced up from her water. "Why'd you come over, anyway? You didn't call."

He shook his head. A musical laugh escaped his lips. "I missed you. Why don't you seem to believe it?"

Whenever Richard moved closer to her, Naomi got nervous. He did so now, sidling across the couch like a crocodile advancing on his prey. She saw a threat in Richard that she saw in no one else, but it wasn't a threat against her own well being, like the threat of the stalker. It was a threat against her emotional stability, her heart, her mental capacity—it was a threat of temptation, of attraction. That was something that Naomi wasn't ready for. What Richard was willing to give her was too much for her. She had already lost so much. In Naomi's mind, physical love only led to commitment and attachment— and *any* kind of attachment could just as easily lead to abandonment.

She shied away when Richard tried to kiss her. She had to admire his determination.

"What's wrong?" he asked.

"Nothing." Her hands clenched up. Her heart beat faster. She could feel a tingle rising along her spine, every hair on the back of her neck standing on end because he had put his arm around her.

"I don't believe that for a second." His face was so

283

close to hers that she could feel his breath on her cheek. "It's not me, is it?" He recoiled, but only slightly.

"No, it's not you. I . . . ." Naomi glanced at him, but only briefly. "I've never, I mean . . . I've never had a boyfriend before."

There was a long silence. The closed door to the bathroom was nearby and they heard the shower turn off. Richard nodded and allowed his arm to slide away from her shoulders. He clasped his hands in his lap. "I understand," he said. "You've been through a lot."

His blue eyes were so deep, so beautiful. Naomi saw a lot of words in those eyes, words that Richard elected to keep to himself. She thought of her mother, lying dead on the kitchen floor. Somehow, she knew that he really did understand.

Alexis came out of the bathroom wearing a white terrycloth robe. "Oh, hi!" she exclaimed as she dried her hair with a towel. "What'd I miss?"

That night, Naomi had to work. Alexis stayed in the trailer, slept in Naomi's bed and kept the curtains shut. Her car wasn't there; only Roy would know of her presence.

Naomi hadn't been working during her stay at Alexis's apartment. Her father had informed Keith of the situation and Officer Brockman had called to back up the story.

When Naomi returned to work, everyone looked at her with hesitant words on their lips, apparently afraid to ask Naomi about what had happened to her. They all knew— it had been in the papers. If it hadn't been for her father warding off the press, they would have tried to get to Naomi. Thankfully, people were relatively tame in Witchfire, and mostly kept to themselves. It wasn't the kind of town that bred nosiness.

Uneventful days went by, and Naomi began to think that her stalker had disappeared. It was certainly a possibility. The chase through the woods, the gunshot, and the cops had probably given him second thoughts. How obsessed could a person possibly get before their common sense began to kick in?

Several days before her birthday, Naomi pulled into the parking lot at work. Oliver met her by her car and the two of them walked into the building. She turned on her cell phone at first break and noticed that she had a voicemail.

Cigarette smoke drifted through the air and Naomi stepped aside, bringing the cell phone to her ear. She blocked out the voices of her coworkers and listened. What she heard made her shiver; goose bumps rose on her flesh.

"Naomi, my love, don't think that I have forgotten about you. I miss you. Perhaps I'll bring you another rose." *Click.*

285

Naomi found herself pacing the household aisle an hour later. She would put up a case of detergent and then kick the empty box away. Then she would stand there wringing her hands for a moment, after which she would glance toward Ramsey, who was listening to a CD player and too lost in his musings to notice her distress.

Oliver was working in aisle six. Geoffrey had the night off. Naomi left the household aisle and searched out Oliver, desperate to talk to someone. She found him at the end of aisle six, stocking salad dressing. He was placing each bottle of ranch onto the shelf in a dreamy sort of way, as if pretending he were elsewhere.

"Oliver."

Naomi tapped him on the shoulder, which seemed to startle him. He glanced up at her.

"Sorry," Naomi mumbled. "I need to talk to you."

"What's up?" Oliver stood from where he had been kneeling on the floor and dropped the box he had been holding. "Naomi? Are you okay?"

It was easy to tell that something was wrong. Her breathing was labored, as though she were about to cry. She glanced behind her, as though someone might be watching. "He called me."

"What? Who?"

"The stalker."

Oliver seemed to pale with the news. "You talked to him?"

"No. At break time, I checked my phone and I had a voicemail. He got my phone number somehow." Naomi's eyes widened. She shook her head, disbelieving. "How could he have gotten my phone number?"

"You should have told me as soon as this happened. That's scary, Naomi."

"You're telling me. I need to call Alexis."

"Maybe you should have stayed at her apartment a while longer."

"No." Naomi shook her head. "I know what she'll want to do. This is the opportunity, as horrible as it sounds." She looked at Oliver, clearly frightened, but holding herself together as well as she could. "He's gone too far, now. They'll be able to catch him."

Oliver pulled Naomi into his arms. "And they will," he assured her.

"The question is," Naomi mumbled, her voice muffled by the sleeve of Oliver's hooded jacket. "Will they catch him before he catches me?"

Chapter 35: The Birthday Party

July eighteenth began with a rainstorm. The heat of the
previous day had culminated and burst, sending forth
thunder, lighting, wind and a pouring rain that tore at the
landscape in the early hours of the morning.

Roy was aware of a sudden sense of disappointment in
himself. He had driven away the man who might have
exposed his daughter's stalker, and he felt that he hadn't
done as much as he should have to protect her. Now,
Naomi was more upset than she had ever been, having
heard the man's voice on her phone. She was smart; she
saved the message, knowing that it could be used against
her attacker in court. The police had been notified, and
they were watching.

Most people would have lost their minds, but Naomi
was the epitome of cool, calm and detached. Moments of
insanity would grip her and she would need the embrace
of a friend more than anything, but for now, she was okay.
Roy knew that she was safe; she had spent the last few
nights at Oliver's house. Alexis had been staying in
Naomi's trailer, hoping to lure the stalker back for another
round. So far, she hadn't had any luck. Officer Brockman
lurked around the property in jeans and a T-shirt, driving
his dented Ford Explorer, chain-smoking cigarettes, and
spending most of his time fishing in the creek near the

289

house. Brockman wasn't having any luck catching a suspect, and he wasn't having any luck with the fish, either.

July eighteenth was special, because it was Naomi's birthday. Roy had been planning a party for her. Roy's friends were coming, some cousins, and some relatives by marriage. The Vogler family was very small, but those that lived nearby would be present. Brockman would be there, as well as a few other police officers that Roy knew through his business. Over sixty people had been invited. There had been a lot of planning. Roy was expecting the guests at around one in the afternoon. Richard was keeping Naomi occupied. Eventually he would bring her back home for the party.

Despite the fact that this was supposed to be a happy occasion, Roy grew tense as the caterer arrived and set up the tables. He watched three women and four men work in unison, tense and hurried, nimble fingers handling dishes, setting out covered plates and going back and forth, from their hulking white van to the covered tables, like a bunch of worker ants returning and emerging from the nest.

Roy knew that the stalker had attempted to contact Naomi. The police had tracked the number, the voice had been analyzed, and the recording had been saved, but his identity was still unknown. The number came from a prepaid cell phone, which left them at a dead end, and the police could find no suspects and no leads. It was as though the man simply did not exist, a figment of Naomi's imagination turned drastically real.

Alexis and Frank hypothesized that the stalker had already broken the law in the past. They thought he might have been arrested for another transgression, perhaps molestation or rape. Unfortunately, no amount of investigation revealed anything. Officer Gibson and even Brockman looked into the police records and quickly found any possibility exhausted. They concluded that the mystery man was in hiding, a clever lurker who knew when it was time to step back and remain temporarily in the shadows.

And that was just it. *Temporarily*, Roy thought. *He was smart enough to figure out her schedule, find out who her friends were, listen in on her conversations and pay someone to sabotage her car. If he's as intelligent as he seems, he'll know how to evade the police.*

Roy was well aware of these morbid facts, and even more aware that his daughter's stalker was likely to strike again. He thought of sending her out of town for a while, but he didn't know anyone that she could stay with, and the idea of not being able to look after her himself pained him.

What if, while out of town, the stalker discovered her location and decided to strike? What if, rather than help Naomi, the plans of hiding her were to backfire? And, worse yet, Roy had to admit that Alexis's plan, although shaky, was a good one. Waiting was the best thing to do at this point. Alexis was convinced that the stalker would return—and when he did, they would ready for him.

It was nearing twelve o' clock. Soon, Naomi's birthday party would be in full swing. Roy had to wonder if she would even enjoy it, after all she had been through.

"Happy birthday to you, happy birthday to you . . . ."

Naomi stood in the afternoon sun, blinking, feeling exposed and embarrassed before a crowd that covered the lawn. Her father stood there with an accomplished look on his face, as though he had conquered the world in one day.

Richard's hands were on her shoulders as though to keep her from running. She turned her head. Between her teeth, she mumbled, "You brought me over here for *this*?"

She had known there would be a party, but she hadn't realized how many people had been invited. Oliver was standing next to her. He patted her on the back. Naomi couldn't stand something unexpected. Oliver was pleased that she had held herself together so well over the last few weeks. A lesser person would have allowed herself to be crushed by the pressure, but not Naomi.

"Happy birthday, dear Naomi, happy birthday to you!"

The entire crowd burst into a cheer and people ran forward to wish her well, a sea of flesh and smiles adorned in their summer clothes. An hour later, Naomi was

standing in the side yard eating a piece of cake. The icing
looked sickly and off-white under the sun, melting in the
heat. The rain had cooled the air only a little, and the
humidity was like a blow to the head, strong and
unyielding.

In the back, friends of her father were playing
volleyball, and in the front, some older folks were milling
about, drinking lemonade. In retrospect, it seemed sort of
strange; all of these smiling faces, this huge celebration,
was all in the midst of one woman's misery. She was
twenty-two years old and Naomi had never felt closer to
death.

Her memory kept flashing back to that first night when
she had seen the faceless man bound across the driveway
in front of her car. How long had he been watching her,
memorizing her movements, licking his lips as his eyes
took her in, as his imagination took more of her than she
would have willingly given? It was hot, but Naomi
shivered, a chill traveling down her spine.

Oliver, clad in a black T-shirt, jeans and sneakers,
peered into her eyes. "Are you all right?"

Naomi looked up at him, squinting in the sun. "Oh,"
she mumbled. "I'm okay. I was just thinking."

Oliver frowned. "I know you're scared. I am, too.
Did you tell your dad about the voice mail?"

"Yeah."

"What'd he say?"

Naomi shrugged. "He's scared. The cops couldn't do

293

anything, yet again. Nobody who's been arrested within forty miles seems to match this guy. He must be so shrewd that if he's ever done this before, he never got caught."

"I don't think he's done it before, Naomi. I think he's obsessed with you, period. I don't know." Oliver shook his head and poked at the last bit of his cake. "What does somebody do when they're obsessed?"

Naomi stared down at her feet, lost in thought. "I don't know, Oliver. I guess they keep going until they get what they want."

"That's what I was afraid of," Oliver said solemnly.

Naomi snuck away around three o' clock, ducking around the side of her father's house and stepping beyond the tree line. She followed a little path that wound its way to the edge of the creek and sat down on a large boulder. She took off her sandals and dipped her feet in the cool water. She could hear the laughter and conversation behind her. Naomi doubted that anyone had seen her disappear. The water rippled coolly around her toes. Across the creek, two ducks paddled to a stony shore. Behind Naomi, a twig snapped. She startled.

"It's okay," a voice said. "It's only me."

Naomi swung around, her fingers clenched. "Oh! Geo, you scared the hell out of me!"

He walked purposefully to the edge of the creek and crouched by the water, his long black hair falling around his shoulders. "That's what all the girls say," he said, smirking. He pulled a pack of cigarettes out of his shirt pocket. "Want one?"

"I . . . I don't smoke." She watched him light the filterless American Spirit and began to wonder if smoking tobacco really did make a person feel calm and collected. "Oh, let me try one," she said nervously.

"Are you sure?"

"Well, why not? Things can't possibly get any worse, can they?" Her blue eyes drifted lazily over the water, taking in the ironic peacefulness of her surroundings.

"Try mine first," Geo said, handing her the smoldering paper and tobacco.

Naomi took the cigarette tentatively. The smell wasn't all that appealing. "Is it like good liquor?" she wondered. "Does it taste nasty at first, but give you a warm feeling afterwards?"

"I'm not sure. I don't know if I agree with your definition of good liquor. To me, it always tastes good."

Naomi stared at the thing for a moment and then brought it to her lips. She wasn't sure what happened next, except for the fact that she spent the next thirty seconds coughing. A moment later, Geo was holding his cigarette again and patting her on the back with his free hand.

"It's not always like that," he said.

"I hope you're right," Naomi gagged.

"You don't mind me being here, do you?"

"Are you kidding? It's all those people I can't stand."

"I guess your dad didn't realize," Geo said forlornly.

"No, I'm sure he did. He was just trying to distract me. I don't blame him." Naomi slumped forward and picked up a small stone. "I just hate surprises. Ever since I found my mom dead on the kitchen floor, I've hated surprises." She tossed the stone and watched it hit the water with a resounding 'plop.' When Geoffrey didn't say anything, Naomi turned and looked at him. He was staring across the creek. He slumped into a cross-legged position on the stones and rested his arms on his knees. "I'm sorry," Naomi said.

"For what?" Geo asked.

"Bringing up my mom. It tends to destroy a conversation."

"It doesn't bother me," Geo insisted. "It's just hard to know what to say. But don't worry; even if I don't say anything, I'm still listening."

Naomi knew that was true. Geo was a man of few words, except when he was singing or playing music. Then, and only then, did his soul seem to burst across a crowded room like a piercing scream, capturing the wide eyes of every person present. Naomi considered this and said, "You listen better than anyone I know."

"Thank you." Geo took a long drag from his cigarette.

For an hour or so after that, the two friends sat in

silence, watching the clear water trickle around the rocks. A little while later, they climbed to their feet and walked back toward the yard.

"I have something for you," Geo announced as they neared the party guests that mingled behind the house.

"Oh yeah?"

Geo nodded. "Oliver wanted me to wait for him, though. He has a present for you, too."

"Oh, boy," Naomi mumbled unenthusiastically.

"Hey, can't some good friends celebrate a birthday?" Geo clapped her playfully on the back.

"Sorry, Geo, I just don't feel like now's the time to be celebrating life, if you know what I mean."

Geoffrey stepped ahead of her, barring her way. "Naomi, listen to me. You are going to be fine."

They were still a good distance from the party guests. Naomi peered over Geo's shoulder, watching her father laugh with a few of his friends. She wondered if he was truly as happy as he looked. "I have this horrible feeling, Geo. Like it's all going to be over for me."

"Now you sound like some drippy suicidal teenager."

Naomi raised an eyebrow. "Drippy?"

"Never mind. You know what I meant. All of a sudden you've got this defeatist attitude. I *know* you don't really feel that way. That's not you. Now, tell me what you would do if you were face to face with this stalker of yours, right now."

Naomi felt her fists clench. She considered the

question carefully. "I'd pick up the nearest lead pipe and let him have it," she snapped, gritting her teeth.

Geo laughed. "There's the Naomi I remember! Come on, let's go have a beer."

Naomi grinned, suddenly unable to suppress her laughter.

Geo and Naomi met up with Brian; he was enjoying the snacks on the buffet table and drinking a Guinness. Geoffrey and Oliver had invited him the last time they had seen him at the Night Kitchen.

The young musician had brought his guitar. Naomi was beginning to wonder if he ever went anywhere without it. "How have you been?" he asked.

"I'm okay," Naomi said.

Geo shook his head. "She's lying."

"I am not." Naomi glared at him. "Things have been rough, but I'll be fine." She looked back at Brian. "I was just telling Geo that the next time I see my stalker, I'm going to beat him over the head with a lead pipe."

"That's a very vivid piece of imagery, Naomi." Brian picked up his guitar and slipped the strap over his shoulder. "Care to take a little walk with me? Maybe I can try to write a song about it."

"What, the lead pipe?" Geo laughed. "If you sell us the rights, we can play it at our next Jargon show."

Brian smirked. His soft eyes looked back to Naomi, betraying an honest and sincere concern for her well-being. He gestured to the side yard. "Shall we make our way through the throng?"

Naomi didn't think that fifteen people mingling in one area of the yard constituted a throng, but she shrugged and said, "Sure, why not."

"Good." Brian walked purposefully among the people, Geo and Naomi following behind.

Naomi had opened the door to her little garage. In it was a 1978 Thunderbird that she had been working on for the past few days. Oliver wandered over to join them, a gift in his hands. Naomi opened the presents on the hood of the old car, glad to be away from the crowd again.

Oliver had brought Naomi some CDs—Aerosmith, Alice in Chains, and a new Michael Franti album. Geoffrey had thoughtfully framed a photo of the three friends, one that had been taken earlier that summer during an outdoor Jargon show.

Brian handed her the last gift, one that he had wrapped in an old newspaper and carefully taped. Naomi unwrapped it while Geo, Oliver and Brian watched.

"A portable CD player." Naomi smiled. "Thank you, Brian." She carefully placed the gift onto the hood of the car and embraced him in a short hug.

Geo scowled, and then laughed. "That's a lot better than my present, and he hardly knows you."

Brian smiled warmly. "I just know that you're going through some tough times, Naomi, and I've always felt that music is the best escape. So this way, you can escape any time you want."

Naomi didn't know what to say. Oliver took care of it for her. "I have to admit, Geo, I knew that he was going to get her that. That's why I bought the CDs."

Brian grinned. "I did tell you, didn't I?"

"Yeah. When we were at the diner and Geo went outside for a smoke."

Naomi picked up the framed photo. She gave Geo a hug. "I've never gotten a better present," she told him.

They spent the next few moments arguing playfully over whose present was better, and Naomi sat on the hood of the Thunderbird, inspecting the CDs. She imagined herself driving down the road, far away from Witchfire, escaping her nightmares—escaping the nameless man who patiently stalked her. She turned to Brian and watched him as he tuned his guitar. She climbed off the hood of the car, clutching her presents to her chest.

"Brian, did you really mean it?"

"What?" He glanced up at her.

"Are you still going on that road trip?"

"Yeah."

"Can I still come?"

"Certainly." Brian plucked a string. A sharp note

300

permeated the thick air. Geoffrey and Oliver exchanged a curious glance.

When the evening came to a close, Alexis was nowhere to be seen. Naomi wasn't sure where she had gone. At that moment, she was only aware of one thing; all of the guests had left and she was sitting with Richard in the trailer, alone.

The air conditioner had cooled the room considerably, not at all to Naomi's liking. She was already aware that Alexis preferred freezing temperatures. Naomi turned off the air conditioner, opened a window, and went to the kitchen to get a cold beer. It was a different kind, one that she wasn't used to; Alexis had apparently stocked her fridge. She remembered the detective offering to buy her a case of beer because she had eaten most of the food Naomi had bought the week before. Alexis knew how much Naomi liked beer.

"Want one?" Naomi asked.

Richard shrugged. "No, thanks. Your father supplied me with plenty earlier."

"Yeah, I guess he did," Naomi said, remembering that she had seen Richard and her father knocking back beers together in the front yard.

Richard had been sweating profusely from the heat, but he had cooled down after entering the trailer. The beads of moisture had disappeared from his forehead. He scratched through his hair and at some point, mentioned that he needed a shower. Naomi wasn't listening. She was staring at the black screen of the television, scrutinizing her vague reflection.

"Are you okay?" Richard sighed. "I seem to be asking you that a lot lately."

"Most people ask me that a lot." Naomi took a long, deep gulp from her beer. It was strong and bitter. "I never know what to say."

"What are you going to do?"

She knew what he was referring to. "I don't know. What am I supposed to do? I gave a description of the stalker to the cops, we have that photograph, and we know his face—but we don't know his name. He doesn't match a single person that's been arrested around here. They're checking elsewhere, too, but nothing's working. And as far as anyone at Whellaby's can remember, he was going into the store regularly since long before I ever worked there."

"Which implies that he's lived around here for a long time."

"Exactly. They're questioning everyone, though. Someone must know. If he's lived around here for this long, there must be someone who would remember him."

"It stands to reason." Richard watched as Naomi swallowed half of the beer in a few more gulps. "Do you know where Alexis went?"

"No clue." Naomi sunk back against the couch. "Maybe she got an idea or something."

Richard sat beside Naomi, eyeing the beer in her hand. "Naomi, Geo told me something that kind of worries me."

"What's that?" Naomi drank some more of her beer.

"Are you sure you should be drinking that so fast?"

"I haven't had a beer all day," Naomi grumbled. "What was it you were going to tell me?"

"Geo said that you're heading off on a road trip with Brian, that guy that always hangs out at the Night Kitchen."

"I might. So what?" She turned to look at him and couldn't help but notice that her vision swam a little.

"Is there . . . I mean, is there anything between you two?"

"What?" Naomi was beginning to like the beer. She took another gulp and noticed that it was almost empty. She began to wonder how much she had eaten that day; the alcohol seemed to be affecting her more than usual. She turned and looked at Richard. "What did you . . . ."

"You heard what I asked you."

He seemed to be growing frustrated with her, and she wondered why. "I hardly know Brian," she said incredulously.

"Which is exactly why I'm wondering why you would be running off with him on some road trip."

"Excuse me? Running off? Who's running off where? I only said I *might* go. It'd be nice to get away for a while."

She looked at the bottle in her hand and realized it was empty.

"Why don't you read the label on that?" Richard said, pointing.

Naomi squinted at the bottle. "Oh," she mumbled.

"It's over ten percent alcohol," he said, sighing.

"I see that." She set the bottle down on the coffee table, swaying slightly. "But, Richard . . . ."

"Yeah, Naomi?"

"I just like Brian as a friend, that's all. I swear." She belched, and then covered her mouth as an afterthought. "Sorry."

Richard laughed. "That's okay."

"Now I should be the one asking if *you're* okay," Naomi said pointedly.

"I'm fine. I guess I was just a little bit jealous."

"There's no need to be." Naomi leaned over and kissed him.

Chapter 36: A Dark Night at Whellaby's Grocery Store

Frank drove Alexis back to Vogler's Auto Repair in his own car. He didn't want anyone to think that there were cops sneaking around the Vogler place. After all, Alexis was still hoping that the stalker would show up there and accidentally give himself away.

The sun had yet to rise on the nineteenth of July. Frank yawned and rolled down his window, letting in the muggy morning air. "I'm trying to cut the coffee habit, I really am. But when you get me in on these all-nighters, it's a wonder I make it home in one piece."

"You'll live, Frankie."

"Hey, I never asked you, but if you're allowed to give me a nickname, why can't I call you Lexxy?"

Alexis cringed. "First of all, *Frank*, most people call you Frankie. Second of all, 'Lexxy' sounds like the name of a barely legal porn star."

The smirk that spread across Frank's face was almost sickening. "Sounds good to me."

"You're disgusting."

"Oh, come on!" Frank exclaimed. "You know I'm only kidding. I wouldn't touch a porn star." He paused. "Unless she was *at least* nineteen."

"Frank." She shot him a look that sliced through his

retinas like a knife. "I wish you would start drinking coffee again."

"Why?"

"Without caffeine, you are grumpy and irritating."

"You're probably right."

This time, when Frank yawned, Alexis yawned, too. "You're like a disease, Frank."

Frank leaned back, closing his eyes briefly. "Does that mean you're going to catch me?" His eyes immediately snapped open, as though expecting Alexis to punch him in the face. She had been especially nasty lately, ever since Thurston had almost strangled her to death, not that he blamed her. "I was only kidding around, Alexis."

To his surprise, Alexis sighed heavily. "I know. Thanks for driving last night. I feel like too many people have seen my car lately."

"You could be paranoid, but you could also be right."

"The last thing I want is for a friend of that Thurston Davis to see me sneaking around his house. That's why it was essential that we went at night."

"And that's what I told them when I got the warrant." Frank held out his hand; he and Alexis shook. "Congratulations, Detective Nevid. You found what you were looking for."

"And remember, you promised you wouldn't tell a soul. Not yet."

"I know. I promised—and I meant it."

"Thank you, Frank." Alexis climbed out of the car and

began her trek up toward Roy's house and the trailer that sat behind it. For once, she felt as though she had actually accomplished something.

Naomi had a dream that her mother came home from work with groceries, her arms full and her hair disheveled.

"If you want my advice, Naomi, don't ever work in a grocery store. I was a cashier once, and that place I worked in was like a zoo during the day." The woman's nose scrunched up and for a moment, she no longer looked like Naomi's mother. "Once you walk into a place like that, you just join the rest of the animals." She dropped the groceries onto the table. One of the bags fell over. Oranges and onions rolled off the table together, collecting around Naomi's feet. "Let me tell you something, Naomi, a grocery store is just like a slaughterhouse. And that's all you are, when you walk in there, just a piece of meat . . . ."

Naomi felt her body jump amongst the sheets. Her eyes snapped open. She was lying on her side and staring at the bookcase across from her bed. "Slaughterhouse?" she mumbled. Her dreams were getting stranger. At least in this dream, her mother had been alive. She shivered, suddenly aware of the fact that the room was chilly and she was naked. The sheet and blanket were only covering her legs and she immediately reached down to correct the

problem. Then she heard something move beside her.
Naomi gulped.

As she turned, she pulled the blankets up to her chin.
Her jaw dropped. She caught sight of a pair of brilliant
blue eyes. She took in the soft features and the neatly
trimmed goatee.

"Good morning," Richard said. "I've been awake for
the past hour or so, but you looked like you were having a
dream or something, so I didn't want to wake you."

Richard drew closer to her. She could feel the heat of
his body against her. He began to kiss her. She didn't
know what to say. He touched her and—

Naomi jumped, again. She opened her eyes. This
time, she was lying on the couch in her living room.
Richard was asleep next to her. Naomi's head had been
resting on his chest. She noticed that he was looking at
her. This time, his eyes were more real, *deeper*—although
just as brilliantly blue.

"Richard," she breathed.

I'm still dressed, Naomi thought. *I'm wearing clothes,
and he's wearing clothes and . . . I guess I must have had
a dream, and then I had a dream that I thought was real,
but it wasn't.*

"Hi," Richard said.

"What happened?" Naomi mumbled.

"Last night?" He sunk down a bit so that his face was
level with hers. She was aware of his arms wrapped
around her. "Last night, you had a beer, something that

Alexis left for you. Then, you had another beer."

"I did?"

"Yes."

"That would explain why my stomach feels funny."

"It would, at that. Anyway, you told me all these things I didn't know."

"Like what?" Naomi gulped.

"I'm kidding. You didn't really." He kissed her gently on the lips. "Actually, I wouldn't let you have another beer, and then you fell asleep on me. Eventually, I fell asleep. And just now, you jumped, and woke me up."

"Oh." Naomi relaxed against him. "So I'm not dreaming, right?"

"No. Unless I'm at my house, and you're in your own bed, and we're both having the same dream."

"Is that possible?"

"I'm not sure. It could be."

Naomi sat up. Richard straightened his clothes and pulled himself up next to her. "Are you sure this isn't a dream?" Naomi asked.

"Positive. If this were a dream, my neck wouldn't hurt so badly. Remind me not to sleep on your couch again."

"Then, I just had the strangest dream I've had in a long time."

"What was it?"

Naomi blushed. "Nothing. Another one about my mother." She told him about the first part of the dream, leaving out the second part. The last thing she wanted to tell Richard was that she had dreamt that they'd been in bed together. Naomi suspected that he would want to make the dream a reality as soon as possible, and she wasn't ready for that.

"That's really weird, but are you sure it's the strangest dream *ever*?"

"Not ever—just in a while."

Suddenly, the front door to the trailer opened. Alexis walked in. "Oh, hi . . . Uh, the door was unlocked. I thought you would be staying in the house." She gestured to Roy's old farmstead.

Naomi was beginning to wonder if Alexis's talent—second to detective work—was interrupting tense moments between Naomi and Richard. She seemed to be rather good at it. Naomi scowled.

It was five minutes to ten o' clock at night. Naomi was sitting in her Buick in the parking lot at Whellaby's. She had five minutes until she would have to get up and go inside to start her shift. For a while, she stared at the shadows the headlights made on the grass. She thought about Richard. She thought about the strange dreams she'd had that morning, and about how she had woken up in his arms.

She knew why the second dream had seemed so real to her. She wanted it to happen. Richard had been patiently chasing after her since the night he had seen her at the Coral Reef Tavern. She had been so frightened that he was her stalker. He surprised her by being exactly the opposite—he was an attractive, intelligent man who seemed genuinely worried about her. He seemed to care for her. She had to think about that for a while before she actually believed it. *I guess not enough people have cared about me in the past, so it's hard for me to grasp the idea.*

Naomi knew that he wanted her, and she definitely wanted him. On the other hand, was she ready for a relationship? Naomi had always preferred being by herself. She fumbled with the CDs that Oliver had bought her. She took the Aerosmith album out of its case and placed it in her new CD player.

And what if I do get together with Richard? What then? Naomi wondered. *After all, I'm a virgin.*

All of a sudden, the passenger side door opened and Naomi startled. She turned and looked just as Geo sat down beside her. "Hey, what's up? I didn't know you were working tonight," he said. "You okay? You look freaked out."

"That's because you just scared the crap out of me!" Naomi exclaimed. She sunk forward, leaning her head against the steering wheel. "Damn it. I was deep in thought, Geo."

"Sorry. About what?"

Naomi blushed for the second time that day. "Nothing." She turned off the headlights and took her keys out of the ignition.

"It's ten o' clock."

"All right. Another exciting night of stocking shelves, coming right up."

As the night wore on, Naomi became more and more uncomfortable. She was stocking aisle eight with Ramsey, and she stopped and listened, as though waiting for her subconscious to tell her where her unnamed dread was coming from. The Aerosmith CD was playing through for the second time. She had skipped a song or two at first, but now she didn't bother; she had left her other CDs in the car and wouldn't be able to get them until break time.

It was eleven fifty-five. Break time was in five minutes.

Maybe a minute or two passed before it happened; she wasn't sure. She was stocking a case of cat food when, without warning, the power went out. All of a sudden, everything was black.

Whellaby's had been through several incarnations, but it was a big, square building and whoever had designed it in the first place hadn't seen a need for any windows. At the end of aisle eight, toward the front of the store, Naomi could see a dim sliver of light.

"Ramsey?"

"Naomi?"

She slipped off her headphones, but she could still hear the music. She didn't bother to turn it off. "Aren't there

312

supposed to be some kind of emergency lights?"

Several long seconds went by. "Yeah. I don't know why they haven't turned on yet."

Naomi heard Ramsey's footsteps. She heard her coworkers asking the same questions in various parts of the cavernous store. Finally, after a minute or so, somebody yelled, "Everybody just head for the front, where we can at least see each other by the doors. I think the pole lights in the parking lot are still on." That sounded like Keith.

Naomi started to walk down aisle eight, but she stopped when her cell phone rang. In the inky darkness, she picked up the phone. "Hello?" There was a pause. "Hello? Is someone there?"

"Naomi."

She froze. It was him.

"Naomi," the voice continued. "Go to the back room. I'm waiting."

She heard a muffled sound, and the man on the other line hung up.

Naomi was only vaguely aware of the song that still played as she stood in the pet aisle, hoping that her eyes would adjust so that she could at least see shadows—not this impenetrable wall of black that surrounded her.

Naomi found the stop button. She pulled off her headphones and fumbled around until she found a shelf. She deposited the CD player in the first empty spot she could find, shoving it behind what felt like a bag of cat food.

She stood there for a long moment, wondering what to do. "Is anyone still there?" She was surprised at how quiet and meek she sounded. She realized that she was frightened. Although she had experienced varying degrees of fear over the past month, she was certain that this was the worst kind. She couldn't see. It occurred to her that she wasn't sure what scared her more—the fact that the stalker had come for her, or the inescapable reality that the darkness was quickly closing in on her.

It was at that moment that her childhood claustrophobia came back to her. She remembered that her bedroom had been especially small. She remembered that her mother would close the door whenever she tucked her in at night. As a small child, Naomi had known that when your parents close the door and the shadows disappear, and the inky blackness sets in, that's when the monsters come out—that's when you aren't safe anymore.

Naomi felt like a child again. Her bedroom door was shut, she was trapped, and the monster was coming out from under her bed. She was suddenly aware that her breathing was becoming frantic. She sounded like an animal caught in a trap.

"Calm down, Naomi," she told herself. "It's just darkness, it can't hurt you." Even as she said the words aloud to herself, she knew that there was something *in* the darkness that could hurt her—something in the back room, waiting for her.

Her cell phone rang again. She pulled it out of her pocket and answered it. Her voice came out tiny, afraid. "Hello?"

"Naomi. I know you are scared, but there is nothing to be afraid of. Imagine that I am the flower and you are the sun."

"What?"

"Come to the back room. I'm still waiting. Don't bring your phone. You won't need it here."

Naomi brought the phone away from her ear. For a moment, the glowing screen lit up a very small area of her surroundings. The screen read 'call ended.' Everything turned black again. With a sudden steadfast resolution, Naomi stepped silently down aisle eight, away from the dim light at the front of the store, and toward the empty darkness of the back room. She found the end of a set of shelves and left her cell phone on the floor. There was no reception in the back room, anyway.

Alexis had walked up to Whellaby's grocery store and sat on the bench out front. She had parked her car a half a mile down the street and hung a plastic bag out the window to make it look as though it had broken down. It was a breezy night, so she was wearing her trench coat over a black T-shirt and black jeans. Her fedora was tipped slightly over her eyes. She crossed her legs in front of her and waited.

When Alexis didn't want to be noticed, she had a talent for disappearing. As the sounds of the night settled in and bats fluttered in the overhang, Alexis sunk into the bench and became a statue—a part of the shadows. When the time came, she would be ready.

No one seemed the notice the dark shadow on the corner of a bench until it began to move, straighten, and become a human being. The night crew turned collectively and saw Alexis emerge from the darkness, smooth and snake-like, much like some denizen from another world.

"Where'd you come from?" Keith asked.

"I've been here," Alexis explained. "I've been waiting."

"Not for this . . . I mean, you didn't know the power was going to go out, did you?"

"You're quick, Mr. Ryan. I had a pretty good idea something was going to happen, but I didn't know what. Now, if you'll excuse me." Alexis pulled a nine-millimeter out of a holster on her belt. "I believe there's something in there waiting for *me*."

"What's going on?"

"I'll tell you later." Alexis walked toward the front door.

Naomi knew that aisle eight was directly across from the swinging doors that led into the back room. It didn't take her long to find the doors. She pushed through them and knew that she was standing in the area where all the pallets were kept. This was also where the trucks unloaded the products that Naomi and her coworkers spent all night putting on the shelf, and she guessed that the bins where the damaged goods were processed were somewhere directly ahead of her.

She had always been afraid of the dark, for as long as she could remember. As a child, she had been afraid that some kind of monster was lurking in the shadows, waiting for someone to turn out the lights. That nightmare had suddenly become very real. There *was* something waiting for her in the shadows.

Naomi took a step forward and heard something crunch under her foot. When the power went out, so had the machines that groaned and chugged throughout the day, supporting every freezer and cooler in the building. Without those background noises, the sound that emanated from under her boot seemed altogether too loud.

"Hello?" Her voice was quickly swallowed by the darkness. Naomi gulped. She took another step. As far as she could tell, she was alone. Then, she saw a glimmer of light somewhere to her right. She followed it.

The light became a little clearer as she pursued it. It led her to an even larger area of the back room, a place where she had never needed to go during her shift. She

317

passed through two more swinging doors and knew that she was in the corridor where some of the vendors stored their products. The glimmer of light was coming from the end of the hall and somewhere to the left.

As Naomi drew closer to the light, she saw something in her path. It was a single red rose, delicate and wilted. "Hello?" she mumbled.

Naomi heard a voice. It was him—whoever he was. "In here, Naomi."

Her entire body went rigid. A tremor of fear passed through her. The voice spoke again. "I know you're frightened, but don't leave. We have something we need to discuss."

"Who are you?" Naomi gasped. The shadows around her seemed to be closing in. All she could see was that tiny shred of light, beckoning her.

"Come here, Naomi. You will see."

A little voice in her head told her to turn and run, but she denied it. She was so scared she could hardly breathe, but she felt that running now would be waste—he would still come after her, he would still want her, perhaps more so. She had to face him. She had to end it.

She walked toward the light. She was standing in front of a door and in that door, she saw a figure, dim and shadowed, watching her from behind a pair of thin-rimmed spectacles. There was a movement of light. Naomi blinked. "Who are you?" she repeated. She took a step back.

"Don't walk away," the man said. "Come here."

"I'm not coming any closer," Naomi said firmly.

"*Yes* . . . you are." A nimble hand reached out and grabbed her. Before she knew what had happened, he had pulled her into the little room where the vendors kept records and clipboards and shut the door. An old swivel chair and a desk sat in the corner. "Sit down." Naomi was shoved into the chair. When he trained a gun on her, she was glad that she had gone to the bathroom recently— otherwise, she might have peed in her pants.

Naomi looked up, forcing herself to face him. He had set the large flashlight on the desk. In the yellowish light, she saw the man who had chased her into the woods. His soft brown hair hung around his forehead and was parted in the middle. Behind his glasses were a pair of brown eyes, and he had a goatee and a mustache. He was wearing dark clothes and a wristwatch, and the gun he was holding had a homemade silencer on it. Naomi didn't know much about guns, but she knew enough about them to know that if he killed her now, no one would hear the shot.

"What . . . what do you want?" she stammered.

He leaned forward. His smile was disturbingly sincere. "*You*. I want you."

"You can't have me!" Naomi growled, grasping the edges of the seat, her fingernails digging into the cloth. "Why can't you leave me alone?" Naomi was surprised at the fact that she was able to hold back her terror long

319

enough to snap at her assailant. He appeared perturbed, perhaps even hurt.

For a moment, he turned, shaking his head, but he kept the gun pointed at her. Then he stared back at her. "Naomi, why can't you understand? I love you." When Naomi could find no words to reply, he continued. "The first day I saw you, here in the store, I thought you were the most beautiful thing I'd ever laid eyes on. I knew, right then and there, that I loved you *more than anyone* would *ever* love you." The tone of his voice had grown sinister. "I want you to love me back. That's all I want."

"Are you kidding?" Naomi couldn't keep the disgust out of her voice. It dripped from her lips like stale vomit. "I wouldn't love you if you were the last man on earth!"

Suddenly, he flew forward. His right hand tightened around her shirt, his left hand kept the gun trained on her head. She felt her body hit the ground as he threw her against the cement. She knew that it was in her best interest to remain limp, or else he might shoot her. She felt the cold cement against her. He straddled her, his hand at the base of her neck, the shaft of the gun against her forehead.

"What are you going to do, rape me?" she hissed. "They'll find me soon, you know that. Did you plan all of this? Did you turn off the power?"

Another smile spread across his pale skin. "I knew I couldn't go to your house anymore. I knew they would find me there. But here . . . I had a chance. I can finally

320

see you face to face, talk to you . . . I can finally . . . ."

He threw himself forward, imposing all of his weight against her. He pressed his lips against hers, violently stealing a kiss. He was tall and thin, but he was muscular and heavy; Naomi pushed against him, but found herself floundering helplessly. Her desperation was evident and she knew he was enjoying it.

She felt his free hand pulling at her clothing, trying to undress her. She was wrestling with the question of whether or not it would be wiser to give in when suddenly, he jumped back and shrieked, the fingers of his right hand splaying as they went to his face, grasping his forehead in an expression of pure agony. At first, Naomi thought he had hurt himself. She scrambled back, taking her chance to escape. Then, she realized that there were tears on his face. The gun looked as though it had a mind of its own, hanging limply from his fingers, yet still pointing dangerously in her direction.

"God damn it!" he screamed. Naomi wondered if someone had heard him. She pushed herself against the wall, her heart pounding.

She found words. "What?" The single syllable emerged in a hushed squeak.

"I can't, I can't." He stumbled back, pulling himself to his feet. "I can't hurt you. Naomi . . . ."

He stood above her, legs spread, his pants loosened and his fly down, tears streaming down his face. His arms were thick and long, and he pointed the gun at her as though it were an extension of himself, reaching for her. For a split second, she stared at the dark barrel, wondering if this would be her last moment on earth.

Then, as though he had planned it that way all along, he turned the gun on himself and fired. His skull broke and his brains dashed across the wall behind him. His body stood for a moment longer, shuddered, spasmed, and fell. In the throes of death, his limber form resembled the body of a Greek warrior, bowing to kiss the feet of a Goddess.

Chapter 37: A Rose for Naomi

With a resounding grumble, the motors stirred back to life
and the harsh lights in Whellaby's replaced the darkness.
Police sirens blared. In the back of the store, someone had
fixed the fuses; electricity had returned.

Two limp forms lay motionless in a little room in the
back of the store. Alexis surveyed the damage, cringing.
She quickly checked Naomi's heartbeat and pulse; she
was fine, but she was unconscious. The blood and bits on
the wall were ghastly. The man's hand still held the gun
in a death-grip, and although his face was gone, Alexis
knew who he was.

"Hitcher Chandler," she mumbled to herself. She saw
something poking out of his back pocket. She knelt down
and took a brown leather wallet from the dead man.
Inside, she found his license, which confirmed her
suspicions. Height, six feet, two inches—brown eyes.
Alexis read the address beneath the name Hitcher H.
Chandler. "I was right," she told herself.

She looked through the wallet and found a photo.
There was no mistaking the identity of the girl in the
picture—it was Naomi. On the back of the photograph,
neat handwriting proclaimed, *'Vacation in the mountains
with Dad.'* Alexis slipped the photo into a jacket pocket
and knelt down next to Naomi. She pulled the limp girl

into her arms and carried her out of the little room.

"I'm ruined!" Spencer Whellaby shouted. He slumped forward at the manager's desk in the office, suddenly appearing a lot older and more broken than he ever had in the past. Alexis watched the owner of the grocery store run his fingers through his gray hair, cursing. "How is this possible?" he gasped.

He had arrived shortly after receiving the news. His clothes were disheveled; it was clear that he had dressed hurriedly. The man's eyes were red and puffy and he seemed unable to stop moving his hands. After scratching through his thinning hair, he twisted his fingers together and rocked back and forth like a mental patient.

Keith was sitting in the adjacent armchair and Alexis was standing in the corner imitating a coat rack. A moment later, she rejoined the human life in the room, scratching her chin. "No, no, I think not," she said sternly.

"What?" Whellaby glared at her. "After hearing about this, who will want to shop here? No one! After they clean that man's brains off the wall, what company will want to supply me with products? No one!"

"You're mistaken," Alexis insisted.

Keith had a curious expression on his face. He looked up at the detective from where he sat. "You know, I think you're right," he said.

Whellaby nearly exploded. "Are you both insane?" He stared through the glass door of the office, where police officers talked amongst themselves. They disappeared from view. The night crew had left and Naomi had been taken to the hospital. An ambulance was outside, ready to transport the body, and Alexis presumed that a crew had been called to do the dirty work.

Keith leaned forward. "Mr. Whellaby, think about it. Murder is sensational. The news of this is spreading, and people aren't going to shop somewhere else, they're going to come here. People are screwed up; they love this stuff."

Alexis nodded in agreement. "That's what I was trying to say, Mr. Whellaby. I couldn't have said it any better than that." She leaned her hands on the desk. "People are sick. They *love* murder."

"Hm?" Whellaby looked up at her, hope dawning in his eyes. "You think so?"

"Certainly. If anything, you'll get more customers."

Keith agreed. "People always say they're against killing, but they can't help but be interested in it. Almost everybody's got a fascination with sick shit." He and Alexis exchanged a knowing glance.

"Maybe you're right." Whellaby almost smiled.

Someone knocked on the door. Frank walked in.

Alexis turned and slipped out of her trench coat, hanging it over her arm. "How goes it, Frankie?"

"They're cleaning up the back right now. It's on the

books as a definite suicide."

"A blind man could've told you that."

Keith stood slowly and mumbled something about his gout acting up. "If the overnight cashier is still here, I've got to go talk to him," he said. "See you later, Mr. Whellaby." Just then, a short blond-haired young man appeared on the other side of the glass door. He looked particularly nervous. He was gesturing to Keith, who said, "I'm coming, Nick, keep your pants on," and walked out the door.

Frank followed Alexis outside. They went to where her car was parked and she lit a cigar.

"I've gotta say, Alexis, you were right about everything." Frank leaned against the hood of the car. "He tried to cover his tracks, but you figured it out."

"It was that pay stub that did it, the one from the electric company. You were the one that found the photo album. I was surprised about that."

Hitcher Chandler had stolen Naomi's photo album from her car on the night that he had gone to Whellaby's and broken the driver's side window of the Buick. Frank had found the album while they had searched through the upstairs rooms at Thurston's house. Hitcher had put a new cover on the album, making it look like something else, and had hidden it in the open. Hitcher was only a roommate; it seemed that none of the bills for the house had his name on them, and none of the neighbors knew him very well.

Alexis stared up into the sky. "It smells like rain," she observed.

"It's supposed to rain, tonight," Frank told her. "There's been a chill in the air."

"I feel horrible," Alexis mumbled.

"Why?"

"It's my fault Hitcher got her cell phone number. Naomi's, I mean."

"I don't follow you."

"Sure you do. You were there."

"Oh!" Frank realized what she was talking about. During the struggle at the Davis house, Alexis had dropped her cell phone. At the time, she only had a vague idea that Thurston had a roommate. The roommate—Hitcher Chandler—had come back to the house unseen, found the cell phone and accidentally come across Naomi's phone number stored in the SIM card. It was no wonder that Alexis was feeling guilty. "It was just an accident," Frank said. "He would have done this anyway."

"I know. I just feel partly responsible. But I also knew that I couldn't just barge into Whellaby's and watch for him; I had to wait for him to make his first move. If he had seen me, nothing would have happened, and Naomi would still be in danger. I just wish I could have done it

differently. I knew it would happen here, though. He
figured out that someone would be watching her house.
This was his only chance."

"I wouldn't worry about it too deeply if I were you."

"I know, but—" Alexis turned and looked at Frank.
She blew a ring of smoke into the air. "She could have
been killed."

To Alexis's surprise, Frank laughed.

"What's so funny?" she demanded.

"*You*. Alexis, you knew he wasn't going to kill her.
You knew all along that he wouldn't be able to, even
before you knew his name. You knew that he was too
obsessed with her to hurt her. He thought that he loved
her."

"I know."

"So what's bothering you?"

"Naomi. She's not dead, but this'll follow her for a
long time."

Frank nodded. A long silence passed between them.
Frank spoke. "That garden at the Davis house, it was a
nice one."

"Then you saw the roses?"

"Yes, I assumed they were the same ones."

"My mother grew roses," Alexis said. "She was a
genius horticulturist. She won prizes for those roses. The
roses in the Thurston's yard—those were prize roses. Did
you notice?"

"No."

"I knew Hitcher had taken them from that rose bush, I just knew it. After I didn't have any luck at the florist shops, I realized Naomi's stalker was a gardener. There were three pairs of shoes near the back door at Thurston's house; that gave me a clue, too. If Thurston really had lived alone, chances were good that he would have had only one pair of shoes sitting by the back door. I made a big mistake leaving my phone there, but I didn't realize it until later. That was stupid." She took another drag on her cigar. "I should have noticed sooner that Thurston Davis was somehow connected to Naomi's stalker."

"Everyone makes mistakes, Alexis."

"No." She put out her cigar. "I *can't* make mistakes. In some cases, it could be deadly."

In the back room of Whellaby's grocery store, another red rose lay crushed on the floor. Someone picked it up and threw it in the trash. Naomi would never know that Hitcher had left it for her, that she had stepped on it upon entering the back room, or that it had been meant to lead her to him—a beacon in the inky darkness.

Chapter 38: Aftershock

Over the next few weeks, Naomi became oddly complacent. She was relieved that she wouldn't have to go to court over the entire affair, but the image of Hitcher Chandler blowing his brains out was not an image that she would ever forget.

In her nightmares, she saw the bullet cut through his skull in slow motion.

While she slept, she heard his sobs.

And while she worked, toiling through the night, she saw his body slumping to the ground. She was unable to expel the memory.

The first night that she returned to work, Keith came up to her while she was stocking in aisle eight.

"Naomi, when you get done, fill the cat food up from the end display."

"Okay." She finished a case and broke down the cardboard box.

"And go through the back stock, most of it should go up."

"Okay."

Keith eyed the CD player that was sticking out of her pocket. She had her headphones on. "Did you hear all that?"

She took off her headphones and turned to him.

"Yeah, I heard you."

Keith stared at her. Naomi stared back at Keith. Keith felt extremely uncomfortable all of a sudden. Death, murder and suicide weren't things that normally bothered him. His grandfather had died, and he had wept, but that was normal. When it was someone you cared about, death wasn't an easy thing to deal with. Seeing someone die wasn't easy. He had been with his grandfather, Tom, when the old man had passed and it had made him depressed. That was normal.

What wasn't normal, Keith knew, was when someone witnessed a person commit suicide, and then came back to work at the same place where it had happened a week later, seemingly unaffected by it. Naomi looked just as she had before it had happened—calm, thoughtful, perhaps even bored. Considering the fact that the dead man had stalked Naomi for a month or two prior, this wasn't an attitude Keith had expected.

"Are you okay?" he asked.

"I wish people would stop asking me that." Naomi picked up another case, seemingly annoyed, and cut the box open. As she put the cans on the shelf, she felt Keith's eyes on her. Finally, she turned and looked at him. "What? What is it? You're looking at me like I just grew a second nose or something."

Keith fidgeted where he stood. "I'm just wondering, I mean—I didn't think you would come back here."

"Huh?"

"I thought you would quit. You saw him shoot himself, didn't you?"

Naomi's gaze shifted to the floor, then to the shelves, and finally back to Keith. "Yeah, well. I need to make money somehow, don't I?"

"That's your reason?"

Naomi put a few more cans on the shelf. Her brow furrowed. She frowned. She looked back at Keith. "You know what; I don't really know why I'm here."

It was an aftershock. That was how she explained it to Richard when he came over the next morning. They sat on the couch in her trailer and drank tea together.

"I would have quit, if I were you," Richard said.

She looked at him, blinking, her eyes heavy with the prospect of sleep. "A friend of mine died when I was in high school," Naomi mumbled. "I always felt like he was the only person that made any sense. He was smart and fun to be around. I loved him like a brother. His name was Ali." Naomi paused and sipped her tea, staring off into the distance.

"What happened?" Richard asked carefully.

"He killed himself. I don't really blame him, actually. He didn't have a great life, and things had happened to him that I wouldn't have wished on my worst enemy." She sipped her tea again and put her feet up on the coffee table. "When I was in high school, I had a job at a little deli. Someone called me when I was at work one day, the same day that Ali's body had been found, and they told me what had happened. I could hardly believe it. I didn't know what to think. I wanted to believe that it was a different Ali who had died, that it wasn't the Ali that I knew. I kept working. I rang people out at the register and I made hoagies. About an hour and a half later, I got a call from another friend who asked me if I knew. I told him, yeah, I did. I said I was at work."

"What'd he say?"

"He asked me what the hell I was still doing there, and that was when it hit me. I didn't really know what I was doing there. I was just working." Naomi turned and looked at Richard. "After I talked to him, I realized that Ali really was dead, and that was when I had to leave. My boss was short-handed. I felt almost selfish."

"But you weren't."

"No, of course not. It's natural to want to go home and be by yourself if your friend dies. But, I felt like it was almost . . . *silly*. I mean, I was physically capable of working. But I was sad. I guess part of me just didn't think that death was a good enough reason to stop working."

"I think I know what you mean."

"You don't think that's stupid?"

"No, it's not stupid. It was your reaction, it was . . . ."

"Aftershock," Naomi said.

"Hmm?"

"I didn't want to believe what had happened. In that hour and a half, I operated like I was in a dream, like somebody was playing a trick on me. I didn't want to believe that Ali was really gone."

"Denial, you mean."

"No, not necessarily. I was just in shock. And I guess I am right now."

"If you can say that, can't you move past it?"

"I guess not. I went to work, didn't I? It's the same thing. You keep doing what comes naturally to you until you realize that you can't anymore. Until you realize that something is bothering you so much that you have to stop."

Richard reached over and took her hand. "When are you going to realize that you have to stop?"

A tear rolled down her cheek. "I don't know. I keep reliving everything, as though it's a long, drawn-out nightmare."

"It was, Naomi."

She nodded. "The worst kind of nightmare. But now, what do I do?"

Richard shrugged. "Only you can decide what's right for you. But no matter what you decide, I'll be here for you."

"I know that." She squeezed his hand. "And I won't forget it."

Chapter 39: Check Out Time

A week later, Naomi finished a work night only to realize that she wanted to leave, badly. She had been seeing a therapist, one that the police had supplied. The therapist mostly dealt with rape victims, and Naomi had gotten close enough to require counseling. She had been going to this person for a couple of weeks now, and the woman couldn't understand why Naomi was still working at Whellaby's. As the therapist described it, it was as though Naomi was trapped in a dark room, and rather than look for the door, she sat in the corner trying not to think about her situation.

As she realized that she had this great need to find the door, open it, and leave, Naomi clocked out for the night and grabbed a shopping basket. There were a few things she needed. As she shopped, she thought about various trivialities, trying to ignore the desperate voice in the back of her head that told her to walk out and never turn back.

When she reached the front of the store, the overnight cashier who was currently on duty walked over to one of the cash registers. Naomi didn't know him very well. He was a little bit younger than her and had short blond hair and glasses. She set her things by the register.

"Hi, Nick."

"Need to check out?" he asked.

"Yes."

"How are things?"

Naomi couldn't help but recognize the concern in his eyes. He knew about what had happened, and although Naomi was only an acquaintance to him, he seemed worried about her.

"Um, as good as they can be," she said vaguely.

Nick scanned the last of the items. "Twelve twenty-seven," he said.

Naomi dug through her wallet, a nagging thought in her mind. She pulled out a twenty and handed it to Nick. He gave her the change and bagged her groceries as she stared thoughtfully toward the manager's office.

"Can I leave this stuff here for a minute?" Naomi asked.

"Sure." He had seen her looking toward the office. "What are you going to do?"

"I think it's time I moved on." She and the cashier exchanging a knowing glance. Nick seemed to understand. Naomi walked purposefully toward the office, content that she finally knew what she wanted to do.

It's time that I checked out of this place . . . for good.

"You quit?" Roy looked up at his daughter from across the kitchen table. He dug into his eggs with a fork, hurriedly eating his breakfast.

"It was time."

"I'm glad. You shouldn't be there anymore." Roy took a sip from a glass of orange juice. "I've been worried about you, Naomi."

"I know, Dad."

"I could use another mechanic. I've been keeping the position open for you. What do you think?"

Naomi picked at her nail and stared at the table. "I don't think so."

Roy finished his eggs and pushed the plate aside. "Look, I know you didn't want to work for me when you first moved here. I understand that. But you've been here quite a while now, and this would be easy for you. It would give you some time to rest, let you figure things out, and I'll pay you well."

"I appreciate that." She looked up. "But . . . ."

"But what?"

"I already know what I want to do. I'm going to leave for a while."

He crossed his arms on the table. For a moment, they both stared at each other. All they could hear was the ticking of the clock. Outside, it was raining. "Are you sure about that, kid?"

"Yeah, I'm sure."

At a Jargon show that week, a guest singer nearly broke all the beer glasses with a powerful voice while Geoffrey Harp played the drums. Naomi sat in the corner with Oliver and smoked a cigarette. She blamed Geo for the habit, but it wasn't all bad. It was true what they said: it calmed her nerves, and that was what she needed more than anything.

Geo came over to her table after the first set and sat down across from her. "So, what'd you think?"

"It was great," Naomi said.

"It was awesome, Geo," Oliver echoed.

There was a tense moment between them. Geo ordered a beer. "Oliver told me that you're leaving soon."

"That's true."

"Where are you going?"

"I don't know, actually. I'm leaving with Brian and his friend on a road trip in a few days."

"Brian? The musician that hangs out at the Night Kitchen?"

"The very same." Naomi sipped Magic Hat 9 from a glass.

"I didn't think you two knew each other very well."

"We don't." She shrugged. "He offered, he said there was room in his van. So I'm going. I need to get out of here for a while, maybe indefinitely."

"You mean you don't know if you're coming back?" Geo sunk back in his chair, a disappointed look on his face. On the stage, Jargon's bass player tuned his instrument. All around them, people laughed and talked.

Naomi hung her head and stared into her beer. "I need some time, Geo."

"I know. I guess I was just hoping that you would spend it with friends."

"I'm sorry. I can't. I just can't stay here. Maybe wherever I go next, I'll have better luck. Maybe I'll come back, maybe I won't. I already told Alexis, and I told her I would send her a postcard sometime. I'll do the same for you two."

"Well . . . ." Geo lifted his beer. "To you, Naomi. I hope you find what you're looking for. Cheers."

Oliver lifted his own drink. "To Naomi."

The three glasses clinked together, and Naomi took a long drink.

On a hot summer morning, Naomi loaded her bags into Brian's old VW van. The thing was rusty and had seen a lot of action, but Brian seemed confident that it would take them wherever they wanted to go.

They stood in the driveway at Brian's little house. A sign in the yard read 'For Rent.' Brian planned to be gone for a long time, and he had his entire savings tucked away in a safe under the driver's seat.

Naomi had told Richard to meet her at Brian's house. She had already told him about the trip, but he didn't quite believe that she was leaving until he pulled into the driveway and saw her standing there with Brian and his friend. She walked over and met him by his car. The two of them embraced. The hug lasted a long time, and Naomi was sad when it ended.

"So, when will I see you again?" he asked. The two of them fidgeted where they stood.

Naomi could hear Brian talking to his friend on the other side of the van. "I don't know. I think we might head west, maybe go to Arizona, or maybe even all the way to California."

"I thought we had something, I mean . . . ." He seemed to be struggling with his words.

"We *do* have something," Naomi said, taking his hand. "But I need to get away for a while. Okay?"

"Okay." Richard hugged her again. As shadows of night began to recede, Richard and Naomi kissed.

Naomi looked him in the eye. "I'll be back. I promise," she assured him. "I just don't know when."

"I'll miss you."

"I'll miss you, too." Naomi went and joined Brian.

Brian's friend was a musician as well, and Naomi already felt comfortable around him. He was short and had long hair and a beard. He reminded Naomi of a mountain man.

They climbed into the van just as the sun was rising. Richard stood watching. They could see the sun peeking over the tops of the trees. Mist clung to the ground, and the day was sure to be sweltering. Brian started the engine and they rolled down the windows.

"Well, off we go," he called to Richard. "Goodbye, Witchfire."

"See you, Brian," Richard said, waving.

Naomi leaned out her own window and said, "Remember, I'll be back! If not for anything else, I'll come back to see you."

Richard laughed, stepping toward his car. "I believe it."

In the front passenger seat, Naomi breathed a sigh of relief. She felt as though a heavy weight had been lifted from her shoulders. Although it would be a long time before the thoughts of Hitcher Chandler's suicide would leave her, and even longer before she finally stopped blaming herself for her mother's death, Naomi knew that she was taking a step in the right direction.

http://oaklightpublishing.com

CPSIA information can be obtained at www.ICGtesting.com
Printed in the USA
BVOW03s1718080114

341210BV00001B/4/P

9 781613 920152